WANNA BE SCARED?

LEE MOUNTFORD

FREE BOOK

Sign up to my mailing list for free horror books...

Want more scary stories? Sign up to my mailing list and receive your free copy of *The Nightmare Collection - Vol 1* as well as *Inside: Perron Manor* (a prequel novella to *Haunted: Perron Manor*) directly to your email address.

The novel-length short story collection and prequel novella are sure to have you sleeping with the lights on.

Sign up now.

www.leemountford.com

1. THE LIGHTHOUSE

Are there places people don't belong?

John had always thought so. There had never been a doubt in his mind. Why, for example, did humans need to venture miles and miles beneath the oceans, where the water pressure was so intense it could turn their bones to mush?

Or what of the endless void of space? The lack of oxygen was a clear indicator that humans had no business up there. So why go?

John understood the reasons put to him whenever he'd asked that question: *but John, pushing ourselves to further our knowledge. By conquering the unconquerable. By going to places we weren't built to go.*

Benjamin, John's old friend, was of that opinion. In fact, those were Benji's exact words.

Benji doesn't think that *now*, of course. Benji doesn't have opinions. He doesn't have anything.

Doesn't even exist.

Or… maybe he does. He exists with the others. His thoughts and opinions are currently implanted into him by vast, unknowable things.

The answer is, there *are* places people should never tread. The places your mind and body scream at you to get away from if you accidentally stumble across them. John had always thought there was something to that instinct: people could sense the *wrongness* of a place.

And of course, Benji had always dismissed it. Said it was something in our programming left over from when we were cave people. There was no need to fear the unknown any longer. It had kept us alive then, he said, but humans had outlived the usefulness for that instinct. That 'programming,' as he'd called it.

Benji was wrong. Poor fella had only realised it right at the end.

Dear reader, you are no doubt aware a story is coming: a cautionary tale about listening to yourself when you feel something isn't quite right. That notion could save your life one day.

Didn't save Benji. Didn't save John. Not really. It only prolonged John's life, though he will forever be haunted. Eventually, the things from that day will come for him.

John still sees them in his sleep. Drawing ever closer, night by night.

Would you like to go back to the start? Well, the most appropriate place to begin is the weeks leading up to the trip.

Benji had always wanted to visit a very specific place. Unfortunately for John, it was *his* job to accompany his friend, as much as he didn't want to. Benji, you see, explored old buildings. He even wrote books about his expeditions. John had no interest in that pastime. None at all. He did, however, know the owner of Whitburn Lighthouse: one of the few lighthouses in the UK that was still private and not under the control of the Trinity House charity.

The structure, which stood like a concrete spear erupting

from the choppy waters off the eastern coast, had not been in use for a long time.

It had a bit of a history. Many tragedies had befallen the lighthouse in the short time it had been operational, which had garnered the building something of a reputation.

So to Benji, it was a holy grail. Not because he believed the ghost stories, of course, but because that building had a story to tell, one that needed to be documented.

The whole estate had first been commissioned and built by Archie Whitburn, another rich man with maritime business interests. It was during Archie's time as custodian that the tragedies Benji had read about had all occurred, ending with the death of Archie's family and him going missing.

The whole estate then fell into disrepair, until finally it was purchased for a snip by Mr. Barrow in 2018, fifty years after it had been abandoned.

Why is all this relevant?

Well, it brings us to the current ownership of the lighthouse. Augustus Barrow was a very wealthy landowner who had bought up quite a lot of properties across the United Kingdom. The purchase of the estate included the main house, the surrounding buildings, the small dock, and the lighthouse.

John was a solicitor, and his company had handled many of Mr. Barrow's affairs, including the purchase of Whitburn House.

Benji had been in John's ear for years after finding this information out. 'Use your contact to get me access, John. Please!' The American property owner had done nothing with the estate since buying it, though there was talk of major redevelopment. Ever since that talk had come about, Benji had become more insistent.

It was during a conversation with Mr. Barrow that John mentioned in jest the incessant pleading of his friend. To

John's surprise, Mr. Barrow was more than amenable, saying it would be good for someone to document the place one last time before it was gone forever. In fact, he'd insisted.

That blindsided John—he certainly didn't *want* to facilitate the expedition. Somehow, it seemed somewhat unprofessional. But Mr. Barrow, with his usual carefree attitude, had said John's friend should contact him directly to set things up. The only caveat was that John must be there as well. That way, Mr. Barrow had someone to punish should things go wrong.

John cursed himself for ever having brought it up. But he was stuck.

His employers had been less than impressed, but made it clear John would ensure Mr. Barrow was kept happy, and that he would accompany his friend during the trip. If anything went wrong, John knew his job was on the line.

Benji, of course, was elated.

So everything was arranged. John and Benji had access to the estate for three nights, scheduled to arrive on a Friday and leave on Monday.

John should have listened to his gut when it told him to cancel, regardless of professional fallout. Even on the drive out there, his body was telling him to turn back, to run—those stories existed for a reason. Plus, he was worried Benji might damage something and get him in trouble. In an age when health and safety were probably going overboard, letting two people loose and unsupervised in an abandoned estate, with an old lighthouse attached, seemed irresponsible.

But that was the exact position John found himself in as they pulled up to the gated entrance of Whitburn House.

Turn back, his body told him.

---

1 - 2

DUSK WAS SETTING IN. JOHN AND BENJI SAT IN THE SUV, with the vehicle stationary. Both stared out the front windscreen at the gates. The car swayed gently from side to side as the coastal winds whipped against it.

The mesh wire gate ahead was secured with an industrial-sized lock. Tall, close-boarded fencing ran off either side of the gate, completely enclosing the estate. Augustus Barrow had installed the security fencing immediately after his purchase, to ensure no one wandered in and got themselves hurt. Though in truth, the place was so isolated John didn't see it being a problem. The nearest town was over fifteen miles away, so it wasn't even like bored youths would venture out this far.

'Just be careful while we're here,' John said to his friend as he opened the door.

'I'm *always* careful,' Benji shot back. 'This isn't my first time doing this, you know.'

John didn't respond. He just got out of the car and dug into his pocket, retrieving the key he had been given by Mr. Barrow. He then unlocked the padlock and heaved both leaves of the gate open, gesturing for Benji to drive their vehicle inside. Once Benji had, John refastened the lock, this time on the inside of the gate, and trotted back over to the car, the hem of his long raincoat whipping around his shins.

'As I was saying,' Benji continued from the driver's side as John got back in, 'this isn't my first expedition to places like this, John. This is my *job*. The whole estate will remain undisturbed. There'll be nary a trace of our being here after we've gone. Don't worry, I'm not going to break anything and get you in trouble.'

'Please don't,' John said.

Benji chuckled. 'Be more worried about your own clumsiness, dear boy. You're the one more likely to do some damage.'

John didn't say anything in response, mainly because he knew Benji did have a point.

The sight of the estate before them was an eerie one, especially as it was framed by the darkening sky in the distance and the expanse of rough sea behind it.

There was a large house directly in front of them, sitting at the end of the cracked road. The house was two stories high, clad entirely in white render that had dulled over time, with weathered streaks of greens and sickly yellows running down the surface. There were other smaller outbuildings as well, in addition to a long, low warehouse structure to their left. That building had a heavy-looking industrial door to the front. John knew it to be a workshop and storage unit, and a track led from it out to the pier behind the house.

Then there was the lighthouse. It was within sight, but farther back in the distance, jutting up to the sky. The tower was accessible by a long stone walkway, which rose out of the sea, supported on thick columns all strung together by sweeping arches of stone. Drooping chain balustrades were the only protection from falling into the sea on either side of the walkway. When staring out, John found himself wondering if the tide would rise high enough to engulf the route completely. The thought of being out there, stuck in the moss-covered tower for hours at a time, filled him with dread.

What are we doing out here?

Like many lighthouses John had seen—or rather, the *pictures* he'd seen of them—this one was mounted on a small rock island. The stone shaft of the structure was thicker at the base, and the building had a domed top with glass walls around the head. The glass looked black with dirt and grime.

John looked down the length of the building and noted there were no windows other than the glass at the top.

'We shouldn't be going in there,' he eventually said.

'Relax,' Benji told John. 'You told me yourself all the structural surveys stated the buildings and lighthouse are all safe. Nothing is going to fall down on us.'

That's not it, John thought, but didn't voice it.

They drove the car down to the house, being careful on the asphalt road, which didn't seem as sound as the surrounding buildings. Driving slowly, Benji carefully manoeuvred the car across the ridges and cracks. There were even areas where grass had forced its way through the uneven black asphalt.

Eventually, they came to a stop and got out of the vehicle.

Three nights of this, John lamented glumly as he stared at the house. The ridgeline of the building ran left to right in front of him, though there was a single peak on the front elevation just above the entrance. The slate tiles on the roof were all intact, but layered with thick green moss and bird droppings.

All the windows were also in good order, each with stone sills, which helped break up the expanse of the white render. The main door was black, with no glass, though there was a full-height window just next to it. A long, covered porch ran the full length of the front elevation from right to left, jutting out from the main building and supported on square columns at regular intervals. The building seemed like a standard large house, though in John's opinion it was somewhat lacking in architectural flair.

'Should we unpack now?' John asked, turning back to the car. The boot and back seat were both crammed with supplies: food, drink, changes of clothes, sleeping bags, and blankets, as well as Benji's cameras and other equipment. There were also candles, electric lights, lanterns, and even a portable generator.

John hadn't been to the estate before but had seen photos, so he knew there were beds still inside the main house. He was hoping that with a change of blankets, those beds might be good enough to sleep in for a few nights, rather than having to bed down on the floor in sleeping bags.

He couldn't help but sigh at the thought, however—he *hated* that he had to be here.

'Let's have a quick look around before we unload everything,' Benji said. John could see the glee on the face of his friend, who seemed like a child at Christmas.

'But it'll be dark soon,' John replied. He didn't fancy the idea of heaving their supplies inside under the cover of night.

'That's why we'll be quick,' Benji said, smiling. He started to dig through the pile of equipment on the back seat and soon stood upright, holding an expensive-looking camera with a mounted flash. 'Need this, though,' he said. 'I always like to photograph a place as soon as I arrive. Just shoot it from the hip, you know, see what jumps out.'

John didn't want *anything* to jump out.

'If you're taking photos,' John said, 'then it isn't going to be a quick tour. Let's just—'

'Let's just get on with it and be quick, I agree,' Benji insisted, cutting off his friend. He started to walk forward. A moment later, John shook his head and followed.

I don't like this, he told himself again. His eyes were drawn to the lighthouse beyond them. Standing out at sea, maybe a hundred feet from the house, it almost felt like the structure itself was lonely, removed from everything else. An odd thought for something that wasn't sentient, John knew, but it struck him all the same.

The pair soon reached the main door of the house. John shoved his hand into his coat pocket and pulled out the keys, all bound together on a thin steel ring. He thumbed through them until he found the correct one. Once the door was open, he pushed it inward, and the two men stepped into the yawning house.

The air seemed stale, which was to be expected given how long the building had sat abandoned. John reached to the side of the door and flicked the brass light switch.

Nothing.

That didn't surprise John. He had known Mr. Barrow had cut the electricity to the estate a while ago. Still, he'd felt compelled to try anyway—his heart had dropped a little when it hadn't worked. Night still hadn't claimed the sky, and natural light poured in through the windows. John suddenly dreaded the sun going down, knowing they were going to have to rely on the candles and lights Benji had packed. Just being able to see their surroundings seemed like it was going to be a lot of work.

And that was saying nothing of staying warm. The gas had been cut off as well, so they would need to keep wrapped up. There was a log-burning stove in one of the rooms; of course, they hadn't brought wood with them.

I want to go home.

He also didn't like the silence. It wasn't *total* silence—

9

John could still hear the wash of the sea, and the cawing of seagulls—but there was still an eerie heaviness to the quiet.

A single staircase stood before them, pressed against one wall. A green carpet runner sat in the centre of the stairs, and John spotted exposed treads with lacquered oak on either side of the thick material.

He followed Benji, allowing his friend to lead the way. Benji already had his torch in hand, though it wasn't quite needed yet.

Once out of the entrance lobby, John saw the flooring underfoot switched from marble tile to timber boarding, though the corridors had runners of thick carpet central to the hallways. As the two men moved to the left side of the house, their footfalls kicked up small plumes of dust.

Benji ducked his head into each room that they passed. John, however, was happy to just peer inside from the hallway. As they moved, he noticed a study, a lounge, and some storage rooms. At the end of the corridor was a large open space, which housed living, dining, and kitchen areas. Many full-height windows had been punched into the walls, giving something of a panoramic view. That might have been a nice, tranquil sight for residents at one point, but was now ruined by the wooden fencing that circled the estate. Benji poked through the kitchen cupboards, where the two men also found a small pantry, though it was devoid of food. *Thank god,* John thought. Spoiled food was a smell he didn't think he'd be able to put up with. There were some old mugs, glasses, and plates, but all were covered in a fine layer of dust.

Lastly, in the dining space was a large table, complete with six chairs around it.

On the other wing of the ground floor the two men found another lounge, more storage spaces, rooms that were bare and had no obvious use, and at the end a rather grand sunroom, the roof and walls of which were a mix of timber posts and large expanses of glass. That space still had some furniture inside, with a long, low sofa, armchairs, and even high-backed wooden chairs around a waist-high circular table.

Upstairs was a collection of bedrooms, some with en-suites, bathrooms, and a space John presumed had once been an office.

Two of the bedrooms still had their beds; both were large, and one was a four-poster. The sheets were made, but the dust and cobwebs showed how long they had been left without use. During the entire tour, Benji had continued to snap pictures of everything he saw.

There was a sadness to the house. John knew it was just an emotion he himself was projecting onto the structure, of course, yet he couldn't help but feel like he was standing in an echo of time, in a last fading memory of a life once lived.

'Right,' Benji finally declared. 'We best start bringing our things inside, eh?'

For John, it wasn't a moment too soon. The light outside was fading quickly, and Benji was already using his torch to guide them. John doubted they would get everything inside and set up before the night was on them.

They worked quickly, but John's hunch was right. It was indeed dark before they got the small generator going, which they put outside, near the living space to the far left of the house. That living space was to be their headquarters, according to Benji.

They had set some electric lights on the dining table and dotted some candles around the perimeter of the room as well. The white hue from the electric lights was almost sterile: pure and clinical, which cast the immediate area in an almost spectral glow. That blurred with the warmer light from the candles at the extremities, creating an odd effect.

From one of the windows, John was just able to make out the lighthouse, aided by the moonlight. The skies were clear and the moon was full, which only added to his feeling of unease. Seeing the full moon sitting high behind the lighthouse caused a creeping chill to work its way up his spine. He thought about telling Benji to get a snap of it, as it would be a perfectly gothic photo for the book. However, he stayed silent.

At that moment, Benji was staring out the window while both men sat at the table. They were enjoying a coffee Benji had prepared with his portable electric stove. They'd already finished some of the pre-packed sandwiches.

The warmth was welcome, but John still felt too far removed from the comforts of everyday life. It had the same vibe as camping, something John hated.

'Should we go out there tonight?' Benji asked, still staring out of the window—John almost dropped his cup.

'What... out to the *lighthouse?*' he asked, incredulous. Benji nodded with a grin. But John shook his head. 'Are you insane? It's pitch black out there. *Anything* could happen. If I have to shadow you out here, then by God I'm going to make sure we don't do anything stupid. And that,' he said, pointing out the window, 'is just stupid.'

Benji just laughed. 'You need to lighten up, John. But fine, we won't go tonight. However, we *are* going out there at first light. I need to get some shots of the lighthouse at sunrise during that magic hour. The photos will look stunning. A perfect, double-spread background image for the book. Maybe I'll use it for the introduction pages.'

John stifled a sigh. 'Fine,' he said. 'First light. But please be careful. You have a tendency to be a little... well... bullheaded when you get excited, always charging in, often with little thought beforehand.'

Benji just laughed again. 'Interesting you say that, dear

friend. Because I often think you are *far* too timid and hesitant in life. Lord knows how many opportunities have slipped through your fingers due to your inaction. No offence intended, of course.'

'None taken,' John replied with a tight-lipped smile. He knew offence was very *much* intended; such was the nature of their relationship. 'Regardless of that, though,' John went on, 'I want to get through this weekend without falling into the sea and drowning. Or without breaking something that will be too expensive to fix. So... a little restraint, if you please.'

'Point taken,' Benji said, raising a hand. 'Though didn't you say this place was scheduled to be demolished? What does it matter if—'

'Benji, please,' John interrupted. 'Just take the point on board.'

'Fine,' Benji said with a grin. 'I'll be good. You have my solemn promise.'

'Thank you,' John replied. He took another sip of his coffee and let his eyes wander around the room.

A slight shudder passed through him.

John wasn't sure whether it was from the cold or the unnerving way the shadows sat in between pockets of light. He looked back at his friend to see Benji eyeing him.

'Uncomfortable?' Benji asked.

'I'm fine,' John replied. 'A little chilly, but I'll cope.'

'No, that's not what I mean,' Benji went on. 'You seem... uneasy. You know this house is just a collection of blocks and mortar, right? And the lighthouse out there is the same, just a man-made thing. All the stories about this place are merely folklore and fantasy.'

'Of course I know that,' John replied.

But Benji cocked his head to the side. '*Do* you, though? I can tell by the way you're looking at the shadows that you're expecting something to jump out and yell boo. There's nothing here, John. Nothing except the two of us.'

John sighed, not bothering to hold back his annoyance. 'Is there a point to this, Benji?'

Benji shrugged. 'Just an observation. For a solicitor, supposedly a man of reason, it always surprises me how you believe in the illogical. How many times have you refused to come with me to a place just because it has a bit of a reputation?'

'Nothing illogical about self-preservation.'

'Well, I've always come back safe and sound, haven't I? And I can tell you now I've never seen anything so odd that I couldn't explain it away. No ghosts or spirits. Only empty buildings.'

'So why do it?' John said. 'I mean, what do you get from visiting and cataloging these places?'

'I get plenty from it!' Benji replied, eyes widening. 'Some of the places I've been to are no longer here, so I was able to capture their final days, a kind of echo of their essence. It's sad, in a way, rather melancholy, and each time I've done it I can almost feel the history seep into my soul. But it's the same reason I can walk into a church and be awed by the architecture, design, and just the *feel* of the building, while knowing there is nothing divine about the place.'

'Very good,' John replied. 'Quite the speech. Did you rehearse it?'

Benji chuckled. 'Nope. Completely off the cuff.'

'What about the people who buy your books? Are they all of the same belief? Or could it be part of the appeal? Do some of them conflate these old places with the supernatural? Don't forget, I've read some of your books—you definitely go into dark histories and things like that.'

'Of course,' Benji said. 'Charting the history of a building is the very point of the book. If there are dark elements, there's no reason to shy away from them.'

'Ah,' John said, raising a finger. 'But those grisly stories are *always* front and centre, overshadowing everything else. And the typeface you use on the covers… well, let's just say it wouldn't look out of place on a ghost story. You can grandstand all you want, but that very belief you mock is what gives you a livelihood, and you have no qualms about leveraging it. So if I may, perhaps drop the holier-than-thou attitude. Because if it comes through in your writing, you may lose your audience.'

Benji just looked at John. *Did I finally do it?* John asked himself. *Have I beaten him?* Benji, always self-assured and quick of tongue, usually got the last word when the pair verbally sparred. John waited for the other man's response.

'Well played,' Benji eventually said, surprising John. 'But,' he went on, 'the point is there's nothing in the shadows here to worry about. I still stand by that.'

'Well, you keep focusing on your pictures, and I'll keep an eye on the shadows.'

'You'll drive yourself crazy,' Benji warned in a sing-song voice before draining the last of his coffee.

John didn't answer. He knew Benji had a point, though: the weekend would be almost unbearable if John kept unnerving himself over nothing.

Still, that feeling in his gut, the one that had taken hold after they'd first arrived, was refusing to let go.

You shouldn't be *here, Johnny-boy.*

He checked his watch. Eight-thirty. Though technically nighttime, it wasn't late enough to turn in just yet, as much as John wanted to. The journey had tired him out, and the idea of sleeping through as many dark hours as possible was a comforting one.

'We should have brought a board game,' John mused. 'Something to kill the time.'

Benji nodded. 'Yeah, it would have helped. Though, I'm going to spend a bit of time making some notes, if you don't mind. Organising my thoughts on what I've seen so far.'

'Of course, don't let me get in your way. Do you mind if I stay here with you? I won't watch you work if it makes you uncomfortable, but I—'

'It's fine,' Benji said. 'Watch all you like. I don't mind. I tend to keep notes and diaries on trips like this, just so I don't forget specific feelings or first impressions. Actually, I also have some notes on the history of the estate. Would you mind reading over them? Given you'll know some things due to your dealings with legal matters, you may spot something important: things that are incorrect, or events or details I have perhaps overlooked.'

'I… yes, that would be no problem,' John said. He didn't exactly want to dive into the morbid history of the estate, but the task would at least keep him busy for a little while, and let him focus on something besides what lay in the shadows.

Benji handed over the notes. A moment later, John finished the last of his coffee, set the papers down before him, and started reading.

3

1-3

BENJI'S NOTES WERE PRINTED OUT ON THICK, GOOD-QUALITY paper, not the cheap flimsy stuff John had expected. That paper was a light yellow, rather than standard white, and looked relatively expensive, especially just for notes.

'Regular paper not good enough for you?' John asked, waving the collection of sheets.

Benji laughed. 'Only the best. I like the yellow. Feels aged, somewhat. Fitting, given what I do.'

John nodded, then began to read. He had to give credit to Benji's writing style; given the books were predominantly photographs, plans, and diagrams, Benji had to keep whatever text he did have succinct while still being punchy and conveying all that was required. *Seems like he's mastered that,* John thought, reviewing the notes.

They began by describing the land before Whitburn House had been built. In truth, there wasn't much to tell. It was simply open space, with the only landmark of note a section in the cliffs that dropped down sharply, allowing access to a small stone beach. That, the notes claimed, was the precise reason Mr. Whitburn had bought the land, as it was the perfect place to construct a small dock.

Initially, the construction of the estate had proceeded without incident. Then work on the lighthouse had begun…

The pier out to the rock island was the first step in the creation of the lighthouse, which would allow the workers to reach the rocky island the tower was to be built on. The work underwater to plant the footings of the pier had gone slowly, especially after digging on the seabed at one point caused an unexplainable black plume of inky liquid to erupt from the ground. Soon after, one of the men who had been caught in the explosion fell ill. No more than a month later, he died.

Building work had continued, and the stone walkway was finally finished, standing a few feet above sea level when the tide was in. Steps had been formed from the cliffs down to its surface, and a rung ladder was fixed to the side so people could reach the small stone beach and dock below.

After that, work had begun on the structure of the lighthouse itself. Benji's notes referenced documents he'd apparently found, which claimed the construction had taken longer than expected, this time due to a high turnover of staff, with workers reportedly walking off site and refusing to carry on. Not much information was given beyond this.

There was even a report of another worker dying, having leapt off the very top of the lighthouse to land on the rocky island below.

When the structure was finally finished, the Whitburns moved in, and Mr. Whitburn got to work growing his business.

Less than four months later, the entire family was dead.

'How are the notes?' Benji asked, drawing John's attention. 'All accurate so far?'

John shrugged. 'I'm sure your research is more detailed

than the meagre information I had to work with. I knew of the deaths of the family, but the problems faced during the construction of the estate are entirely new to me.'

'But nothing strikes you as incorrect?'

'Nothing so far,' John said. 'Again, though, I'm taking your word for much of this.'

'Good. Do tell me if you spot anything. How far through are you?'

'The Whitburns are in the house. They've just moved in.'

'Ah,' Benji said, eyes wide. 'You're just getting to the good bit.'

'Good bit?' John asked. 'People died, Benji. There's nothing good about it.'

Benji waved a dismissive hand. 'You know what I mean, don't be so sensitive. It was a long time ago. The Whitburns are dead and gone. They aren't going to be offended by the way we talk about them.'

'Unless they're still here listening to us,' John added, unable to keep the grin from his lips.

Benji laughed. Then, raising his hand, he spoke aloud to the room around them: 'Well, if the Whitburns are listening in, please let it be known I'm sorry that I'm profiting off your tragedy.' He looked back to John and winked.

John shook his head. 'You aren't sorry in the slightest.'

'Shhh,' Benji snapped, feigning annoyance and bringing his finger to his lips. He then pointed to the air. 'They'll hear you.'

John was going to reply, but a sound stopped him. He quickly turned his head to one of the back walls, which over-looked the sea.

'What… what on earth was that?!' he asked.

Benji gazed at the wall as well with a frown of confusion. 'The wind,' he eventually said, though to John the response seemed forced.

To John, it had sounded like a low cry, or even a moan, carried over on the wind to the house. While the noise was admittedly faint, to John it had still sounded human.

'It wasn't the wind! That was a—'

'Don't!' Benji quickly said, shaking his head. 'I'm not going to entertain whatever you're about to say.'

'And what was I about to say?' John asked as he folded his arms.

'That it was a person,' Benji shot back. 'I can tell by the look on your face.'

'I wasn't going to say it was a person.'

'Well, that's good. I apologise for... Wait, you're going to say it was a ghost, weren't you?' John didn't answer, just grinned. Benji sighed. 'That's even worse.'

John didn't answer. It *had* been his first thought, even if he'd wanted to play it off as a bit of a joke. He couldn't help how his brain was wired, and at that moment it again told him to leave.

'Just... don't let your imagination run away with itself,' Benji said. 'If you claim every strange noise is a spirit, then this trip will be unbearable. We're perfectly safe, so I just need you to be an adult about this.'

'Excuse me?' John asked. 'An *adult?*'

'You know what I mean,' Benji said. 'This is a great opportunity for me—'

'And an inconvenience for me,' John was quick to add. 'Best you remember that. I never wanted to come.'

'I know, but you're here for a reason, so as to not upset a client. Like it or not, you're staying. And in order for me to get my work done in good time, I can't be worrying about your mental condition. I want to work, not babysit.'

'I'm not a bloody child!' John seethed, quickly rising to his feet. 'And do *not* talk to me like one. Keep it up, and career be damned, I'll take the car and go. You can have fun here on your own. Good luck on your walk back.'

Benji just scoffed. 'You won't leave me, so stop with the act. Just busy yourself with my notes like a good little helper and make yourself usef...' However, Benji trailed off and looked down at the table, brow furrowed. 'I...' He then looked up. 'Sorry, John, that was uncalled for.'

The apology surprised John. He slowly sat down again. 'I... Thank you. And I'm sorry too,' he said. 'I think we escalated a bit quick there, eh?'

Though Benji had always been fond of needling and teasing his friend, John couldn't recall things ever having gotten quite so personal.

'Maybe we're just tired from our day of travelling,' John said.

'You might be right.' Benji rubbed at his face. 'In fact, you *are* right. My eyes feel like they have sand in them.'

'They look red,' John said after Benji moved his hand away—they were definitely bloodshot.

Benji checked his watch. 'A little early, but perhaps we should turn in for the night. What do you think?'

John checked his watch as well, seeing it was now nine-thirty. 'Actually, I think that's a good idea. If we're to be up at the crack of dawn, getting some shut-eye now makes a lot of sense. Though I don't know how easily I'll fall asleep in a sleeping bag. Haven't used one of those since I was a child.'

'You'll be fine,' Benji said. 'The bags are really warm and well insulated.'

'Well, I suppose that's a bonus.'

'Are you taking the floor, or are you going to use one of the beds?' Benji asked. 'I'll be honest, the beds look comfy. Don't fancy getting under the covers, but I'll happily sleep on the mattress.'

'I... don't know,' John replied. 'I've been considering it,

but it seems strange lying in a dead person's bed. Especially after what happened here. It... I don't know... feels disrespectful, somehow.'

'I understand that,' Benji said, his empathy surprising John. 'But try to remember that it's *just* a bed.'

'You may have a point,' John eventually conceded. 'Plus, I don't know if I have the energy to blow up one of the inflatable mattresses.'

'I hear that! I feel strangely drained. Like you said, probably the travel. Plus, I'm always excited when I first arrive at a new place. But once the adrenaline wears off, the fatigue hits hard. After a full night's rest, we'll both be ready for action tomorrow, I promise.'

With that, the two men did a little tidying before retiring to their respective rooms, each taking a lantern with them for light.

To John, there was something quaint—and eerie—about being guided by the lanterns. They each gave off a warm, orange glow that was much more pleasant than the harsh, clinical white from the lights in the living area. John imagined himself in an old Victorian manor, stalking around at night, clad in sleeping robes and a nightcap with a tail and a puffball at the end.

The adjacent rooms they had chosen both had views out over the sea and the lighthouse, but once inside, John quickly pulled his curtains closed. The idea of waking up and peering out at that structure filled him with unease. He also ensured his door was closed as well, as he didn't fancy looking at the creepy, empty hallway either.

The bedroom was a good size, with some other furniture left behind beyond just the bed: a large wardrobe with ornate carvings on the wooden surface, and a chest of drawers. Both looked in good order, despite being old, and John guessed they could potentially fetch some money at an auction. *I can't understand why they've just been left.*

He regarded the bed, holding the lantern high to let its light fall over a larger area. When he saw the coating of dust, he shuddered. Still, the idea of blowing up the inflatable mattress seemed somehow worse, so he bundled up the sheets, coughing as the dust was kicked up, and placed them in the corner of the room. Then he pulled off the under-sheet and added that to the pile.

Thankfully, the mattress beneath looked clean, but he wiped it down anyway. Then John unfurled his sleeping bag, set his pillows at the head of the bed, and placed one of his thick blankets over the bag, just for an extra layer.

After using the toilet and pulling on some jogging bottoms and a plain t-shirt, John climbed into the sleeping bag and tugged the blanket up to his chin. He then leaned over to the nightstand and flicked off the lantern before letting his head fall back to his pillow.

He could hear Benji moving around from the next room, but soon those sounds fell away, and the only sound remaining was the noise of the sea outside. The continuous, gentle hum of the rolling waves was relaxing, and given how tired he was, John was asleep in less than fifteen minutes.

---

4

1 - 4

JOHN'S EYES OPENED. HE BLINKED A FEW TIMES. A STRANGE sound echoed in his head: the creaking of a door. However, he couldn't determine if it was just the remnants of a dream, or real.

He lifted his head and squinted towards the door, trying to gaze through the darkness while listening intently. There was only the sound of the sea. Eventually, John's tired eyes began to focus, and through the darkness he just barely made out the end of his bed, the far wall, and even the door.

Which hung open.

John drew in a sharp breath and sat bolt upright. Just beyond the opening, in the thickest of the shadows, John swore there was the impression of a person, just standing in place and staring back at him. He tried to call out for his friend, but the only sound that came out was a choked croak.

The figure turned, and John heard muffled footsteps on the carpet, as well as a creak on the floorboards as the person moved away. Free of the previous paralysis, John quickly leaned over and switched on the lantern. The light pushed back the immediate darkness, which let him see the now-empty corridor beyond the door. Though the space was still heavily shadowed, the lantern offered just enough light for him to be able to spot the far wall of the hallway outside.

The light brought with it renewed bravery, and John quickly grabbed the lantern and untangled himself from his sleeping bag. 'Benji,' he called out, finding his voice. 'Was that you?'

He got no response, but did hear footsteps continue down the hallway.

It has to be Benji, John told himself. *But... why didn't he answer?*

John was unsure if Benji was prone to sleepwalking, or if he was deliberately trying to scare John.

Is someone else here with us?

John pushed the thought down. The mere notion caused ice to flood his veins.

It's Benji. Of course it's Benji.

Determined to prove himself right, and terrified of being wrong, John swung himself out of bed, placing his feet on the floor. The air was cold around his exposed ankles and feet. He shivered, but got up and slowly padded over to the door. After taking a breath to steady his nerves, he peeked his head out and gazed down the corridor, holding the lantern before him.

No one was there.

However, Benji's door was also open. John slowly crept down the hallway... then stopped. Whispering was coming from inside Benji's room.

Though the voice was quiet, and the words incomprehensible, John was *certain* it was Benji. He snuck forward, staying light on his feet, and peered into his friend's room.

Benji was inside, standing before one of the windows. The curtains had been pulled back and he was facing outside. John could see the moon beyond the window and just make out the lighthouse standing in the darkness.

'Benji?' John asked, his voice not much more than a whisper itself. 'Are you okay?'

However, Benji just continued his quiet mutterings. John concentrated, but couldn't make out the words. They sounded like a foreign language, though not one he was familiar with. John slowly moved over to his friend.

'Benji, old boy,' he said, a little louder this time. 'What are you looking at?' He placed his hand on his friend's shoulder, and in that instant Benji's whispering ceased. The man drew in a sharp breath and John felt Benji's body stiffen beneath his palm.

John circled around a little and saw that Benji's eyes were only half open—the whites of his eyes were completely bloodshot.

Sleepwalking, John told himself, *has to be.* He felt a wash of relief at the realisation. John had never witnessed it first hand before, and seeing Benji skulk about and whisper to himself like that had certainly been unnerving. But at least there was an explanation.

Then Benji's head began to turn. The half-open eyes seemed to look at John, and a weird, almost sinister smile crossed Benji's lips a moment before the man began to giggle.

John had to force himself not to take a step away. A shudder ran up his spine.

'Come on,' John said soothingly. 'Let's get you back to bed.'

John set his lantern down on Benji's nightstand and then tried to usher the man away from the window. After the slightest bit of resistance, Benji allowed John to guide him. John was then able to assist his friend into the sleeping bag.

It surprised John, seeing just how much Benji was still able to do while obviously still asleep.

Such a strange thing.

Once Benji had laid down, his eyes fully closed. Soon, it looked as if he was fast asleep.

John straightened up and was about to retrieve the lantern, but paused when his eyes fell on the window. John approached it to close the curtains, and as he grabbed a length of cloth in each hand, he looked out.

'What in the world…' he uttered.

John then leaned closer to the glass and squinted. Though the moonlight helped some, much of the lighthouse, and particularly the walkway over to it, was shrouded in darkness.

Even so, John was able to see something standing out on the pier, about midway along its length.

There's no way, John said to himself.

To John, it looked like a person. Little more than a shadow, but with a definite humanoid shape to it.

Whoever it was stood completely motionless, much as Benji had been when he'd been outside of John's room.

However, as John stared, he continued to doubt himself. The shadows seemed to mix together, and his eyes blurred a little. He rubbed them. A soft murmuring from Benji briefly drew his attention, but after seeing his friend settle once again, John turned back to the window. He stared a second time, still unsure.

No, he thought to himself eventually. *There's nothing there.* Try as he might, he couldn't make out the figure any longer. *Because there was nothing there in the first place.*

Satisfied, John closed the curtains, retrieved his lantern, and moved away from the window. The adrenaline from waking with such a start was starting to fade. He realised he didn't even know what time it was, only that it was still the dead of night.

He walked back to his bedroom and checked his watch, which was on the nightstand—a little after three-thirty in the morning. John groaned to himself. *So much for getting a full night's sleep.*

After setting the lantern down, John climbed back into bed, though he kept casting glances toward his curtains. The idea of the lighthouse looming outside played on his mind, as did the figure on the walkway.

There was never a figure there! John was quick to tell himself. Again, the notion that it was a mistake to come to the estate weighed heavily on him.

Once inside his sleeping bag, John pulled the blanket over himself and tried to relax. However, sleep was infuriatingly slow to welcome him, despite the tiredness in John's bones. He lay awake in the darkness, accompanied only by his thoughts. After about thirty minutes of tossing, turning, and staring into the black, John heard something: shuffling, coming from Benji's room. Then there was a *creak* of an opening door.

What now?

Light footsteps on the carpet followed. They drew closer. Then John's own door opened.

Benji, go back to bed!

This time, John didn't hesitate. He sat up and immediately switched on the lantern. The glow emanated far enough to reveal Benji standing in the doorway. John sighed. He had heard you weren't supposed to wake people who were sleepwalking, but this was getting ridiculous.

Benji was now motionless, just staring into the room, eyes again half open. John couldn't be certain, but it seemed like Benji was looking directly at *him*. John just continued to stare right back, waiting for his friend to do something, all the while fighting the urge to get up and shake the man awake.

Eventually, Benji started to shuffle forward. The man's focus seemed to stay with John, though he didn't move towards the bed. Instead, Benji walked to the window, though he kept his eyes trained on John.

He then stopped and took hold of the curtain, hesitated for half a second, then slowly pulled it open.

To John, it seemed like Benji was being careful, as if trying not to wake John, despite him sitting upright with his light on.

So strange.

John wondered what kind of dream his friend was currently lost in. In fact, John realised his anger and unease had faded, and he now watched his friend with something approaching amusement. He suddenly looked forward to telling Benji about all this the following morning. It then occurred to him that maybe he should film everything, so that Benji would have no choice but to believe him, but he stopped himself from reaching for his phone—it didn't seem right. *He's already going to be really embarrassed about this.*

Finally, Benji's head slowly turned away from John and towards the window. The man stared through the glass, swaying slightly.

Then the whispering began again. As before, the words were incomprehensible—certainly not English. John tried and failed to place the language. It wasn't French, nor German, and didn't seem to have any other kind of European feel to it, as far as John could tell. However, John knew he was far from an expert in other languages. But Benji wasn't either, which made things all the more puzzling. Benji's mutterings just sounded like gibberish.

Though that in itself made sense. *He's just babbling in his sleep.*

But the longer John listened, the more unsure he became. Somehow, the words sounded... deliberate. Sometimes repeated, and spoken with a kind of quiet confidence. It did sound like Benji *knew* what he was saying, even if John didn't.

No, it's babble, John told himself confidently. It was the only explanation. He again thought about recording his friend, and again felt guilty about it, so held off.

Benji leaned his face closer to the glass.

The man's hand raised, and he began to... wave. John couldn't help but smile. *Who does he think is out there?*

A sudden urge to look outside as well overcame John. He slowly wiggled from his bag and stood up, careful not to startle his sleeping friend. Benji continued his waving. The gesture wasn't large or sweeping, just a simple curling and uncurling of his fingers, over and over again. Benji then chuckled. It was almost childlike.

John moved as close as he could to his friend and stared outside. It was difficult to make anything out in the darkness, especially with the light from the lantern reflecting on the glass before him. John quickly switched the lantern off and looked out again. It was still hard to see much. He glanced to Benji, then back outside, and tried to gauge Benji's eye-line. The man seemed to be staring at the lighthouse. Specifically, at the top of the lighthouse. John leaned closer to the glass, trying to discern more, but the lighthouse itself was little more than a silhouette.

John felt a breath on his neck.

He froze, then slowly turned his head. Benji was looking directly at him. The man's head had twisted ninety degrees, with his body still facing forward. A chill ran up John's spine as a manic grin spread across Benji's face.

John backed up.

More childlike giggling came from Benji, but this time it seemed to carry a sinister undertone.

He's... laughing at me.

Both Benji's hands were down at his sides. The waving had stopped, and now he just continued to stare at John with half-open eyes, giggling. John shuffled back even more, and Benji's head followed, though his body still didn't turn, meaning Benji's head continued to rotate farther and farther around unnaturally.

'Benji!' John suddenly bellowed, yet Benji continued laughing. 'Benji!' John yelled again. His friend still didn't snap out of it.

Enough of this.

John grabbed Benji by the shoulders and shook him, gently at first, then with more vigour. 'Wake up!'

Suddenly, Benji's hands shot out and grabbed hold of John's t-shirt. In the same instant, his eyes snapped open, startled, and he sucked in a sharp breath.

John felt his friend's fingers dig into his skin at the same time the grip tightened.

'Wha...' Benji slurred. His eyes then darted around. 'No! Stop!'

John saw Benji's body stiffen until he focused back on John. There was no recognition there. 'Leave me alone!' Benji shouted, causing John to jump in shock. 'Just leave me...' But then Benji trailed off, and his grip loosened ever so slightly. 'J... John?' he asked in confusion.

'It's me,' John replied, breathing heavily. 'Are... are you okay?'

Benji then looked around. He frowned. 'Where... where am I?'

'You're in my room, old friend. You've been... well, sleep-walking.'

Benji's head snapped back to John, his frown deepening. 'Huh?'

John gave a forced chuckle. 'You didn't tell me you were prone to wandering around in the night.'

'I...' Benji shook his head, clearly confused. 'I *don't*,' he finally said. He looked around again. 'At least... I don't think I do.'

John knew Benji was single and lived alone, so it made sense he might not be aware of what he did in his sleep, especially if it happened infrequently. *Twice in one night isn't infrequent*, John then told himself.

'What say we get you back to your own bed, eh, old boy?'

Benji paused for a moment, his expression still plagued with confusion. He eventually nodded. 'Yeah, that would be... good.' John made sure to pull the curtains closed before the two of them moved out into the hallway. Just as they stepped out, Benji turned to him. 'It's okay,' he said, sounding more confident. More like himself. 'I can go back on my own.'

'I don't doubt it,' John replied. 'Just wanted to help in case you were a little disoriented.'

'I... was, I guess.' Benji gave his head a little shake. 'But I'm okay now. Just... perplexed. I had no idea I did that kind of thing.' He hesitated for a moment. 'Was I... doing anything else?'

John cocked his head to the side 'What do you mean?'

'You know,' Benji replied. 'When people sleepwalk, they sometimes do other things. They talk. I've heard some can have full semi-coherent conversations. I even knew of one fella who unfortunately urinated in his closet, thinking it was a toilet—' Benji stopped and his eyes went wide. 'Oh God. John... I didn't *piss* anywhere, did I?'

John had to stifle a laugh. 'Of course not,' he said. 'At least, not that I noticed.'

32

Benji nodded, obviously relieved. Then he frowned. 'But who knows what I was up to before I came to your room.'

'Ah, well,' John began. 'This is actually the second time tonight you've been up and about.'

'The *second?*' Benji asked.

'Afraid so. A little while ago, I woke up to find you standing just outside my room, staring in. I took you back to bed, but it seems you had unfinished business.' John tried to keep his tone jovial and playful, but his friend didn't smile at all.

Benji shook his head. It almost seemed like he was disappointed with himself. 'Is there... anything else?'

John was torn, unsure if he should share more, if only to save his friend's pride. But in the end, he decided to be honest. 'Well, you were... whispering quite a bit. Having some kind of conversation. Though, it was just gibberish. Don't worry, you didn't divulge any deeply buried secrets.' John had said it with a grin, but again, Benji's face was serious.

'Whispering, huh? Brilliant.' He sighed 'That everything?'

'Well, almost,' John said. 'You... seemed to have a fascination with the windows.'

'The windows?'

'Actually, that isn't accurate,' John said. 'You were looking through them out to the lighthouse, I think. After I woke and found you looking at me the first time, I followed you back to your room and saw you looking out at the lighthouse. And then after I put you back to bed, you came in and went over to my window. You were even... waving.'

'Waving?'

'Yes,' John replied with a nod. 'No idea who to. Someone at the top of the lighthouse, I think. In your dream, of course. There was no one out there.'

'No… no, of course not. I'm just surprised and confused. Bit of a worry, really. Is this going to be a regular thing?'

John just shrugged. It was a hypothetical question, of course, yet he couldn't think what to say. It was only then John realised the same could happen again the next couple of nights, making the creepy vibe in the house even creepier.

Oh God.

'Not to worry,' John said with a forced smile. 'I'll just tie you to your bedposts.'

That, finally, elicited a chuckle from Benji. 'Thank you,' he said drily. 'Most kind. Keep me leashed like a dog, eh? But what about when I go home? What will I do then?'

'Not my problem,' John joked. 'You'll have to tie yourself up.'

'You're a real good friend, John, you know that?' Benji said as he rolled his eyes. However, he was smiling.

'When you get back, go to the doctor,' John suggested. 'See what they say. Lots of people sleepwalk. As long as you're aware of it, then I have no doubt it will be manageable. Just, maybe put a lock on your closet, so you don't go peeing in your shoes.'

'Again… a good friend. Thank you.'

John playfully slapped him on the back. 'I'm here to help. Now go and get yourself back to bed. Try to sleep some.'

'What time is it?' Benji asked. Then his eyes widened again. 'How long until dawn?'

John felt his stomach sink—it wouldn't be too long now. He quickly went to check his watch and sighed. 'We have around an hour and a half before it starts to get light, I'd say,' he called back.

Pointless trying to sleep now.

He walked back to Benji. 'I'm going to be honest,' Benji said. 'My mind is wired at the moment. I don't see me falling asleep anytime soon. At least, not quick enough to make it worth it.'

'No,' John said with resignation, 'I agree. It's a waste of time even trying. So... I guess we're up?'

'You don't sound very enthused.'

'I'm not,' John stated. 'I feel like I'm running on empty, and the second day hasn't even started yet.'

'Good thing I brought lots of coffee.'

Cheap, instant coffee, John thought to himself, but just nodded. 'Let's hope it does enough. Now, I'm going to wash up and get ready. I'll give you a knock when I'm done.'

'Sounds good,' Benji said and stepped out of the room. He paused, then turned back. 'John,' he began, sounding sheepish.

'Hmmm,' John replied.

'Would you mind... keeping this whole thing to yourself? The sleepwalking, I mean. I have to admit, I'm a tad embarrassed about it, and the thought of our friends finding out isn't a pleasant one.'

John smiled. 'Of course.' Then he raised a finger. 'Though next time you're hopping on your high horse or getting too big for your britches, just remember this. I can keep a secret... as long as you don't annoy me too much.'

A worried look flashed over Benji's face. 'Oh... erm, of course. I—'

'I'm kidding,' John said. 'Now go, get yourself set for the day. I'll see you in a few minutes.'

'Will do,' Benji replied, expression relieved. 'Thanks.' He then set off.

John let out a long exhale and rubbed the back of his neck. *Come on, John,* he said to himself. *Just get through it. It's only a few days.*

Just a little bit longer.

35

5

1-5

MOVING ALONG THE PIER MADE JOHN UNEASY. ESPECIALLY looking down at the sea on either side. The stone structure was easily fifteen feet wide, so he stuck to the centre and had no worries about falling in. He just didn't like being surrounded by so much water—it was unnatural. John had never been one for pools or swimming, either. He preferred the solid certainty terra firma offered underfoot.

Still, he couldn't deny Benji had been right about what he'd called the 'magic hour' of dawn. The sky behind the lighthouse was a mix of dark pinks and burning oranges, and John had just spotted the sun cresting over the horizon. It set the lighthouse against a glorious background that would no doubt look fantastic when photographed.

Benji was currently crouched down beside John, snapping away on his camera and aiming the long lens out toward the lighthouse.

Though the sound of the sea had been relaxing while inside the main house, out in the open it was much louder and more immediate. Even threatening. And the constant cries of circling seagulls were annoying as well, though John knew that was mostly because he was tired and irritable. The one good thing about being outside was the refreshing blasts of salty sea air regularly hitting him, filling his lungs, and helping energise him.

He looked again at the towering lighthouse, remembering how Benji had waved at it the previous night.

Doesn't matter, it's empty, John told himself.

However, he then remembered the figure he'd also seen out on the pier, roughly where they both now stood.

There was no figure. What are you doing to yourself?

John rubbed his eyes while his hair was whipped about by the wind. He waited patiently for Benji to finish. Eventually, the other man rose to his feet and let the camera hang by the strapping around his neck.

'Get what you need?' John asked.

Benji nodded. 'Oh yes,' he said as he started out towards the lighthouse. 'A perfect morning. The shots will come out brilliantly.'

Maybe not 'perfect,' John thought. But it certainly was a fine morning, weather-wise, if not for the wind. There were some clouds in the sky, but John had a feeling they would add to the atmosphere of the shots, not that he really had an eye for that kind of thing.

'Okay,' Benji said. He turned to John with an excited grin. 'Let's check out the inside. You have the key?'

John pulled the long iron key from his coat pocket and jiggled it. 'Unfortunately,' he said dourly.

Benji just laughed and motioned the way forward. 'After you.'

The two men continued on while John surveyed the small island the lighthouse sat on. He was able to see a huge stone plinth that had been cast into the rock to give the building a foundation. John couldn't imagine how much work had been involved in hollowing out the rock and placing such a large footing. He suddenly imagined entering the tower, only to have it topple from the plinth the moment he was at the very top. He quickly chastised himself. *That thing has been standing for a long time. I hardly think it's going to fall now.*

The iron door at the base of the lighthouse was old and rectangular, big enough only for a single person to pass at a time. A large ring handle and keyhole was set at waist height. John slipped the key in the door and found it unlocked easily. He looked to Benji—who still wore an excited grin— then pushed.

The heavy door creaked and squeaked as it swung inwards, opening up to the dark interior, though most of the shadows were quickly pushed back by the invading sunlight. Once his eyes adjusted, John was able to see the back wall.

He guessed the inside diameter of the lighthouse was around ten feet. He and Benji both pulled out their torches, flicked them on, and stepped inside.

The air had the same stale quality that the main house had, only worse. The walls inside were bare red brick, and a spiral staircase corkscrewed up the centre of the space and cored through the concrete ceiling overhead.

The ground floor was mostly sparse, save for two old-looking crates, each with dirty cloth draped over them.

'Everything you'd hoped?' John asked his friend. 'Because there isn't much to see.'

'It's great!' Benji replied. 'I can almost *feel* the history seeping out of the walls around us.'

John couldn't feel anything, but slowly cast his light around in an arc.

'What's that?' Benji said. John turned to his friend and

saw him pointing to the cast concrete floor and gesturing between the two crates. John aimed his light.

The uneven, blemished concrete was covered in a thin layer of dirt and dust, so he was quickly able to see what his friend was referring to: marks in the dirt, as if someone had quickly run their fingers back and forth over the surface.

'Looks like someone was clawing at the floor,' John said.

'It does,' Benji agreed.

'How long do you think those marks have been here?'

Benji shrugged. 'I have no idea.'

John stepped closer and saw dark stains in with the claw marks, and he had the horrible notion they were the stains of old blood. An image of someone digging into the concrete so hard their fingers bled popped into his mind. *It's not blood, though. It's just dirt. Has to be.*

'Let me get some more shots,' Benji said.

John looked at his flashlight. 'Do you need me to switch off my light?' His question was answered as Benji quickly clicked off his own light.

John moved behind his friend and leaned against the far wall. Benji then started to snap away, checking the screen of the digital device after every shot. After a moment, the man ushered John to a different spot so he could get more photos.

'Happy?' John asked while Benji stood staring at the LCD screen. But Benji's face was fixed in a frown. 'The light comes out weird,' he said while nodding to the open door. 'Some of the shots are okay, but most look weirdly smudged. Not sure why. I thought the stream of daylight would cast a nice effect.' Benji then pulled out a flash accessory and clipped it to the top of the camera. 'Hey, pull the door closed, would you?'

John cocked an eyebrow. 'Closed?' he asked. 'But then it will be pitch black. We won't be able to see a thing.'

'It'll only be a few minutes,' Benji replied. 'I just want to take a few shots with the flash.'

'But… how will you know what you're pointing at?'

'John, we're standing in a circular room with barely anything in it. There isn't much to think about. Just pull the door closed.'

John sighed and pushed himself off the wall before walking to the door. He placed his hand on it, then hesitated. He knew it was irrational, but deliberately plunging themselves into utter darkness, even for a short space of time, seemed *wrong*. It was like they were inviting trouble.

Regardless, he swung the door shut. It settled into the frame with a dull *thud*.

John was pleasantly surprised to see some light from the glass structure at the tip of the lighthouse had found its way down through the spiral staircase, though it wasn't quite enough to illuminate the outer perimeter of the space they stood in.

Click.

A bright flash quickly lit the area for an instant.

Click.

Then again. The explosion of light lasted less than half a second, though it was enough to disorient John each time.

'Can you turn down the strength of the flash?' John asked. 'If you keep going like that, you'll burn out my retinas.'

'Fair point,' Benji said. 'It's too bright for the images, anyway, so I'll dial it back.'

After fiddling with his camera for a second, Benji began to snap again, and while the light was still bright, it was much easier to handle. Regardless, he still saw small motes float about in his vision. He blinked a few times to clear them.

Click. Click. Click.

'Okay,' Benji said, 'Circle round a little, please, so I don't get you in the shot.'

John shuffled around as ordered, keeping his back pressed against the wall. He felt like a spare part. 'Wouldn't it be easier for you if I just head back to the house? I feel like I'm in the way.'

'You can go back, certainly,' Benji replied. 'I don't mind. Do you trust me enough to leave me alone here, though?'

John sighed. *Damn it.* 'Maybe. But... I'm not going to.'

Benji laughed. 'Thought you'd say something like that. Let me get a few more images, and then we'll head up to the next level.'

'Can't wait,' John quipped.

As he stepped around a little more, John hit a cold spot. It was enough to make him shiver, but he held his ground as Benji took more shots.

Click.

A flash.

Click.

A flash.

Click.

A person.

John's body locked in fright.

'What is it?' Benji asked.

Though darkness had again settled, in his mind's eye John could still see the figure. He stood frozen, locked with fear.

John had only gotten the tiniest of glances, but had seen a tall, looming, and shadowy person in his peripheral vision. He pressed his back firmly into the wall as he struggled to breathe.

It can't have been, he told himself. *You're wrong. You have to be.*

'I... I saw someone,' John eventually choked out, his voice a strained whisper.

'You... what?' Benji asked, confusion evident.

John's heart hammered in his chest. His throat felt tight. The logical part of his brain tried to argue that what he'd seen was impossible.

That was no illusion. He was sure. He even remembered seeing the reflective glint of two eyes.

'John, you didn't see—'

'I did!' John shouted, still pushing himself back into the wall, almost willing himself to be able to phase through it to get outside.

He heard Benji sigh. There was another bright flash, causing John's body to lock up again, expecting to see the figure.

But... he saw no one. Only Benji. Who looked at him sceptically.

Click. Another flash. Nothing.

Just an empty space. He then saw Benji cross to the door, and there was a long *creak* as the man pulled it open. A wash of daylight again flooded inside, filling the space. Benji then clicked on his flashlight and slowly shone it around the room, revealing every dark area.

'See, John,' he said, sounding annoyed. 'Nothing here.' Benji's judgmental eyes then settled on John. His eyebrows were raised expectantly, waiting for an answer.

'I... I saw someone. I know I did,' John insisted.

'You didn't,' Benji replied. 'This room is... what... ten feet across. There's nowhere for anyone to hide. *No one* is here with us, John.'

'But—'

'*No,*' Benji snapped, holding up a hand as he shook his head. 'You didn't see anyone, because no one is here. And don't even start to explain it as some kind of supernatural occurrence. The light startled you and caused you to see a weird shadow. That's it. The only explanation.'

But John was unwilling to accept that—*I know what I saw.* He quickly remembered the previous night, when he'd spotted a figure out on the stone walkway as well.

'I'm not imagining it,' John said, though he could feel the doubt in his voice beginning to creep in. Benji just continued to stare, unbelieving, clearly annoyed. 'I'm not!' John insisted.

Benji gave a slow, disappointed nod. 'Then go back to the house,' he said. 'If you're so unnerved, just leave. I'll be fine on my own.'

John opened his mouth to respond. In truth, he *did* want to get out of the lighthouse. He was still pressing himself back into the wall, worried that the figure might reappear. After a few deep breaths, he began to force himself to calm down.

Am I just being stupid?

His gut was again telling him to flee. For *both* of them to flee.

But Benji's judgemental stare had started to wear down John's certainty. The fact he hadn't gotten a clear look at the shadowy person, that it had all been in his periphery, was difficult to ignore. Could it have been a trick of the light as Benji had said?

'Well?' Benji asked. 'Am I working here alone this morning? Because I need to keep moving, so if you're going to slow me down—'

'I'm fine,' John eventually said, and pushed himself away from the wall. He took a breath. *It* was *in your head. Get it together, John.*

He hadn't wholly convinced himself, but Benji had lit the whole area, and no one had been there. As worried as John was, he knew Benji was likely right. So he decided to press on with the job at hand: standing around and watching Benji work.

'You sure?' Benji asked, cocking his head to the side and narrowing his eyes on John. 'You look a little shaken.'

'Like you said, trick of the light or something. I... erm... I'm sorry for causing a scene. I think I'm still tired.'

Benji gave a tight-lipped smile. 'Yeah, which is my fault for wandering around all night. Apologies, my friend. Sounds like you're running on empty because of me. Seriously, if you need to go back and rest—'

'No, that won't be necessary.' John shook his head, both in emphasis and also to shake loose the last fog of worry he was feeling. 'I'm happy to press on.' Benji continued to look at John, clearly unsure. John made a gesture with his hands to hurry Benji on. 'Come on,' he said, 'Let's keep going and get what you need. Don't worry about me.'

Eventually, Benji nodded. 'If you say so. I'm finished down here, so we can work our way up. Leave the door open for now.'

John was happy to hear that, not wanting the lighthouse to be any darker than it was. 'Well, it's your show,' he said, trying to hide his relief.

The two men proceeded up the spiral staircase; Benji took the lead, moving with slow and steady steps. John had expected the staircase to feel wobbly as they climbed, but it was firm and secure.

While the ground-floor space didn't have any obvious use besides maybe storage, the utility of the mid-floor was clear: it was a living and sleeping space.

A small, single, wood-framed bed was present, though it had only had a mattress set on it, with no covers or blankets. On the other side of the space was a basic desk that consisted of a flat wooden surface set on thin metal legs. A wooden seat was set just in front of it, with two other seats nearby. There was also a small chest of drawers, which Benji immediately began to look through, pulling each of the three out from top to bottom.

'Empty,' he said.

One thing John did notice was that the internal circumference of the tower remained constant between stories, whereas externally, the lighthouse was conical in shape. It meant the walls thinned out as the building rose up.

Also, now they were in a living space, John again became aware of the lack of windows.

Benji took more of his photos. 'How's the light here?' John asked. Being on the middle floor, they were getting more light-spill from the glass on the storey above them.

'Not bad,' Benji said. He clicked his flash again, then turned it down, snapped some more, and checked the screen again, giving a satisfied nod. A moment later, Benji looked up. 'Should be quite a view up there,' he said.

John nodded. 'On one side, maybe. Nothing but sea out to the other.'

'Still a nice view,' Benji insisted. 'You don't find watching the ocean waves calming?'

John shrugged. 'Can't say I've ever thought about it.'

His friend chuckled. 'You need to get out more.'

They began their ascent and soon reached the top. John paused for a second. Benji was right: the sight around them *was* impressive, especially considering the dawn skyline around them.

'Okay, fine,' John said. 'I guess you had a point.'

To the west, John could see the land stretch away from the shore, which only served to remind him just how far away from civilisation they were. The nearest buildings looked like little white dots on the landscape.

'We're in the lantern,' Benji stated.

John turned to him and cocked an eyebrow. 'Excuse me?'

Benji held his arms out wide and looked around. 'This enclosure with the glass walls,' he said. 'It's known as the lantern.'

'Ah, good to know,' John said, not really meaning it.

Benji then gestured to the huge light in the centre of the room. 'And that's the lamp.'

John stared at the apparatus. He'd never seen the actual light in a lighthouse before. It stood on a rotating plinth, and the top of the light was about as high as his head. He noted the lens was roughly disc shaped, with lots of overlapping lenses held together by thin sections of metal bracing. Staring close, he saw large bulbs inside the dust-covered lens.

'Don't suppose this thing still works,' John said, tapping the glass.

'No, I don't suppose it does,' Benji said. 'Still fascinating to see. Now, please keep out of the way. I want to get the last of my photos. Just *look* at that sky. Amazing, no?'

John just nodded. He had no doubt the shots up in the lantern would be fantastic. Though he had initially been resistant about such an early start, John now completely understood Benji's thinking. In a book where the images inside made all the difference, shots like the ones he was getting were pure gold.

As Benji was working, John frowned and tilted his head to listen—he heard a long, slow *creak*.

Is that the...

The door beneath closed shut. John cast a confused frown at Benji, then moved to the staircase to look down. He couldn't see the door from his position, but there was no light below other than what washed down from the lighthouse's glass walls.

'The door!' John exclaimed.

Benji just looked at him and shrugged. 'So? It's probably just the wind.'

John looked down again with a frown. 'But... the door swung inward. There was no wind *inside* the lighthouse.'

'John!' Benji snapped as his head dropped back. He sighed. 'The wind probably blew in, whipped around, and shut the door. It's no big deal.'

'The door is pretty heavy.'

'And the sea winds can get pretty strong.'

'But we would have felt it from up here.'

'No!' Benji stated through gritted teeth. 'We *wouldn't*. We're three floors up. Now, will you just calm down? You're starting to panic again. I can see it on your face.'

John stared at his friend, then took a deep breath. *He's... he's right,* John told himself. *Your mind's running away with itself.* The door had closed slowly, as if drifting shut. Still, his point about the door being heavy was valid. It would have taken a considerable gust to force it to move in the first place. John was certain he would have heard that, regardless of how far up they were. But he knew he was alone in his fears, and letting himself needlessly worry wouldn't help him get through the rest of the trip.

Just let it go... for now.

'Fine,' John eventually said. He gestured to Benji. 'Keep going.'

Benji hesitated for a moment, watching John, before he got back to work. The man took far more pictures on the top storey than on the other two, which made sense, given there was more to see up there. However, it was still a small space, so it didn't take long for Benji to finish.

'I want to get back out here later today as well,' Benji said. 'Get the same kind of photos, but in normal daylight. Just for variety.'

John gave a quick nod. He didn't look forward to coming

back, but knew that was why they were there. He couldn't avoid spending time in the lighthouse… unless he wanted to leave Benji to work alone. However, his employers had ordered him to be alongside Benji at all times.

Guess leaving him alone isn't an option.

'So… what's next?' John asked.

'I want to tour the rest of the estate. It would be good to have a snoop around, see what we can find, get some more photos. We do have free rein here, right?'

'Yes,' John confirmed. 'Mr. Barrow said there was nothing of value left, so as long as we don't damage any of the buildings or structures, we're fine.'

'Then let's get to it.' Benji paused for a moment. 'You're… okay, right?'

John frowned. 'Of course.'

'Just… with what you thought you saw downstairs, and then with the door—'

'Honestly, I'm fine,' John stated. 'I just freaked myself out, but I'll be fine. Like you said, there's nothing here.' As John spoke, he felt like he was trying to convince himself more than Benji.

The pair moved slowly back down the stairs, Benji leading. John didn't like being at the rear. He kept glancing back up, expecting to see something behind them, maybe a figure just standing there looking back at him.

However, they reached the ground floor without incident. Once there, Benji approached the door and took hold of the handle.

He pulled, but nothing happened.

John saw Benji frown in confusion. The man pulled again, hard, and the door shunted on its hinges… but it didn't open. John felt panic rise, though he made a concerted effort to keep it in check.

'Everything okay?' he asked.

Benji pulled again with the same result. 'Stupid door is stuck,' he said. Though he was obviously trying to keep his voice even, John picked up on the first hint of doubt and worry in his friend's tone since they'd arrived.

'Strange,' John said. He looked at the handle to see if there was any kind of thumb-turn lever, but there wasn't. The door hadn't been locked, so there was no good reason it wouldn't open.

'Maybe the weather made the door expand in its frame,' Benji said. John frowned. *Only heat makes metal expand,* he thought to himself, *and it isn't hot.* He didn't say anything, however.

A cold sensation then crept over John. He held out his torch and slowly moved it around the room, though he saw nothing.

Keep calm, he told himself—the icy, snaking tendrils of worry began to work their way up his spine.

Benji pulled again and again, harder and harder each time. The door juddered in its frame but still wouldn't open. 'What in the...' Benji said, before giving. He crouched down to examine the handle. 'Maybe the latch is broken, from when the wind blew the door closed.'

John considered that. Though the door hadn't closed particularly hard, he supposed if the lock was old enough, it was certainly a possibility.

'That doesn't help us get out of here, though,' he said. 'And the door's too thick to break down. With no windows here, we're stuck.'

Benji cast John a disapproving frown. 'We aren't stuck,' he replied.

John just shook his head in annoyance. 'What else would you call it? We can't open the door and it's our only way out. We're stuck!'

'*Temporarily,*' Benji replied. He shone his light in the small gap between the side of the door and the frame, obviously trying to look at the latch.

'What can you see?' John asked.

'Not much,' Benji replied. 'The gap is too thin.' He stood back up and sighed. 'Okay, we need to find something long and thin. Once we do, I'll try to wiggle it in the gap and ease the latch open.'

John looked around the near-empty space. He held back a sigh. 'Not exactly an array of instruments here to choose from, is there?'

'We'll check upstairs too,' Benji replied. 'There might be something we missed.' He then led the way over to the stairs again.

The main door suddenly shifted in its frame, startling the two men. John's body immediately tensed up and he sucked in a breath. Both of them sent their flashlight beams over at the door.

'Did… did someone *kick* it?' John asked in shock. 'Sounded like someone kicked the door from outside.'

'Don't be ridiculous,' Benji replied, though the doubt was back in his voice. 'Just the wind beating against it.'

John didn't say anything. *You're using the wind to explain an awful lot here,* he thought.

Both men waited for a moment, with John fully expecting something else to happen, but after about twenty seconds, Benji turned to the stairs again. 'Come on,' he said, 'let's find something to use on the door. The quicker we do that, the quicker we'll be out of here.'

John didn't like it. He didn't like any of it. And it was getting harder and harder to explain away what was happening. However, he forced his worries back down. At the end of the day, panic would help neither of them, and it *was* possible Benji was right: that everything was completely explainable.

The two men searched the mid-floor, but as John had expected, they found nothing usable. Then they ventured back up to the top. However, that space was almost completely bare, save for the large lamp.

Shit, John cursed internally. He'd already known they wouldn't find anything, but even so, his spirits deflated. 'Now what?' he asked, letting his irritation show.

Benji moved his light uselessly around the area, as if that would magic up a usable tool. Finally, he looked over to the lamp.

'Think we can get some of that metal framing off?' he asked with a nod over at the apparatus.

John paused. 'We can't start dismantling things like that!' he stated. 'That's certainly within the bounds of breaking and damaging the buildings. I'll be fired.'

'We'll put it back together once we get the door open,' Benji said, still looking over the metalwork.

'Would you even know how to begin?'

'Can't be that hard.'

John shook his head. 'And do you have tools with you to fix it? No, you don't. We don't even have anything to take it apart. It's pointless to even think about.'

Benji stood back up and sighed. 'Fair point,' he conceded. 'But we need to figure something out, bec—'

'Shhh!' John quickly said, cocking his head. His eyes widened. 'Do you hear that?' he asked, dropping his voice to a whisper.

Benji frowned and tilted his own head to the side as well. Both men listened. A second later, John saw Benji's eyes widen a little.

He hears it too.

John was somewhat relieved he wasn't imagining it... and also unnerved.

'What *is* that?' Benji asked quietly.

John continued to listen. 'It's... whispering,' he replied, keeping his own voice low.

He peered down the staircase, looking at the stairs spiral down into the darkness. The voices were coming from below.

The words were indecipherable, and so quiet he could barely hear them. John was reminded of how Benji had been talking in his sleep. After a moment, Benji moved up next to John and looked down over the handrail as well.

'How do you explain that?' John whispered, pointing down.

Benji continued to stare, yet he didn't answer. The man then slowly tilted forward. John saw Benji's face and noticed a weird expression wash over it. Benji's eyelids dropped so that his eyes were only half open and he had a far-off stare— it was like he wasn't focusing on anything, just... staring. To John, it almost looked like his friend had fallen into a trance.

'Hey,' John whispered and nudged him. 'You okay?' Benji didn't respond, didn't even seem to notice the question. The strange whispering continued. Then, John was certain he heard the shuffling of feet. His heart froze.

'Jesus Christ,' he uttered. *Am I imagining this?* Part of him dearly hoped he was. Summoning all the mental strength he could, John lowered his arm over the railing and shone his flashlight farther down into the inky depths. The light pushed some of the shadows away, allowing him to just make out the floor far below. He then slowly rotated the light to reveal more of the space on the ground floor. Other than the crates, it seemed empty. As he was concentrating, John suddenly realised the whispering had stopped.

After a moment, John heard the *creak* of the main door slowly drift open, allowing daylight to spill inside once more.

What the hell?

He thrust out an arm, grabbed Benji by the collar, and shook his friend. 'We need to go!' he shouted.

Benji shook his head. His eyes fell on John, regaining focus once more. 'Huh?' he asked, clearly confused.

'Didn't you hear that?' John asked. 'The whispering and movement?'

'I...' Benji frowned and lowered his eyes. 'What do you mean?'

'The *whispering*, Benji!' John exclaimed. 'The bloody whispering that was just happening down *there!*' He jabbed a finger over the handrail. 'You heard it—I know you did.'

Benji continued to stare down. 'The door's open,' he said, as if realising for the first time.

'Yes,' John said, and pulled at his friend, 'which means we need to go. We have to move, before the bloody thing closes on us again.' Without waiting for a response, John pulled Benji over to the stairs and hurried down, careful not to fall, but going as quickly as he safely could.

The two men descended, spiralling down past the mid-floor and finally arriving at the ground floor. John had kept his eyes on the door the whole time, half-expecting it to slam shut again, while at the same time willing it to stay open. He also didn't want to look into the shadows, for fear of what he might see.

Eventually, the pair emerged outside into the daylight. John didn't stop running until he was halfway down the long pier, where waves crashed on either side of him.

'John, stop!' Benji shouted.

He finally pulled up, gasping for breath, legs weak. He turned to face his friend, who still looked utterly confused. Beyond Benji, John could see the lighthouse, where the door still hung open.

'What's going on?' Benji demanded.

'What do you *mean* what's going on?' John asked, incredulous. 'The... the bloody whispering. We heard it! Down onto the bottom floor. *You* heard it!'

Benji hesitated, frowned, then shook his head. 'You sure? I... don't remember that.'

John's eyes widened. He almost gasped. *He's lying. Has to be.* 'What do you *mean?* How can you not remember? It was only minutes ago. We were standing at the top'—John pointed over at the lighthouse—'and heard voices at the bottom. You heard it. You *did.* You even asked me what it was, so don't you try to deny it.'

Benji held up his hands. 'John,' he said calmly, 'I don't know what you're talking about. I remember hearing... something... at the bottom, but it definitely wasn't voices. Maybe the wind or something.' John clenched his teeth. *The fucking wind again!* 'So just slow down,' Benji went on.

John just shook his head and gave a humourless laugh. 'Then explain the door opening on its own? That doesn't make sense, you saw how stuck it was.'

'I...' Benji paused for a moment. 'I don't actually remember what happened when it opened. I... kind of have a black spot in my brain from back there.'

'And don't you find that strange in itself?' John asked. 'You looked like you were zoned out, like you were in a trance. You were just... staring. It reminded me of when you were sleepwalking last night.'

'I just... don't remember.'

John threw his hands up. 'It doesn't matter,' he said. 'We're out. And we're going home. Now. Come on, let's pack up and get on the road.'

Now Benji's eyes widened. 'What?'

'We're going!' John stated firmly. 'I'm not arguing about it, Benji. That's just what's happening. Make your peace with it and let's move.'

John turned and began to walk away.

'Wait,' Benji called. John heard his friend's hurried footsteps, then felt Benji take hold of his shoulder and spin John around. 'You can't be serious,' Benji said.

'Of *course* I'm serious!' John shouted. 'Why on earth would we stay after what just happened?' John turned, yet Benji quickly spun him again.

'But nothing actually happened, John. I told you, I didn't hear any voices.'

John balled his fists in anger. 'Because you weren't with it!' he snapped. 'You were in dreamland. But *I* was with it, Benji. *I* heard it all.'

'John,' Benji said, hands up again as if trying to calm a hysterical child, which only served to anger John all the more. 'Let's be honest, you've not really been yourself since late last night. You've been getting spooked out by the littlest things, letting your imagination run away with itself—'

'*I've* not been myself?' John cut in. '*Me?* Is that supposed to be funny? You're dropping into trances for no reason, wandering around at night while asleep, yet *I'm* the problem here?' He shook his head, laughing without humour. 'I can't believe what I'm hearing.'

'So I zoned out,' Benji said, as if it wasn't a big deal. 'I'm tired. We both are. It happens.'

'It doesn't fucking happen, Benji,' John snapped. He narrowed his eyes on his friend. 'Look,' he began, 'I know you want to stay, but you need to face reality here: there are strange things happening. Whether you heard the whispering or not, *I* did. There were voices inside that bloody lighthouse. That's not opinion. There were. So, I'm not staying here any longer.' He turned and started to walk away once more. Benji grabbed him a third time, but John angrily shrugged him off. 'Don't try to talk me out of it, Benji,' John said. 'The trip is done. I'm leaving. If you don't want to, then you need to make alternative arrangements to get home, because I'll leave you behind.'

'You wouldn't,' Benji said, keeping pace.

'Watch me.'

'What about your job?' Benji asked. 'Didn't Mr. Barrow want us to look at the place, so there was a record of the place before it gets torn down?'

'I don't care,' John shot back… though it wasn't quite true. 'Everyone will understand.'

'Really?' Benji asked, suddenly sounding confident. 'They'll understand that you heard some voices and forced us to leave because you got scared over nothing?'

John stopped. He turned on Benji, eyes glaring and jaw clenched. 'Stop it,' he snapped. 'Just stop it. I don't know why you're so dead set on staying, but it's madness. Absolute insanity. And the mental leaps you're making to justify everything make no sense.'

'There's only one person here making mental leaps,' Benji shot back. 'And they're all to justify how scared you are. Scared of nothing, might I add. We can't run away just because you're spooked.'

'Well, that's what's happening,' John said.

'And your employers?' Benji asked again as he folded his arms cross his chest. 'What will you tell them? Surely the truth, if you're so certain of it?'

John paused. 'I'll tell them something,' he replied, waving his hand dismissively. 'I'll say I fell ill and we had to leave.'

'Ah-ha!' Benji explained, raising his finger. 'See, you're too scared to tell people the *real* reason you want to run. And do you know why that is, John? Because you're scared of what they'll think of you.'

'I don't care what people will think of me.'

'Yes you do,' Benji went on. 'Especially your employers and Mr. Barrow. You know they'll judge you if you told them what you think you saw. Because they'll think you imagined it all... which you did.'

'That's not true.'

'It is. If not, feel free to tell them the whole truth. Tell them everything, John.' Benji waited for a moment and gave him a chance to reply, but John stayed quiet, so Benji went on, 'Ask yourself why you're so ashamed of admitting it to them.'

'People will believe what they want,' John said, his voice a little quieter. 'But I know what happened, and I won't put myself in danger by staying. Me lying about why we left makes no difference.'

Benji, with his arms still folded, narrowed his eyes. 'Then I'll write to Mr. Barrow, and your employers, and tell them everything.'

John's jaw fell open. He glared at Benji. 'You... you wouldn't.'

Benji's eyes fell to the ground as he slowly unfolded his arms. John saw shame wash over Benji's face.

'I'm... afraid I would, old boy,' Benji replied quietly. 'I wouldn't be proud of it, but... I need this.'

John's fists tightened by his sides. 'You need your precious work more than our friendship?'

Benji slowly shook his head. 'It's not like that. It's not just my 'precious work.' It's my entire livelihood, John. And things... aren't going so well. In all honesty, I'm really struggling financially—I need *something* to work for me. My last few books haven't sold well.' He raised his head. 'But I really think this one will turn things around.'

John took a step back. 'That still isn't an excuse for throwing me under the bus.' He couldn't keep the bubbling rage from his voice.

Benji just shrugged a second time. 'I need this,' he said again, as if that were explanation enough. 'I'm sorry.'

John continued to glare at his friend. After a moment, he shuddered, with the cold wind taking hold in his bones. He wasn't sure what to say next. All he knew was that he wanted to be away from the damn lighthouse. 'Let's go back to the house,' he eventually said. 'We can talk more there. But I warn you, I consider our friendship finished now.'

Benji raised his eyes to meet John's, looking hurt. 'What? John... Don't be like that. You have to understand—'

'I understand plenty,' John seethed. He then turned and walked away from his friend.

6

1 - 6

JOHN SAT AT THE DINING TABLE, A MUG OF INSTANT COFFEE IN hand. Benji was in a seat across the table with his own drink. Both sipped in silence.

It was clear Benji was waiting for John to begin. The other man certainly looked sheepish, and kept his eyes mostly down, only allowing fleeting glimpses up at John. John himself was still struggling to keep a lid on his anger. He did feel better now that he was back in the house; the main abode didn't have the same weighty, unnerving feel to it, though John was still far from being at ease. His mind was racing, pondering a multitude of different things at once: If he left, how would he explain things to his superiors? What if Benji followed through on his threat? Also, *if* John stayed, could he really go back inside the lighthouse? Could he ever forgive his so-called friend for the betrayal?

And, was it somehow possible that Benji was actually right, that everything was explainable somehow?

To John, that last question seemed open and shut. It wasn't explainable. Not by any logical reasoning. He'd heard the voices, end of story. Even so, John knew he was tired, and he also knew the mind was a funny thing, capable of great self-deception. He'd experienced it before, where people were so convinced of something as to swear their lives on it, only to be proven wrong. Those people weren't liars, just... wrong. And not just in relation to the paranormal, of course, but in everyday life.

John *had* been uneasy the whole trip, from the very moment the pair had set foot onto the estate, in fact. And, whether John had openly admitted it or not, he'd chalked up every strange occurrence to the paranormal.

Even so, John said to himself, *it's hard to mistake actual whispering for something else.*

While his internal struggle continued, he said nothing, just sat and drank. He could see Benji was uncomfortable, waiting for John to speak first, but he was in no rush.

Let him squirm.

Eventually, however, it seemed Benji's patience ran out. 'Look,' the man began, 'again, I'm sorry. I really am. But... the day is drawing on and I want to make the most of the time I have here. How about you stay here, busy yourself with something, and I'll just work as I need to. If you don't want to go back to the lighthouse, you don't have to. I completely understand that.'

John scoffed. 'And when it locks you inside again on your own, then what?'

'*It* didn't lock us inside, Jo—' Benji started to say, then caught himself and took a slow breath. 'Better one of us is out here then, eh?' he said. 'If you don't hear from me for, say, two hours, then you know I'm stuck and you can come and help. So it works out better if you stay here, don't you think?'

However, instead of answering, John fell back into silence. *Let him twist in the wind a little more.* John could sense

Benji's eagerness to get going, and John had every intention of making things more difficult.

'If you want something to occupy you,' Benji went on, 'you can continue reading through my notes, see what you think. That would be a big help. I know you didn't get a chance to finish before.'

Now John raised his eyes to meet his friend, feeling the look of astonishment etched on his. *He's really asking for my help again, after what he threatened me with?*

Benji caught the glare and held his hands up defensively. 'Fine,' he said. 'No need to read them. It was just a thought so you didn't get bored.'

John took another sip. The coffee was bland, with little of the bite he enjoyed from his preferred caffeine. He drew in a breath. 'Actually,' he began, 'why don't you tell me the rest?'

'The rest?' Benji asked.

John nodded. 'The rest of the story. I stopped reading your notes at the point the Whitburns moved in. What happened to them?'

'Well, just read—'

'I'm asking *you* to tell me,' John interrupted. 'I'm curious to hear it.'

'Why?' Benji asked.

John shrugged. 'I just am.' What he didn't tell Benji was that John wanted to know if there were any similarities to what had happened back then and what was happening now. An outlandish thought, perhaps, but in John's current state of mind, it seemed a perfectly reasonable request.

Benji stared at him for a moment, as if debating going along with the request. 'If you say so,' he eventually said. 'Then can we get back to work?'

John gave a noncommittal shrug. 'Just tell me.'

There was a brief flash of annoyance on Benji's face, but it quickly disappeared. 'Fine,' he said before settling back in his chair. 'So initially, no one spent much time in the lighthouse after it was completed. Mr. Whitburn had his hands full setting his business operations up, and it was about a month or so before he started to use the dock and the lighthouse. I think his plan was to eventually hire staff to monitor the sea at night when a boat was due in, but initially he covered the duties himself, spending many a night out there up at the top of the tower.'

'And things soon started happening, I presume?' John asked.

Benji gave a noncommittal shrug. 'Well, so the stories go, but don't put too much stock in that being accurate. You know how things get exaggerated.'

'Surely the stories have a basis in reality, though. And who was telling the stories, anyway?'

'Well, I think the safest source of information is his wife. Apparently, she spoke to people in town when things got bad. She reported that her husband was becoming very distant. More than that, he'd started spending more and more time in the lighthouse on his own, and he was quick to anger. Supposedly, his wife sported a bruise on more than one occasion. She said she'd even heard him muttering to himself, in a language she didn't understand, though at some points English got mixed in with it as well. She said she heard him use the phrase 'the deep ones' more than once.'

John leaned forward, eager to know more—he was also ready to remind his friend that Benji himself had been muttering too, in an unknown language.

'Those accounts all came from police record, with locals making statements after the tragic event and reporting their interactions with the wife. So this is all on record.'

'Okay, then what?'

'Well, all we know is that the family was killed. The wife and child were found in their beds, throats cut. Mr. Whitburn, the obvious perpetrator, was nowhere to be found, though the police say he killed himself by throwing himself into the sea. Those are the only solid facts we have on the case, so the ultimate fate of Mr. Whitburn is obviously up for speculation.'

'What about the stories of ghostly noises from the estate?'

Benji cocked an eyebrow. 'You know about that?'

'A little.'

He sighed. 'They're ghost stories propagated by the locals, nothing more. It happens every time there is a tragedy like that in a small town. Especially in a remote location. Apparently, some youths came up here for a dare and heard strange things. But who's to say they even made it here in the first place, let alone actually heard anything? The legends after such an event tend to write themselves, and usually in the same manner: 'the spirits of the dead remain on the property and come out at night, blah, blah, blah. Some say if you come up here on Halloween, at the stroke of midnight, you will see the events replay themselves.' Utter balderdash. For one, the murders happened in June, so I have no idea why people started to tie Halloween into it all.'

'The reports of Mr. Whitburn muttering to himself don't concern you?'

'Why would they?' Benji replied with a raised eyebrow.

'Because you were doing the same thing. In your sleep.'

Benji held eye contact for a moment, then looked away. 'Nothing is going on here, John,' he said.

'Why are you resisting this so much?' John asked. 'Blatantly ignoring the obvious.'

'I'm *not* ignoring the obvious,' Benji said. 'I'm being rational in the face of irrationality. And I'm also trying my best to keep calm while doing it, but you're making things difficult.'

'*I'm* making things difficult? Are you for real?'

Benji let out another sigh. A moment later, he pushed his seat back and stood. 'Fine,' he said, annoyance in his voice. 'You're still mad. I suppose I can't blame you, considering the ultimatum I've given you. But I'm going to continue my work.' Benji then strode from the room. John didn't stop him, just continued to sip at his coffee, longing to get back to civilisation so he could get a decent cup again.

Alright, now's when I need to decide. Do I stay or go?

Going meant leaving his friend—or ex-friend—behind and facing potential wrath from his employers. John did again think how ridiculous it was that he had been forced into the whole thing in the first place. *Talk about overexerting their authority on my personal life.* But he also knew how business worked in the real world. Taking care of important clients was part-and-parcel of how things worked.

So, leaving early had plenty of drawbacks for John.

The other option, of course, was to stay.

That idea brought with it an innate fear that made John's chest tighten. He couldn't shake the image of that shadowy figure or the horrid whispering he'd heard. To stay would no doubt invite more of that kind of activity, and John didn't think he was brave enough to handle it.

His thoughts were interrupted when he heard Benji rummaging around upstairs.

What's he doing?

After a while, Benji emerged once again and walked over to the table. John watched as the other man flicked through a stack of documents and files. 'There,' he said, pulling out a pad of ring-bound writing paper. 'Found it.'

John frowned. 'That's what you've been looking for?'

Benji nodded. 'I need to take notes. But also...' He opened the pad to show some pages had already been written on. 'I've already noted down some on places around the estate to check out. I just need to make sure I tick these off.'

John looked again at the pile of folders and paper. They'd always been on the table, so he was puzzled as to why Benji would search upstairs for them.

'Have fun,' was all John said, still not making eye contact.

Benji stared at John for a moment. 'You aren't going to do anything silly like disappear on me while I'm out there, are you?'

John remained silent for a moment before answering. 'To be honest, I haven't made my mind up yet.'

Benji just shook his head and walked away again, camera still slung around his neck, notepad in hand. John heard the door to the house open and close, and silence fell. He suddenly felt isolated and exposed, but regardless, he was still eternally grateful to be away from the lighthouse.

The house itself felt empty and unsettling, certainly, but no more than any old, empty building. They all shared that same sense of loss, like they were fading from time.

The lighthouse had been… different.

While in there, he had a separate feeling, though it was harder to place. He thought on it, and then it struck him… *It felt like we weren't alone out there.*

He shuddered and drained the last of his drink, still no further forward in his decision. Part of him wanted to try to call Benji's bluff, but he had a feeling the man would follow through on his threat. Benji had seemed different since arriving at the estate: more driven, and a touch manic. Though now that John knew the truth, it perhaps made sense.

Does it though?

Even if Benji was struggling, did it really explain everything? The fact was, John had known Benji go through hard times before, and the man had never been like this. He tended to be carefree, and while perhaps a little judgemental

65

at times, John could never say Benji was short-tempered or uncaring of his friends.

John rose to his feet and stretched out his back. He felt exhausted, despite the early hour. When deciding whether or not to leave, he knew there was one other factor that weighed most heavily on him.

Can I really leave Benji behind?

As much as John was angry at the man—furious, in fact— he didn't think he could leave Benji stranded somewhere John felt might be dangerous.

Ultimately, that alone made up John's mind for him. He was going to stay, as much as he hated it.

Damn it!

Still, John had no intention of venturing out to the light-house again. As Benji had said, it would be better if one person stayed outside, just in case they had the same issue with the door again. While John didn't exactly have tools to take the door off its hinges, at least he could get help from town if needed.

Then, an idea struck him.

I'll just drive to town now and buy some tools, so we're ready just in case.

It seemed obvious. He might need to go out and investigate the door before going, to see exactly what he'd need, but if he had tools, then Benji couldn't get trapped.

With that, he decided to go grab the car keys from Benji's room, then go and tell Benji his plan. John would stay on the condition Benji joined him in town for a few hours to get what they needed. *I don't want Benji alone here, even if it's only for a little while.*

After climbing the stairs, John entered Benji's room and walked over to the open suitcase. He dug through the clothes, then checked in all the zipped-up pockets and compartments.

Where are they?

After coming up empty, he took out all the clothes that had been left inside and sifted through them, checking between each folded t-shirt and even shaking out some garments in case the keys had gotten tangled up inside.

Nothing.

John was confused. He knew the keys were in the case— or should have been, since Benji had told him where he'd stored them. John quickly checked the rest of the room, searching the nightstand and the chest of drawers, but was left frustrated. He wondered if Benji had left them down-stairs somewhere, then paused. Benji had just been upstairs, under the pretence of looking for a notepad that had actually been in front of him the whole time.

He took the keys!

'Damn him!' John seethed with renewed anger. He stomped from the room back down to the dining space and grabbed his coat, throwing it on as he stepped outside. 'Benji!' John shouted, looking around. 'Benji!' he shouted again. 'Where the hell are you? I need to talk to you!'

His voice echoed out, with no response. While it was possible Benji might not have heard him, John doubted it, considering how loudly he was yelling.

He's ignoring me. He knows I'm onto him.

John began his search. First, he checked in the larger warehouse, then some of the smaller buildings. It took him forty minutes to run from building to building, each time coming up empty-handed. Once he'd finished, he was out of breath and no farther forward. *Where is he?* he thought to himself while sucking in breath. Then, John cast his eyes over to the lighthouse again.

The door of it was closed.

No.

7

1 - 7

'WHAT THE HELL ARE YOU *DOING*, BENJI?' JOHN SCREAMED AS he strode down the pier to the tower before him. The structure seemed to loom higher the closer John got, unnerving him more and more with every step. He dearly didn't want to go back inside.

Why is he even in there? He has the rest of the bloody estate to investigate.

John reached the door. He took a breath. *I don't want to go in. I can't.*

Instead of opening it, he instead banged the side of his fist on the door, over and over. 'Benji!' he shouted. 'Come here at once. We need to talk!'

He waited and listened. Eventually, John drew in a deep breath and sighed. Benji was giving him the silent treatment, clearly too scared to face him. *Which means I need to go inside.*

'Shit,' John seethed under his breath. After taking another steadying breath, he grabbed the handle and eased the door open. He'd half expected to feel resistance, or for the door to be stuck as it had been before, but it opened easily. Part of John wished that wasn't the case, because now there was nothing stopping him from going in. After the door swung open, John poked his head inside without entering fully.

'Benji?' he called, then listened to his voice echo off the walls, working its way up the tower. There was no response. John couldn't even hear any footfalls from above. The ground floor had shadows around the perimeter and he suddenly regretted not bringing a torch with him.

Doesn't matter. I'm just going to get Benji, give him a piece of my mind, get the keys, and go.

Then, he remembered he had his phone. He pulled out the device and pressed the screen to activate it. However, there was no response. *What the hell?* He was sure he'd charged it earlier with their generator. Yet no matter how much he fiddled with it, nothing brought it back to life.

How can it be dead?

John sighed in annoyance. He then put one foot inside and pushed himself farther in, looking up as much as he could to the floor above. Sadly, from his position still within the threshold, John couldn't see too much. 'Benji!' he shouted again. Still nothing. 'Why the hell did you take the keys? *I* paid for the bloody rental car. Come down here and give them back.' No response, which caused John's anger to flare once more. 'Benji, answer me. Come down here now. I know you're in here!'

Shit, John cursed to himself after once again receiving no reply. 'You're a bloody child, do you know that? A petulant bloody kid.' He clenched his teeth together before taking a breath. 'Fine,' he called. 'I'm coming in.'

John touched his hand to the heavy, open door again, making sure it was going to stay in place, then took half a step forward. The memory of the door closing on its own was fresh in his mind. *We could get trapped for good this time.*

John couldn't bring himself to move any farther forward. Though his anger still ran hot, it started to give way to worry. *Just give Benji his time in there. Confront him when he comes out.*

Don't go in.

Better to wait, John realised, than for both of them to get stuck.

A second later, though, John thought he heard footsteps high above him. He looked up, trying to peer through the gap through the stairs.

'Benji?' he called.

The footsteps continued, growing heavier as they started to descend the stairs.

Thump, thump, thump.

John felt his breath catch in his throat. A thought struck him and made his chest tighten: *What if that isn't Benji?*

The footsteps were slow and laboured, and not at all in keeping with Benji's normally hurried walking. They drew closer and closer, and John saw a shadow pass above him. He backed up a little.

That doesn't sound like Benji. He doesn't walk like that.

The icy grip of fear tightened its hold on his heart. He mentally prepared himself, expecting some kind of spectral horror to lower into view, perhaps the same shadowy figure he'd seen earlier. John realised he was shaking.

Thump, thump, thump.

The figure eventually came into view. When John caught sight of the legs, he realised it was Benji. He breathed a sigh of relief. His friend slowly moved closer, now fully in view.

'You bloody idiot,' John snapped. 'You scared the life out of me! Why weren't you answering?'

Benji stopped halfway down, facing John. The man's eyes seemed glazed over again, and he stood almost completely motionless, with only a gentle, almost imperceptible sway.

'B… Benji?' John asked.

Benji just continued to look over in John's direction. A

smile crept over his face. It had a sinister quality to it. Then, Benji held up a hand—he was holding the car keys.

'Those are mine,' John snarled. 'Come down here and—'

John felt a pair of hands shove him forward from behind. He stumbled into the lighthouse and fell to the ground.

The door slammed shut behind him, and a second later, Benji started to giggle.

8

1 - 8

WHILE ON THE GROUND, JOHN INSTINCTIVELY SPUN AROUND
to look back at the door. With it closed, he couldn't see who
had pushed him, but he knew what he'd felt. Panic filled him.
Other than he and Benji, there was no one else on the estate.

He scrambled backwards, moving away from the door to
the stairs, and then looked up to Benji, whose eerie giggles
slowly trailed off.

'What's going on?' John demanded, breathing heavily.
Benji didn't answer. Instead, he slowly turned and began to
walk back up the stairs, again taking slow, heavy steps. 'Benji!' John shouted. 'Benji, answer me!'

But Benji disappeared from sight when rounding the top
of the stairs, then he continued up to the very top of the
lighthouse.

What the hell is going on?

John again gazed over to the door in panic. Whispering
and shadowy figures were one thing, but to be actually
touched, and *shoved,* by... whatever it was... had instilled a
new level of fear in him. His mind tried to look for logical
explanations, but he knew deep down there were none.

He wondered if someone else had managed to sneak onto the grounds. But if so, why? And why sneak up and push John? Also, that didn't explain any of Benji's behaviour.

John even considered if it could be some elaborate prank by Benji—to act strange, then bring someone else in to scare John. But again, that didn't make sense. Who would go along with that, and what would Benji gain from it? A good laugh at John's expense wasn't worth risking the entire trip over.

Nothing made sense.

No... John said to himself. *There's one thing makes sense.*

The shadowy figures, the whispering, the hands shoving him, and Benji's sleepwalking and gibberish...

While he didn't fully understand it, John *knew* there was something paranormal going on in the lighthouse.

Shit, shit, shit.

John's chest drew tighter and tighter as that realisation began to solidify.

Are we going to die out here?

The thought of being alone in the dark, constantly tormented until he died, brought tears of panic to John's eyes.

There has to be a way out!

John scrambled over to the door, still struggling with his breathing, and tried to force it open. As he'd feared, it didn't budge.

'No! No! Please... open!' he said, panting.

Tap, tap, tap.

John stopped and backed up away from the door, eyes wide.

Tap, tap, tap.

Someone was gently knocking from outside.

'Who is it?'

John got a response in the form of a faint giggle, though

it was too quiet to determine if it was masculine or feminine, young or old. The knocking didn't resume.

'Hello?' John called. Silence.

As panic continued to take over, John backed farther away from the door, finally reaching the stairs. Not wanting to be down there alone anymore, he grabbed the handrail of the spiral staircase and pulled himself up, before taking the first two steps in a single bound. Better to be with a strange-acting Benji than completely isolated, he reasoned.

Just as John took the third step, he felt something grab his ankle.

He let out a cry and fell forward—as if in response, the strong, icy grip instantly released. He spun on the stairs and looked down, but could see nothing.

This can't be happening, this can't be happening, he told himself.

John scrambled backwards, keeping his eyes on the floor beneath as he looped up quickly around the stairs, moving higher. As he broke through to the next floor, the lightest of touches suddenly ran over his head, moving John's hair back. He cried out again and whipped his head around, shuddering in fright. Again, there was no one.

He began to sob.

'Leave me alone!' John shouted, then sprang up to his feet and sprinted to the top floor. As he moved, he was *certain* he could feel something coming up behind him, some looming presence closing in on him.

Once at the top, John dove forward to the floor and flipped himself round, hands held aloft to stop what was chasing him. Only... nothing was.

The stairs were empty, and the last reverberations of his rapid footfalls quickly died out. John lay on the floor for a moment, panting, desperately trying to keep from hyperventilating. He then quickly got up and moved around to his left, towards Benji, who stood looking out to the horizon at the edge of the sea.

John cast a nervous glance over the guardrail again, then turned to his friend.

'Benji, w-we need to go.' His voice was shaking. No response. He nudged the other man, but he didn't budge. 'What are you doing?' John asked, hearing the fear in his own words. Benji still didn't respond and continued to stare.

Being close to Benji in this state did little to alleviate John's fear. He was next to his friend, yet was absolutely alone.

The keys were still dangling from Benji's loose grip. In fact, they looked ready to drop at any moment. John slowly lowered his hand, then reached out and snatched the keys away. Benji didn't react.

While John was still terrified, he felt a *tiny* bit better now that he had the keys again. At least now if they got out, there was a way to leave.

The problem there was Benji. *How am I going to get him anywhere when he's like this?*

Moreover, John didn't know how the hell they were going to escape the lighthouse in the first place.

He looked again over the bannister and down into the darkness. It was a struggle to keep his composure, remembering the cold grip on his ankle and the gentle touch across his hair.

He turned to Benji and took hold of the man before shaking him by the shoulders, desperate to wake him up.

'Benji!' John shouted. 'Benji, I need you to come back to me. Enough of this.' Benji's head wobbled from side to side, but he didn't respond, still staring vacantly out the windows before him. 'Benji!' John shouted again. Nothing. Giving up, John let go and cursed.

A thought ran through his head. *Should I hit him?*

John had seen plenty of movies where slapping someone brought them around. But he'd never hit anyone in his life. Even at school, he'd always managed to avoid conflict.

He reluctantly moved in front of his friend, blocking Benji's view of the sea, and even waved his hand just over Benji's face.

Does he even know I'm here?

'Benji,' John asked one final time in the vain hopes of reaching him. Still nothing, which caused John to sigh in disappointment. 'Don't get mad, Benji,' John whispered. 'But I *really* need you to pull round.' He raised his hand high behind his head, palm open, paused for a second... then swung.

The sound of his slap broke the silence, and John's palm immediately began to sting. Benji's head snapped to the side.

John paused, cradling his hand, staring wide-eyed at his friend while he waited for a reaction. Eventually, Benji moved, turning to face John, a red mark already blooming on his face.

I hit him too hard, John thought to himself, worried. However, there was now recognition in Benji's eyes.

'Did you just... hit me?' the man asked in a low voice. He then coughed and then rubbed his cheek. 'Why the hell did you...' Benji then looked around. Confusion clouded his face. 'Wait, why are we back here?'

John tilted his head in confusion. 'You came here your-self,' he said. 'Don't you remember?'

Benji rubbed a hand over his face, a look of panic spread-ing. 'What do you mean? No, I don't remember...' He trailed off and shook his head.

'What's the last thing you *do* remember?' John asked.

'I...' Benji paused, clearly in thought. He then lifted his gaze and looked out of the windows again. 'We were heading back to the house, weren't we?'

'Back to the house?' John asked, confused. 'That was... a while ago. You don't remember getting back? Or our conversation there? Or taking the car keys?'

'Wait... the keys?' Benji asked. 'No, I don't. And what conversation?'

John was struggling to make sense of everything. *How could he forget something so recent?* 'Yes,' he eventually replied. 'I told you I wanted to leave, but you said you'd call my employers and tell them I was spooked over nothing if I did. Then, you took the car keys to make sure I was stranded here with you. You... really don't remember?'

Benji started to sway unsteadily on his feet. 'No,' he whispered and lowered his head. 'I... I don't.' John quickly saw that his friend was about to fall, so he grabbed Benji's hands and guided them to the guardrail.

'Easy now,' John said. He rubbed Benji's back. 'Do you need to sit?'

Benji took a deep, steadying breath, paused for a moment, and finally shook his head. 'I'm okay,' he said. 'Just a bit lightheaded.' He looked over to John once more. 'All that really happened?' he asked.

'Of course,' John said. 'Do you think I'd make it up?'

Benji shook his head. 'No, no, of course not. It's just... I don't remember any of it. Nothing at all. What time is it?'

John checked his watch. 'A little after ten,' he said. *So early, but it feels like I've been awake for days now.*

'Jesus,' Benji uttered. He paused, taking several more deep breaths, and rested his forehead on the rail. 'What's wrong with me, John?'

John hesitated at the question. 'I... I don't know,' he replied, not sure what else to say.

'Sleepwalking,' Benji began, 'muttering to myself, zoning out. Now this. I've lost *hours*. What if... what if it's something to do with my brain? Like a tumour or something.' He

77

turned his worried eyes to John once more. 'Shit, do you think that's what it is?'

John placed a hand on his friend's shoulder. 'I don't think so, no,' he said.

'What... what else could it be?'

Benji was obviously looking for reassurance. And while John had an answer, he knew Benji might not want to hear it.

'I don't think anything is wrong with you,' John said. Benji's eyes widened with hope.

'So then why is it happening?' he asked.

'Well,' John began, considering his next words. *Just be honest. What is there to lose?* 'I think it's this place,' he finally said.

'This... place?' Benji asked. 'What do you mean?'

'I mean this lighthouse—maybe the whole estate. Something's happening here and it's affecting you. Both of us, but you more so. It's causing these blackouts, making you act in a certain way. Benji, I'm sure of it.'

Benji just stared at him for a moment. John could see his friend's mind working, trying to comprehend what he'd just been told.

'John,' Benji began, sounding unsure. 'Please, not this again. I'm not in the mood for—'

'Just listen,' John said. 'I know you don't want to believe me, but you need to at least hear me out, okay? What else could explain it? You don't remember the last few hours, but you were walking around and talking to me like normal. How can you explain that? Plus, you came *straight* back here, to the lighthouse. It's like you were drawn here.'

Benji shook his head, but John went on: 'There's more. I thought you were somewhere on the estate, because you said you were going to look around. When I realised you were here, I came to get you.'

'And then you found me here and hit me?'

'Keep quiet,' John snapped. 'I had the door open, but didn't come inside. I was standing on the threshold. Something *pushed* me in here, Benji, from behind. It couldn't have been you—you were already up here.'

Benji frowned. 'So… someone else is here with us?'

Frustration coursed through John. 'No, Benji. Not *someone*, some*thing*. Something pushed me and then shut the door on us again. It won't open, like last time. But that's not all.'

'Go on,' Benji said, still looking sceptical.

'I ran up to the top but felt something grab my leg. I didn't imagine it. Something grabbed me. And after that, I felt something run a hand over my hair.'

Benji took a breath. 'The wind or—'

'Enough about the fucking *wind!*' John roared. 'Christ, that's your explanation for everything. Enough! The wind doesn't explain this. Now, I need you to listen to me, Benji, and I need you to listen good. We're stuck in here again and we're in trouble. We need to figure out a way to get free. Then, we're going home. We're not staying here any longer.'

Benji was silent for a moment. John fully expected resistance. 'You're right,' Benji said, utterly surprising John. 'Maybe not about what's going on,' Benji continued, 'but we do need to leave. I… I think I should see a doctor or something. You'll need to drive.'

John was stunned. He'd never seen Benji so vulnerable. And while he was still annoyed Benji was refusing to acknowledge the full truth, at least the other man was open to leaving. *Now we just need to get free of the bloody lighthouse.*

'I can drive,' John confirmed. 'Of course. But we need to get the door open, and…' He looked down to the inky depths below again, remembering the spectral touches that had come out of the darkness. 'It might not be safe down there.'

He quickly looked back at Benji. 'I know you refuse to believe me about that, but I don't care. We don't have any lights, and eventually it's going to get dark. Wait,' he suddenly added. 'Do you have your phone on you? It has a light on it.'

Benji patted his pockets. 'No,' he said. 'I obviously didn't think to grab it when I was zoned out. You?'

'No battery,' John said, annoyed.

Benji glanced down over the guard rail as well. 'Come on,' he said, 'we can't just stand up here all day. We'll get the door open if I have to tear it from the hinges myself.'

John appreciated Benji's optimism but knew it was a fool's hope. Plus, the force holding it shut would not likely relent. Not unless it wanted to.

It opened before, John reminded himself. He just hoped it would again. The thought of going back down into the darkness terrified him, but John knew Benji was right—they couldn't just stand up there all day. They had to try something.

'Okay,' John finally said, his body tense. 'Let's go.'

9

---

1 - 9

THE HEAVY DARKNESS PRESSED DOWN AROUND JOHN AS BOTH men stood on the ground floor again. The light from above helped guide them over to the door, though most of it was lost to shadow.

We should be able to see more of this, John thought, now convinced the intensity of the dark was somehow unnatural.

Luckily, Benji was able to find the handle. John heard the man groan with exertion, then curse under his breath, confirming John's fears.

'Stuck?' he tentatively asked, already knowing the answer.

'Stuck,' Benji confirmed. 'But don't jump to conclusions. We know there's an issue with the door sticking, so this isn't unexpected.'

'Probably the wind, right?' John said sarcastically. Benji turned to face him with a disapproving look, but said nothing and instead went back to heaving at the door.

John's mind began to search for an alternative way out. There were no other openings besides the door, though, so unless they were going to break through the solid wall of the lighthouse, there was only one other option: the lamp.

He had no idea how thick the glass was at the head of the tower, though had a feeling it was extremely durable. Also, even if they did get through, it would be one hell of a drop on the other side. And it wasn't like they would plummet down into water, either, but the rocky island at the base of the lighthouse. It promised a grisly, painful death. Images of lying on the rocks, screaming in pain, bones shattered, filled John's mind.

It just wasn't an option.

Which means we need to get that bloody door open!

'Let me try,' John said. He knew he would fare no better, but wanted to do *something* to quell the rising panic within him. As expected, the door didn't obey, no matter how hard John tried—he grew more frantic by the moment.

'Come on,' he uttered. 'Open, damn you.'

John felt Benji's hand on his shoulder. 'Careful,' the man said. 'You'll give yourself a hernia. Just try to stay calm.'

John kicked out angrily at the door. 'Shit!' he shouted, then stepped back.

'We got through before, we'll get through again,' Benji said, obviously trying to sound reassuring. But John knew the truth. The only way they would get out was if the power holding them inside decided to let them.

'I… I can't stay in here,' John said, eyeing the shadows warily. He was struggling to keep it together, expecting another ghostly touch on his body. John moved closer to the centre of the space, into the light, and hugged himself.

But then his body locked up in fright at the sound of a knock at the door. John looked over to Benji, wide-eyed, and saw his friend seeming equally shocked and confused. They both stared at the door in silence for a moment. The knocking then came again—not the light tapping from before, but this time louder, with more purpose.

'H... Hello?' Benji shouted.

John waited, listening intently.

'Who is that?' a male voice replied from the other side. 'Who are you?'

Benji again cast confused eyes at John. The voice sounded... normal. Not sinister or taunting. Just... a person.

'We're trapped inside,' Benji shouted back. 'Could you help us get the door open?'

'*Why* are you inside?' the man asked.

'My friend and I are here taking photos of the lighthouse,' Benji explained. 'Kind of documenting the place before it's torn down.'

'Torn down?' the man questioned. 'What do you mean?'

John was struggling to understand what was happening. He prayed that maybe... just maybe... it *was* a normal person standing out there. Perhaps someone in town had driven by, noticed some people on the grounds, and had come to check it out.

'The owner will be pulling everything down at some point in the future,' Benji explained. 'He has plans for the land.'

There was a pause, then a disbelieving laughter. 'I don't think so.'

'No, I promise you, it's true,' Benji replied.

'No, it *isn't*,' the man stated firmly. 'I have no plans to pull this place down at all.'

John froze. Benji turned to him and leaned his head closer to the door. 'Mr. Barrow?' he asked with a frown.

That isn't Mr. Barrow.

'I don't know who that is,' the voice replied, 'but I want to know why you two are holed up in my lighthouse. Care to explain?'

John felt a creeping dread overtake him. 'Mr... Whitburn?' he asked in a shaky voice.

'Yes, do I know you?' the voice replied. 'You know who I am, so you're no doubt aware that *I* own this estate, not that Barrow fella. Again, *why* are you in there?'

'Jesus Christ,' John uttered and took another step back.

But Benji just shook his head. 'Look, my friend,' he began, 'I'm not sure what game you're playing, but it isn't funny. Mr. Whitburn has been dead a long time, so stop trying to mess with us. Just help us get the door open, please.'

'You think I'm dead?' the voice asked with a trace of amusement. The man let out a single laugh. 'No, not dead.'

Benji sighed in clear annoyance. 'You're starting to annoy me now.' He then grabbed the handle and shook the door again. 'Just help us. The door is stuck.'

'Of course it is,' the man outside replied. '*They* are keeping it closed. You won't get out unless they want you to.'

'They?' Benji asked.

'The deep ones,' the man said, and his voice took on a distorted, gravelly quality. 'And no,' he went on, 'I'm not dead. I'm *far* past that.'

John took yet another step back. 'What... what do you mean?' he asked.

But Benji let out a sigh. 'Utter rubbish,' he stated. 'Look, if you aren't going to help, then get off the estate. Otherwise, I'll call the police when we get free and tell them there's a trespasser out here.'

'I'm not going anywhere,' the man said. 'I've been here the whole time. Years and years. Nice to eventually have more company, by the way. My family, you see, well... they're not very talkative. All they do is scream. Scream and scream and scream. Just like they did that night. It's maddening, you know. And they just. Won't. *Stop.* Can you hear them now?'

The man outside fell silent. John stopped to listen. He

noticed Benji tilt his head to the side, obviously listening as well.

Deafening screams erupted from all around them.

John clamped his hands over his ears, pressing his palms tightly around his head to block out the awful sounds. But it was no good. It was almost like the terrible howls of pain were coming from *inside* his head. Benji was covering his own ears as well, wincing, a look of horror etched on his face.

The screams were those of an adult female and a child, both in terrible pain. Their maddening screeches of agony were constant, just an endless stream of eternal anguish.

'Make it stop!' John shouted, yet he could barely hear his own voice.

After what seemed like an eternity, the howls suddenly blinked to silence. John and Benji continued to keep their hands over their ears for a moment, with John fully expecting the screams to return. When they didn't, he cautiously lowered his hands.

'What... what the fuck was that?' Benji asked, incredulous.

John had no answer.

'Imagine hearing that *all* the bloody time,' the man outside said, sounding disgusted. 'Pathetic screeches of lowly swine, too ignorant to see what their sacrifice has helped bring about. Wretched pigs. But of course, more is needed. More is *always* needed. The hunger is never truly sated.'

The man laughed for a few moments and was then silent. Both John and Benji waited with bated breath, John terrified of hearing those awful howls once more.

They continued to wait.

'Hello?' John shouted a few minutes later. No response came. 'Are you still there?' No reply.

'What *was* that?' Benji asked, eyes wide and full of panic.

'I don't know,' John said, breathing heavily. He realised he'd started sweating. 'But I *told* you something wasn't right about this place.'

Benji shook his head vigorously. 'No,' he said. 'No, there has to be an explana—'

'Stop!' John shouted. 'Enough with the denial! We both heard it. Those screams? We didn't imagine them. So stop trying to explain away what's going on and face up to reality!'

'I... I...' Benji shook his head again. 'I... *can't*,' he said, and John heard the man's voice crack. 'I can't accept it.' He began to sob. 'It *can't* be real. It can't be.'

John paused. The annoyance he'd felt at Benji's denials quickly subsided, replaced by sympathy at watching a man's very belief system break before his eyes.

'I'm sorry, Benji,' John said. 'I know this is hard for you, but you need to come to terms with it quickly, because we need to get away. We don't have time for a breakdown.'

Benji raised his hands to his face and cried into them. 'It can't be real,' he said again. The man was shaking.

John approached his friend and laid a comforting hand on his shoulder. 'Come on,' he said gently, 'We can cry later. Believe me, I want to as well, but for now, let's think. Let's get free and process everything once we're safe. Sound good?'

Benji took a steady breath and moved his hands away from his face. His wet eyes met John's. After a moment... he nodded. 'You're right,' he eventually said.

John gave him a smile. 'Good,' he said, 'then let's work together.'

He found that supporting Benji had actually helped his own state of mind. It gave him something to concentrate on, other than the abject fear he had been battling with.

'But I don't know what other options we have other than the door,' Benji said. 'There are no windows, no nothing.'

'I know,' John said. 'I was considering the glass at the top, but wouldn't fancy our chances on the way down. It's a long drop.'

Benji hesitated for a moment, clearly thinking. 'Do you think it's possible to scale down the wall?'

John frowned. 'Is there a ladder, or maybe some rungs fixed to the wall?'

'I don't think so,' Benji replied. 'But the blocks themselves have weathered, same as the mortar joints between them. Maybe there are gaps we can use for hand and foot holds.'

John held his hands up. 'I don't think we should try that. Not unless we're really desperate. We'd just fall. Especially me. I've never been good at things like that.'

Benji gave a small nod. 'You're probably right. But... be honest, how far are we from being 'desperate enough'?'

It was a fair point. 'Not far, I suppose,' John conceded. 'But let's keep thinking. There might be another way.'

'I'm all ears,' Benji replied.

The men stood in silence, both trying to plot their escape, and both coming up with precisely nothing. Eventually, Benji walked back to the door and tried it again. The results were as expected.

'Shit!' he spat. He kicked the door. 'Shit, shit, shit.'

More time passed. The two men had positioned themselves centrally in the space, sitting on the bottom step beneath the shaft of light from the lamp.

'Should we look around again?' Benji asked, pointing up. 'I don't suppose we'll find anything, but I'm getting restless.'

'Sounds like a good idea to me,' John replied, eager to move around himself. Plus, it was lighter on the upper floors, and he still couldn't shake the expectation something was eventually going to come shambling out of the shadows towards them. He let Benji take the stairs first and followed behind.

'Do you think that really was Archie Whitburn earlier?' Benji asked as they ascended.

'Probably,' John said. 'His spirit, at least. I know you have a hard time with things like that—'

'Those screams definitely made it easier,' Benji stated, reaching the mid-floor.

John nodded. 'Which is why I think it *was* him. Some version of him, anyway.'

'Some version? What do you mean?'

'Well,' John began, moving to stand next to his friend on the mid-floor, 'given what we know about what happened to the family, I'd guess poor old Mr. Whitburn became possessed by... whatever it is that lives here. You heard the way he spoke about them, like his family was nothing more than an annoyance. It's clear some force still has a hold of him, even in death. Which is a terrifying thought: knowing that even death won't bring release.'

Benji stayed silent for a moment. 'He talked about the deep ones,' he then said. 'Did you hear that part?'

John nodded. 'Yes, I heard it.'

'Same as the reports from back in the day. Do you think *they* are behind this madness?'

John shrugged. 'To be honest, I have no idea. I couldn't even begin to guess what the deep ones are.'

Benji took a breath. 'I... think I have an idea.'

'Really?' John asked, raising an eyebrow. 'From your research?'

Benji shook his head. 'It's more... a feeling. Like a dream. I can't explain it, but when I heard Archie mention them, things kind of clicked in my head, as if unearthing a memory. They're under here, I think. Under the lighthouse.

And I'm pretty sure they were disturbed when the lighthouse was built.'

John was in shock. 'How can you know all that?'

Benji shrugged. 'I have no idea. The knowledge is in my head... but I have no idea why.' He shook his head. 'I know it doesn't make sense. I think I'm just nuts.'

John studied his friend, then eventually said, 'No. I don't think you are nuts at all. The way you've been acting... I think there is a kind of link there, somehow. *That's* why you know these things.'

'So... these deep ones are in my head?'

John paused. 'I'm... not sure. Maybe.'

He saw Benji's body sag. 'Well, if they are, how long before they make me zone out again? Or worse!'

'What do you mean?' John asked.

Benji's scared eyes turned to meet his own. 'You know what happened to the family here,' Benji began. 'All because those things got inside Archie Whitburn's head. If the same thing happens to me...'

He trailed off and turned away. John felt his body go tight, a renewed sense of worry flooding.

10

1-10

Hours passed.

The pair had searched the entire lighthouse as extensively as they could, but predictably, found nothing of use. They'd then ventured back down to the ground floor to try the door yet again, but it was still stuck fast.

John was hungry and thirsty. What was more, both men had been forced to answer the call of nature, despite holding it as long as they could. They had taken turns urinating on the ground floor, against the wall and opposite the main door, so the lower level now stunk of ammonia.

John was disgusted at himself, but it had either been that or pissing in his trousers. Worse, the light outside was beginning to wane.

The only good news they had was that in all that time, there had been no other occurrences: no knocking, no voices, no screams, no ghostly touches... nothing.

They were now seated on the top floor, having brought up two chairs from the mid-story, and were looking out at sea. Under different circumstances, the view might have been calming.

'I'm exhausted,' Benji said.

'Me too,' John replied. His eyes had started to grow heavy. 'But we need to make sure we don't fall asleep. The last thing we need is to wake up here in the dead of night.'

Benji gave a humourless chuckle. 'What difference does it make?' he asked. 'Hate to break it to you, but we've made no progress. In fact, I think we've even given up trying and now we're just sitting around. Kind of like we've accepted it.'

'We *haven't* accepted it,' John quickly said.

'Then why aren't we still brainstorming? Don't get me wrong, I'm not having a pop at you or anything, because *I'm* just sitting on my arse as well, but... Well, there's nothing else to try, is there? So here we are, accepting it, and looking at the scenery as we do.'

John... didn't have an answer to that. Benji was right in one sense: there *wasn't* anything else to try. The two men kept intermittently going back to the main door, each time finding it just as stuck in place, and that had been it. *But what else can we do?* Simply conserving their strength wasn't giving up... was it?

Maybe it is, John argued with himself. *Maybe this is what the deep ones want: to just keep us here and wear us down until they finish us off.*

John wondered just how long it would take. Hours? Maybe days? The thought of being trapped in the lighthouse for days on end was terrifying. He wasn't sure how long a person could last without food or water, but already felt himself growing weaker.

If I don't turn up to work next week, people will ask questions, John reasoned. *Then surely someone will be sent out here.*

But even if that was true, it still meant being stuck within the tower for a *long* time.

John eventually turned back to his friend. 'Come on,' he said. 'Let's check the door again. You're right, we are letting malaise set in.' Benji didn't respond, so John leaned closer to the other man. 'Hey,' he said, giving Benji a nudge. 'You awake?'

Still nothing. John shuffled himself around in his seat and looked closer at Benji's face. There was a far-off stare in his eyes, which John immediately recognised.

He felt his stomach drop. He quickly got to his feet and moved directly in front of his friend, yet Benji just seemed to look through John.

Shit!

'Hey!' John said, snapping his fingers in front of Benji's eyes. 'You in there? Hey! Wake up!' No response. John took hold of Benji by the shoulders and shook him. 'Wake up!' he ordered. 'I need you to come back to me. Snap out of it!'

Benji's head wobbled as John continued his aggressive shaking, but the man remained zoned out, utterly unresponsive.

Shit! I'm going to have to hit him again.

It was the only thing John could think of. And it had worked once before.

'Sorry about this,' he whispered to his friend as worry and panic grew. Thoughts of Mr. Whitburn butchering his family swirled in John's head. He raised his hand, took a breath, and swung at Benji's face.

Benji's hand shot up and caught John by the wrist with surprising strength. A second later, Benji's face lifted. *Now* his eyes focused on John. A sinister smile drew across the man's lips, and he slowly shook his head while getting to his feet, still with a firm grip on John's wrist.

'Benji?' John asked in panic. 'Can… can you hear me?'

In response, Benji just chuckled. He let go of John's wrist, but then quickly grabbed him by the collar with both hands before shoving him back into the guardrail.

John let out a cry of shock as his lower back slammed

against the rail. Benji kept forcing John backwards until his top half was leaning over the bannister.

'Benji stop!' he shouted, instinctively taking hold of Benji's arms. 'What are you doing?' John tried to wriggle from his friend's grip, but it was simply too strong.

Benji continued to chuckle. The man cocked his head to the side before saying, 'Shhhhh. Just listen.' His voice was little more than a whisper, but it was enough to make John fall silent. John did as instructed, out of pure fear. After a moment, he heard movement from below.

John started to wriggle again, but it was useless. The sounds of shuffling and dragging from the bottom of the lighthouse were becoming more prominent. He tried to angle his head around to stare down into the void, but was unable to.

'Aren't you going to say hello to them?' Benji asked, his voice dripping with malice.

'Wh... Who?' John asked.

'Just keep still,' Benji said.

'It's them, isn't it?!' John shouted. 'The things that are controlling you!'

But Benji shook his head. 'No, not them. Not... yet.'

John heard a heavy footstep land on the very bottom stair. It was so firm and loud he quickly fell silent. Then there was another. And another.

Thump. Thump. Thump.

Something was climbing higher. He heard a rasped wheezing. Then, there came another footstep on the bottom step again, but a lighter one this time, joining the others.

More wheezing, coming from seemingly two different people both climbing the stairs.

Thump. Thump. Thump.

John's body tensed in panic. 'Let me go, Benji!' he screamed, yet Benji just laughed at him.

Thump, thump, thump.

Closer and closer they drew, steps quickening. The rasps reminded John of people in hospitals taking their last breaths: struggled and laboured.

Thump, thump, thump, thump, thump.

The sounds crossed to the mid-floor and continued higher and higher.

In desperation, John quickly slammed his knee straight into Benji's groin. Benji's eyes widened, and a grimace flashed over his face. The man's grip released only a little, but it was enough for John to push Benji back and slip free. He sprinted away from his friend, moving around to the opposite side of the lighthouse.

'You shouldn't have done that,' Benji groaned. *I hit him hard, why isn't he doubled over?*

Thump, thump, thump.

John looked down. And screamed.

Two... *things...* were coming up the stairs, both looking up, their dead eyes fixed directly on him.

Corpses, John thought in utter terror. *Walking corpses.*

The lead one was a mix of bone and rotten flesh, with most of its skull on display beneath thin, dried skin. It had one remaining eye, which was mostly white, save for the impression of a pale, light-blue patch where the iris should be. The other socket was empty, and a few strands of scraggly hair clung to what remained of the scalp.

The creature had a few loose rags around it—remnants of clothes—but most of its skin was visible, including a single, sagging breast. The other side of its chest showed only an exposed ribcage.

The walking corpse at the rear was in a similar condition, only smaller.

A young girl, John realised, then it clicked in his mind just *who* he was looking at.

Mrs. Whitburn and her child continued their slow ascent. The mother kept her withered, mostly skeletal hand on the bannister as she moved. John noticed a black, sludge-like trail left behind in that hand's wake, smeared against the wood.

'They just want to say hello,' Benji said, smiling again. When John looked over, he saw his former friend was framed by the burning dusk sky through the windows behind him. 'Don't be so rude,' Benji added.

Benji was positioned close to the top of the stairs, which put John as far away as he could get from the two walking corpses. A small mercy... but he was still trapped.

'Benji,' John said, 'Please stop this. Send them away. I'm begging you. Please!'

'I can't,' Benji replied calmly. 'They aren't here because of me. They're here because of *you*. Come on, stop being silly. Go give them a hug.'

Benji then chuckled again just as the woman finally reached the top. She turned onto the circular walkway. Once there, she held her ground for a few moments, allowing the smaller corpse to reach the top as well. John was able to see more of their grotesque features now, such as the blackened meat of their exploded flesh, cracked and yellowed teeth, and the wrinkled, leathery appearance of the skin.

John was horrified to see the older woman begin to advance from one side, while the smaller girl shuffled forward around the other. All the while, Benji stayed still, blocking off the top of the stairs.

John sobbed. 'Leave me alone!' he screamed. The two women continued to move forward with agonising slow-ness, still rasping and wheezing. Seeming to enjoy the display, Benji continued his incessant sniggering.

'Nowhere to run to, dear friend,' he taunted.

The little girl lifted her arms towards John, as if wanting

to pull him in for a hug. She was moving slightly faster than her mother, shuffling forward with an almost excited enthusiasm.

'No, get away!' John shouted in terror. His body tensed, but there was nowhere to go.

Nowhere but down.

Acting on impulse, he quickly swung his legs over the guardrail, placing his feet right on the precipice as he teetered over the edge.

'Where are you going?' Benji asked in amusement.

John looked down, eyes wide with terror. If he jumped and landed on the stairs below, he would only fall a few feet. *I'll have to keep my balance though,* he thought. *It's a long way down after that.*

The little girl was almost on him. He heard her murmur something. It was a guttural noise, and completely incomprehensible. He realised that she was trying to talk.

John leapt, feeling the girl's fingers scrape over his arm.

Oh God, oh God, oh God.

Though the fall took less than a second in reality, it felt much longer, and he watched the stairs get closer and closer.

John's feet collided hard with the wooden tread, impact traveling up his shins—in horror, he also felt his left ankle turn and pain exploded from the joint. He let out a cry and toppled sideways, his side hitting the bannister. A second later he felt himself start to topple backwards, but he was able to quickly grab the rail.

He then looked up to see Benji staring back down at him. The two corpses, however, were gone.

'You scared them away, John,' Benji said, sounding disappointed. 'Do you know how long it's been since they've had contact with anyone? Anyone that's alive, anyway. A *long* time, John. And you ruined it for them. I hope you're happy.'

John started to limp down the stairs, though he kept

casting glances back up at Benji, who seemed content to hold his ground.

'You... sure you want to go down there on your own?' Benji called. 'It's awfully dark, and getting darker by the minute. There are things here that live in the dark, you know, so you could end up with more company soon.'

John stopped. He didn't know if Benji was just trying to trick him, but John quickly recalled the feeling of his ankle being grabbed and his hair being touched. He shuddered. Then, a rumbling sound off in the distance caused him to tense up.

What the hell?

Benji chuckled and turned his head. John could tell the man was looking out to sea. 'Storm's coming,' he said. 'There was a bad one the night Mr. Whitburn's family was offered up, too. Not many people actually know that. *I* certainly didn't... not until the things here told me. Bit of a coincidence we're getting one now, eh?'

'Benji, please stop this,' John said, desperation evident in his voice. 'Just... stop. Snap out of whatever trance you're in. This isn't you. You're being controlled.'

'Of course I am!' Benji said. 'I know that. Somewhere deep down, I'm horrified and screaming in terror for all this to stop. But I *can't*.' He brought a finger to his head and tapped his temple. 'There are other things in here with me now. They're in the driver's seat, you see. I'm just a scared passenger.'

'Try to fight it,' John went on. 'Please. Just... *try*.'

The other man didn't respond for a moment and just continued to stare back down. 'Sorry, old friend,' he eventually said. 'I didn't realise it at the time, but the things here started getting in my head the moment we set foot in the lighthouse. I just kept ignoring the sensations, putting it down to excitement, tiredness... anything, really. I suppose I

97

was easy pickings.' Benji laughed. 'Not like *you*, the one who's afraid of his own shadow. I'm not sure if this information will help you at all, but I'm the one they want, John. And they have me now. There's nothing I can do about it. Still, you'll make a fine hors d'oeuvre.' Benji then turned and moved away. John heard the squeak of a chair as Benji sat down. 'I'm just going to stay here and watch the darkness come. Feel free to join me. I won't hurt you. We can spend a few more hours together before things begin. Or… you can stay down there on your own. Well, maybe not *completely* on your own.'

Benji then fell silent. John remained motionless, just above the mid-floor, looking back up in bewilderment.

It's a dream. Has to be, John told himself. *Please, God, let it be a dream.*

But he knew it wasn't. He looked down at the ground floor once more, gazing into the inky shadows, wondering if there was anything lurking. He knew the door was *right there,* yet had no doubt it would still be stuck, held by the same force that now controlled his friend.

I need to at least try!

John took a breath, clenched his teeth together, then hobbled as quickly as he could down the last flight of stairs. His ankle throbbed, sending jolts of pain up his shin. But John pressed on. His chest felt tighter as the shadows welcomed him.

He then quickly hurried over to the door and grabbed hold of the handle, breathing rapidly, terrified something was going to grab him.

Come on, please work. Please, please, please. He pulled.

The door opened.

John let out a scream.

11

1-11

JOHN FELL BACKWARDS TO THE GROUND, SCRAMBLING AWAY from the horror that stood directly outside the door.

The... *thing*... he was looking at threatened to break his mind.

While having a vaguely humanoid shape, it *wasn't* human. John knew that instantly. It was... wrong. The features were not those of a person, the eyes—*so many eyes*—the *mouths*, and the writhing and pulsating things across its skin, all of it was worse than John could have conjured up in his darkest nightmares.

'No!' John cried in fright, kicking his legs out as he tried to move backwards even faster, the pain in his ankle almost forgotten. The thing outside didn't move, only made inhuman sounds that alternated between chitters and grunts. Just staring at the abomination was enough for John to feel like his hold on reality was slipping away.

He forced himself up the stairs, screaming the whole way, constantly looking back at the open door and the entity on the other side. As he neared the top, John heard the door slam shut once again. He shot out onto the top storey and looked back down, unable to stop from shaking. To his relief, he could no longer hear the awful sounds from the entity he'd just seen. Regardless, John pressed himself against the far wall as much as he could. His heart was beating wildly, and he was bordering on hyperventilating.

'Quite a sight, eh?' Benji asked in a low, mournful voice.

'What… what *was* that thing?' John asked, struggling for breath. His legs felt weak, like he was going to collapse, and his head swam.

'One of… *them*,' Benji replied. 'A lesser one, but one all the same. They're coming. Drawing closer with the night.' He sighed. 'Not long now.'

Despite seeing the thing only moments ago, John was struggling to hold a clear picture of what it had actually looked like. Maybe he hadn't been able to fully comprehend it at the time, or maybe it had been so nightmarish that his mind was trying to protect itself; regardless, any clear picture was lost, leaving only impressions and the odd, horrid detail: flashes of the many eyes, black stalks, inhuman mouths, and the sounds they made.

John pressed his hand to his head and began to pull at his hair, hoping the stinging pain would be enough to wash all memory from his mind.

'This can't be real,' he said, though of course the words were useless.

'Afraid it is, old boy,' Benji replied. He sounded sad.

'You're part of this,' John said with a snarl, jabbing a finger at Benji. '*You're* the same as those things out there. Don't try to fool me.'

Benji slowly nodded. 'I'm both,' he said. 'I'm your friend, and I'm also the envoy of those things. Right now, they're allowing me a little more control. Just to taunt us both, no doubt, knowing how easy it can be pulled away. Still, I really am sorry, for what it's worth.'

'It's worth nothing,' John snapped. 'We're going to die here, all because you wouldn't listen to reason. Because you had to know better and had to keep going. We should never have even come out here in the first place!'

Another nod. 'You're right, of course,' Benji admitted. 'I was too stubborn to see that. So confident that I knew how things were. So yes, we shouldn't have come. You were right: there are places that people should just not tread.'

If Benji had wanted John to be sympathetic to this realisation, he was to be disappointed. 'If that's the case,' John said, 'then just let them take you. This is your fault, so bargain with them to let me go. However you do it, beg for my release. *Then* I'll accept your apology. It's the least you can do.'

Benji gave a surprised smile. 'Nice of you to want to abandon me so easily, John. That is much appreciated.'

'Like I said, penance for you causing this. It's only fair.'

'*Nothing* about this is fair,' Benji replied. 'They don't operate on 'fairness.' They just do what they do. And that *won't* involve letting you go, John. I'm sorry. They have no need to, so why would they?' However, Benji then frowned, cocking his head to the side as if listening. 'Unless…'

'Unless what?' John asked.

Thunder boomed from outside, closer now, sounding like the wrath of God himself. The sun had already begun dipping under the horizon, and the storm only made it darker. 'Not long now,' Benji said as he turned back to the sea.

'Unless what?' John asked again. 'Tell me, what were you going to say?'

Benji hesitated. 'Nothing,' he eventually replied. 'I wasn't going to say anything.'

'Yes you were!' John snapped. He pushed himself away

from the wall, stomping closer. 'Tell me this instant! Is there a way out of this for me?'

'Stop making demands, John!' Benji shot back with a snarl. 'You're in no position to.'

'No!' John shouted and thrust a pointing finger into Benji's shoulder. 'Tell me! If there is a way for me to leave here, then you have to tell me what it is.'

'A way for *you* to leave? Just you, eh?'

John paused. He then crossed his arms defiantly over his chest. 'You said yourself that the deep ones already have you, so I assume it's too late. But it might not be for me.' However, his stern expression then softened as he realised how callous he was being. Regardless, John desperately wanted to escape, and he knew he would leave Benji behind if that was what it took. 'Look,' he began, now speaking softly, 'I'm sorry about all this. I really am. I just… want to be safe. I want to get away from this place. Is… is there a way to make that happen?'

Benji didn't reply. He instead stared out of the window, taking in the ever-darkening view.

'Please,' John added, desperate.

'Sorry,' Benji said. 'They won't let me tell you anything more. I've said all I'm allowed to, so don't ask again.'

'Or what?' John asked, curling a lip and tilting his chin up a little.

Benji slowly got to his feet. He turned to face John, his face becoming dark. 'Or I'll hurt you,' he said in a voice so cold John instantly shrank away. A sinister smirk crossed Benji's lips. John realised he'd gotten complacent around the man. *Those things are still inside him.* He stepped farther away from his friend, who then chuckled. 'Good. Remember your place,' Benji said, sitting back down a moment later with a groan. 'Now,' he went on, 'just shut up and wait. Watch the sunset. It could be your last.'

12

1-12

JOHN POSITIONED HIMSELF ON THE OTHER SIDE OF THE lighthouse from Benji, sitting on the floor, watching his friend the whole time. Constant thunder rumbled outside.

About two hours had passed, and it was now fully dark. Only the slivers of moonlight piercing the clouds outside allowed John to see anything. While he could make out much of the top storey, everything below the stairs was lost. Because of that, the lower levels now seemed cut off to him, as though venturing down there meant certain death.

Which, he realised, it probably did.

John's throat felt like it was clogged with sand, his belly yearned for food, and his eyes felt heavy despite him being terrified. With so much inactivity, his adrenaline levels had plummeted, and tiredness was overtaking him.

The whole time, his thoughts kept running back to the nightmarish abomination he'd seen outside the door. Though by that point John had forgotten its specifics, the feeling of fear and helplessness he'd first experienced in its presence was still just as stark.

He struggled to understand just *what* the entity was.

What were the deep ones? Clearly not human, that much was obvious, but John knew the thing hadn't been a spirit or a ghost, either, not like the two shambling corpses of Mrs. Whitburn and her daughter. At least, that was what his gut told him.

No, that had been something different. Something *more*.

Strong winds battered the lighthouse from outside. Though it might have just been in his head, John was sure he felt a slight sway to the structure as it was bombarded by the violent gusts. The thunder continued, growing in intensity, and John was surprised he was able to feel so tired and drowsy in the cacophony. He also couldn't shake the feeling that the weather might not be completely natural. Like it was there to signify something, or build towards… something.

The arrival of the deep ones, he told himself. They were coming, Benji had made that clear, and with them it seemed they brought the tempest.

There was a louder rumble, then a flash of light out at sea. John was able to watch the fork of lighting spear down from the sky. Rain started to pepper the glass a moment later.

John's apprehension grew.

With nothing else to do, he continued to wait, terrified at what was coming. He didn't dare go back downstairs, and he didn't dare get closer to Benji either, which left John stuck, fearful for his life.

With no choice but to wait for the end.

No, you can't give up, he told himself. *You're fighting for your life! So fight! It's your only chance.*

And yet, John couldn't get his body to move, instead rendered immobile by fear. He felt like a helpless rabbit in the jaws of a predator, simply lying and waiting for the sharp teeth to clamp down harder.

Coward!

John hated himself. If he was going to die anyway, then he knew he should at least try *something,* yet he couldn't find the strength. The memory of that nightmarish thing had quashed the last of his bravery.

Another hour passed. The storm grew closer. More flashes of light exploded in the sky, getting brighter and brighter. The rumbles of thunder grew, causing John's panic to rise with them. The panoramic windows became blurry with the torrent of rain washing down their surface.

Oh God.

It felt like the storm was directly over the lighthouse now, like he was sitting right at the very tip of Heaven's fury.

No, not Heaven.

Slowly, Benji got to his feet, as if sensing the moment as well. His body sagged and his head bowed forward. 'It's time,' he said mournfully.

13

1-13

'Time for what?' John asked. He had an idea, of course, yet couldn't help but ask.

'For their arrival.' John saw that Benji had tears running down his cheeks. The man's eyes looked terrified—it indicated the *real* Benji inside, and yet the man still started to move, walking to the top of the stairs before starting his descent.

'Stop,' John said, desperate. 'Please, Benji, fight against it.'

Benji kept moving, but his eyes flicked back up to John and he flashed a rueful smile.

'Sorry, old boy,' he said. 'I don't have a choice. Neither of us do. We belong to them now.'

'But y-you'll die,' John said, and his voice cracked.

Benji stopped, still staring at John. He gave a slow nod. 'Yes. In a sense. But honestly… it's worse than that. Death won't be the end.' He then turned his head and looked down into the dark. 'It's just the start.' His tears flowed harder. 'Goodbye, John, you really were a good friend. Sorry I dragged you into this.'

'I don't want your apology,' John said as Benji again moved lower. 'I want you to stay here with me and fight it.'

Benji didn't answer. He was soon swallowed up completely by the dark. Above the intermittent sound of thunder and the constant pelting of rain on glass, John could also hear Benji's thudding footsteps get lower and lower and lower.

'Benji!' John called. He got no answer. Eventually, the footsteps stopped on what John assumed was the ground floor. Seeming to know what was happening, the intensity of the thunder dramatically increased. Lightning spears cracked through the sky directly outside. John was certain *some* of them actually struck the lighthouse. The building shook and swayed. The sound of the thunder was deafening, and John clamped his hands over his ears and screwed his eyes shut.

It's happening! It's happening! They're coming!

John realised he was screaming.

Then, almost in an instant, everything grew silent. Not only that, the rain no longer bombarded. The skies outside remained completely dark, though there were no more flashes of light.

Everything was just... quiet. Eerily so.

John waited, listening intently, knowing something was going to happen. His body was tense, his breathing rapid, and his heart hammered wildly.

He kept waiting. Seconds went by, then minutes. Still nothing.

John slowly forced himself to his feet. The sheer act of standing made him feel suddenly more vulnerable. He inched forward and peered over the edge of the guardrail. As before, the dark consumed everything on the lower levels.

He wondered if Benji was okay. He hadn't heard any screaming.

'B… Benji?' John asked in a loud whisper. He didn't get a reply. 'Benji?' he quietly called again several seconds later, even though he knew the result would be the same. 'Are you still down there?'

The silence continued. As well as still being terrified, John was utterly confused. The chaos of the storm had built ferociously, and John had been *certain* that had been leading towards the arrival of those… things. Benji himself had even said it was time.

But nothing had happened. All the chaos had blinked out in an instant.

John gazed around himself, searching the space, just to make sure nothing was up there with him.

There was another flash of bright light outside, causing John to jump in shock. No thunder accompanied it, however, which was strange. The light had been enough to dazzle him, and John instinctively shook his head before bringing his hands up to rub his eyes. He then moved closer to the wall and peered out through the rain-streaked glass. More clouds had rolled in, blocking most of the moonlight, though not quite all of it. The sea stretched on outside, but didn't look angry anymore. There were no roaring waves, just calm, steady undulations.

Another flash lit up the sky and the sea.

John frowned. He looked down to the waters, but darkness had already reclaimed them, making them seem like an obsidian sheet stretching off to the horizon. Still, in the moment of the light, John was certain he'd seen something.

Something massive.

Impossible, he told himself, despite the impossible situation he found himself in. He had been looking up when the flash first hit, so he'd only caught the briefest of glimpses when looking down. But even so… there had been *something* strange under the waters.

Can't have been, John quickly told himself. *Even with the lightning, you couldn't have seen beneath the water from this height.*

He then moved back to the guardrail again and looked down. If there was another lightning flash, he wanted to be able to see his friend. It had remained silent down below, which was almost as bad as if something *were* happening. It was the waiting that was hardest to bear.

Then, finally, John heard something. Movement. Shuffling. Initially, it sounded like one person, then more, as if multiple things were dragging their feet.

A sob followed. *That was Benji!* John was certain of it. He wanted to call down to his friend, but fear held his voice frozen in his throat.

Other sounds then drifted up from the depths. Strange noises that did not sound human. Chittering, gurgles, and something like excited grunting. John narrowed his eyes and lowered his head, hoping to peek through the dark, while at the same time praying he *wouldn't* see what horrors were lurking. Benji continued to sob.

Then… he started to scream.

John's body tensed up at hearing the sudden, high-pitched shrieks of pain.

'Noooo!' Benji cried. The chitters and grunts grew faster, more excited. Benji's pitch grew higher still, to the point he was squealing, like a pig in agony. Whatever was happening to him, it went on for a number of minutes—far longer than John had thought it could—before things grew quieter. The grunts faded, as did Benji's screaming, and all that came then were pained sobs.

Yet again, John wanted to call down to his friend, and part of him even wanted to run down to try to help. But self-preservation—*or cowardice,* John thought—stopped him from doing either. So he did all he could: waited, staring down into the dark.

Soon there was more dragging and shuffling, this time from a single entity. Something eventually reached the stairs. Then, it slowly—incredibly slowly—began to move up higher.

John's heart seized.

No, don't come up here!

He was terrified at what nightmarish horror was now making its way up to see him. He thought of Mrs. Whitburn and her daughter, yet John had no doubt the thing ascending towards him now would be far worse. Like the creature that had blocked the doorway.

The sounds continued up. Not footsteps—it was as if something was actually sliding itself up the spiral staircase. It was only when he heard the accompanying sobbing that John realised who it was.

Benji!

John took half a step forward… but stopped when Benji finally crawled into view, unable to help his gasp of horror. Whatever fear John was feeling before suddenly amplified by a thousand and he struggled not to vomit.

'Benji… What… What…' But instead of finishing, John just began to scream.

How is he still alive?!

'H… Help meeee,' Benji wheezed. The mangled man continued to pull himself up the last of the stairs. He had been stripped of most of his skin, leaving huge swathes of exposed red flesh, which glistened in the moonlight. John could also see connecting tendons and even bone. Much of the skin had been peeled from Benji's face and scalp as well, and blood coated the stairs beneath his form. Large chunks had been taken from his body and one leg was entirely gone from the knee down.

The excited sounds continued from below. Benji was moving too slowly to have escaped on his own—John instinctively knew the things below had *allowed* him to climb up. Which meant they might soon be coming up after him.

'It… hurts,' Benji wheezed in a faint, shaky voice. John saw dirt clinging to the exposed, glistening meat of his friend, and he could only imagine how painful Benji's exposed nerves were.

'What did they do to you?' John asked between sobs.

'E… Eating… me,' Benji stuttered. He managed to pull himself off the top and around onto the walkway, gripping the vertical spindles of the guard rail. 'Help… me.'

How is he still alive? How is he still able to move? None of it made sense to John.

Then, something else started to come up.

Thump, thump, thump, thump.

Footsteps. John realised there were two sets, one lighter than the other. Soon, two disgusting, familiar figures emerged from the darkness and moved out from the stairs, their quick movements taking John by surprise.

Mrs. Whitburn and her daughter scampered close to Benji, standing directly behind him. He desperately tried to crawl away, dragging his body across the ground like a slug while leaving a dark crimson residue behind.

'Time to go back down,' Mrs. Whitburn said with a chuckle. Her voice was cracked and dry. 'Time to see what my husband went through.'

'You'll be with us, Benji' the young girl added. 'For ever and ever.'

They descended onto Benji, lowering their bodies in the blink of an eye and taking hold of the screaming man. As the woman grabbed Benji, she looked up at John, focusing dead eyes on him. 'Just wait. Your turn is coming.'

'No!' John shouted. 'No, please! Not like this! Not like

this!' He looked at Benji's ruined form, knowing that was to be his fate as well. Knowing he was going to feel the same kind of pain was too much for his already weakened mind. 'Please, I beg you, please, just let me go. I'll do anything!'

'We know,' the young girl said.

'Wait,' the woman said again, as if issuing a command to a dog. The pair dragged Benji away, sliding him back down the stairs. He clawed and fought, but it was useless, and he disappeared back into the shadows.

John heard the man's violent screams echo up to him. There was tearing and ripping, followed by awful squelching sounds and prolonged gargles. All of it was accompanied by the inhuman sounds of the feeding entities.

John backed away from the guardrail and sank down to his rear, pulling his knees in to his chest and wrapping his arms around them. He lowered his head to his knees and sobbed.

The utter terror and hopelessness he felt was like nothing he'd experienced before. To know death was coming, and *how* it would come for him, was hard to comprehend.

And impossible to accept.

What's more, the notion that 'death wasn't the end' just further weighed him down with dread.

After what felt like forever, the awful sounds from below died down. Silence once again descended, disturbed only by the wind outside. There was another flash of lightning, though again no accompanying thunder. John was thankful he was away from the bannister and not looking down when the light erupted. The thought of seeing what was below, seeing whatever might be left of Benji, was something John didn't think he could cope with. It would fracture his mind completely.

Maybe... maybe that would be a good thing. Then I wouldn't really be present for what is coming.

John began to pray for his sanity to break. Frustratingly, however, his mind kept clinging to that last thread of lucidity, keeping him present and in the moment. John also hoped for a heart attack. That would end things before he was taken. But although his heart thumped wildly, it didn't look likely either.

John's eyes searched the space, looking for... something, but he didn't know what. Then he realised what he'd wanted to find.

Something to kill myself. Better to go out by his own hand than die like Benji had. *At least then I'll stay dead.*

However, there was nothing around that would work. He then looked at the glass wall. *If I can break that, I can use a sharp edge to...*

John imagined running a shard of glass across his throat. While he knew that would be agonising, it was better than the alternative.

He forced himself to his feet. Facing the glass, John raised his foot, hesitated for a second, then kicked out as hard as he could.

His knee exploded in pain and there was a dull *thud* as his foot connected with the glass. The wall didn't give an inch. It didn't even wobble.

Shit! John tried to ignore the pain and kicked out again.

And again. And again.

His knee throbbed, but John kept kicking, desperate.

'What are you doing?'

John yelped in fright at the voice from right behind him and spun around.

Benji was standing only a few feet away, an amused expression on his face. What's more, he looked... normal: fully clothed and uninjured.

'B... Benji?' John asked in confusion. 'You... But... you were...' John looked at the stairs and pointed.

'I was,' Benji said. 'And eaten. Don't get confused here, though. I *am* now dead. All that stuff really happened.'

John frowned and backed away from the other man. 'Then... how come you're here?'

'It's a weird thing, the soul,' Benji said with a smile. 'It's malleable, pliable. At least, to the things here it is. So, even though I'm here talking to you, I'm also being... what would you call it... digested. Eternally. And though I'm smiling, I can tell you the pain I'm feeling is immeasurable. This grin,' he pointed to his own face, 'isn't mine. *They're* putting it here. I'm just a puppet.'

Jesus Christ.

'Why are you here?' John asked.

'To ask what you're doing.' Benji pointed to the window. 'They want to know.'

'I was trying to break it,' John said.

'That much is obvious. But why? Gonna try to climb down the outside? Bold move. But you wouldn't get far. Even *if* you scaled down to the rocks, you wouldn't get away. They wouldn't let you.'

John stared at his friend. 'I was trying to break the glass. I wanted to get a shard to...' He trailed off.

'Defend yourself?' Benji asked.

John slowly shook his head

Benji gave a slow nod of understanding. 'Yeah, I thought that was it. So you wanted to...' But instead of finishing, he just ran a finger across his own throat. 'That about right?' he asked. John nodded, so Benji went on, 'Yeah, they won't let that happen, either. Sorry, but you don't get to make the choice how you go out. Though... if you really wanna break the window, they could help you with that.'

'What do you mean?' John asked in confusion.

Benji held his smile, yet said nothing. Then there was a sudden roar. It rose up from below, loud enough that John thought his ear drums might burst. It sounded neither human nor animalistic, something different altogether, and brought with it a terrible pressure. John immediately ducked, covering his ears.

The glass walls around him suddenly exploded.

14

1-14

THE BUILDING PRESSURE HAD BURST OUT FROM THE TOP OF the lighthouse as all the glass was blown outwards. John caught sight of shards of glass flying off, all sweeping out to the sea and away from the building.

The roar suddenly ceased. In the ensuing quiet, John heard some of the glass *clink* down on the rocky island below while wind swept in from outside.

Benji was laughing. 'Does that help?'

John gazed around in wide-eyed horror. Every single pane of glass was gone. There weren't even any jagged remains left behind, only intermittent vertical framing. 'What... Why?'

'Does it matter?' Benji asked. 'The glass is gone, so there's nothing stopping you from getting out of there. You could try climbing down. Or, if you've truly given up... just jump.'

John looked out into the night. There was another silent flash of light.

'Waiting for something?' Benji asked.

'This is a trick,' John said. 'They wouldn't let me go free.'

'Of *course* it's a trick,' Benji laughed. 'There's no way out of this for you. But go on and try. I won't stop you. Everything will soon become clear.'

John's mind swam with confusion. *If it's a trick, why bother?* But then, escape—either through death or a managed descent—was *right there*. It was so close. All John had to do was run a few feet and jump. Then, gravity would take over and he could escape Benji's fate.

But what if I survive the fall? John wondered, his mind flashing to the thought of laying on the rocks, broken and helpless, while those things found him.

He stared out at the night sky, wrestling with his decision. Benji watched on.

Fuck it! I have to try.

He then ran forward, hearing Benji laugh, then call out, 'Attaboy!' John quickly reached the edge of the opening and braced himself, ready for the end. A flash of light outside struck at the same time, causing John to instinctively stop. He teetered on the precipice, aware he'd seen something at the edge of his vision below.

Another flash of light flared, illuminating the sky. Then another, and another.

John looked down the face of the lighthouse below as it was repeatedly lit up by the silent spikes of lightning. With every strobe, John was able to see the face of the wall, the rocks at the base of the tower, and the obsidian sheet of the sea.

Only... he could also see *beneath* the sea.

John's heart seized, his body locked, and eyes widened. His mind came as close as it ever had to its breaking point.

Being able to see beneath the water from such a height made little sense to him, but John knew instantly he was somehow being *shown* this. The images under the surface appeared to him like some kind of supernatural projection;

it had sucked out much of the sea's mass, leaving only the thin veil of the surface.

And with every flash, John was witness to the vast, ungodly things that writhed beneath the waves.

Oh... God!

The size of the entities was unfathomable, stretching out to the horizon. John was able to see great and awful eyes, all moving and roving wildly, some focusing on him while others looked up to the sky. Huge openings that he took for mouths were visible, as were swirling, tentacle-like appendages of all sizes. There were spines, horns, pulsating growths the size of houses, and other forms that made no sense.

John guessed there was far more than one titanic entity beneath the water, though they had all seemed to merge into one form. He wanted to scream, but was frozen immobile. And yet, he couldn't draw his eyes away, despite dearly wanting to.

The flashes of light continued, so John was able to make out more. He realised there were other things under the surface as well, bobbing near the top and reaching up with skinless arms.

People.

They were mostly skeletal, like floating corpses, as if their legs were being weighed down and their bodies were upright. There were hundreds of them, and they all reached up to him, mouths open like they were silently wailing underwater.

He felt cold fingers wrap around his shoulder.

'If you jump,' Benji said, 'You won't die outright, and then you'll be taken anyway. *But,* there is another way.' John said nothing. He continued to stare, shaking. Benji continued: 'You asked me before if there was anything you could do to spare yourself. I hinted at something, but wasn't allowed to say more. Well, you *can't* be spared. Sorry. You've spent time here and the things that lurk have licked at your soul and gotten a taste of it. They want it... eventually. However, things can be delayed. It's been such a long time since they've been able to feed, you know, and you may be of use. Most of the souls you see down there are ancient, having been devoured over the centuries. In recent times, however, the area has become secluded; the Gods you see have been forgotten, so their nourishment has been intermittent at best.'

'What are you saying?' John asked, trancelike, still unable to look away.

'Bring more people here,' Benji stated. 'Every few years. One at a time will do. The deep ones don't have to feed often. They don't have to feed at all, really. But they like to. See, they exist in this place and they don't, at once here and somewhere else. It's... complicated. What you see down there is visible only because they want to be. If this were a normal night, the waters would be completely clear. But those things are real, nonetheless.'

'How can that be?'

'Don't try to understand,' Benji said. 'You're still alive, so your living mind won't be able to comprehend it. You'll learn in time, and an understanding will come, as it has for me. But... don't rush to that. Because the price paid for knowledge is eternal agony.'

'I... I can't bring people out here,' John said. 'I can't condemn them to *this*.'

'Then you only condemn yourself,' Benji replied. 'It's up to you. You *do* have a choice, which is more than I had.'

John was finally able to pull his eyes away and turn to Benji. As he did, John jolted in shock.

Benji was no longer whole. Chunks of glistening red meat stuck to his bones, but for the most part the man was skeletal, with small amounts of skin around his chin, chest, and arms. He still had his eyes, which bored into John. When he spoke next, Benji's jaw didn't move. 'Buy yourself some time, my friend. Put this fate off as long as you can.'

John wanted to pull away, but Benji held him firm.

'The police,' John said. 'If I keep bringing people here, they'll suspect me, and then I'll get caught. Plus, the light-house is going to be torn down. There will be people here then, lots of them. Won't that be enough?'

Benji shook his head. 'Bring the owner out here first. Find a way. That way, the lighthouse will remain. After that, it's your job *not* to get caught. If you fail, they'll come for you. There's already a link, so it's unavoidable. In reality, they already have you.'

'How?'

Benji gave a sad smile. 'They just do.'

John started to cry again, even though he felt like he had no tears left. 'Please… please don't make me do this,' he said.

'You have to choose,' Benji said. 'And do it now. You're out of time. What will it be, John? Do I take you down below, or do you want to live a little while longer?'

John stared into Benji's dead eyes. His body shook, but eventually he responded, 'I—I want to live.'

Benji gave a slow nod. 'Glad to hear it. Though I still have to take you down there.'

'What?!' John asked in shock. 'You said that—'

'You will survive,' Benji said, taking firmer hold of John's shoulder. 'Don't worry. But… they want another taste.'

John cried out as Benji's other hand came up and grabbed him as well. The strength of the spectral man was incredible, and John felt himself effortlessly pulled back from the edge of the opening. He was then yanked like a toy towards the stairs—though he fought and screamed, he was pulled down into the dark, where excited grunts and chattering rose in intensity. They soon drowned out John's screams.

15

1-15

JOHN'S EYES SNAPPED OPEN.

A stream of light ran over his body, allowing him to see. He wanted to lift his head... but he couldn't find the strength.

As his mind swam with confusion, it took John a moment to realise that he was lying face down on a cold floor. He searched his memory, trying to recall as much as he could: being dragged down by Benji, cold, slimy things touching him, and his limbs slipping into wet mouths. Chittering. Growling. A mass of pulsating bodies pressing against his own. Then... nothing.

John forced his eyes to focus. There was an entryway in front of him, and he realised he was looking at the open door of the lighthouse. Daylight was streaming in from outside.

All was quiet.

He forced himself up to a sitting position, panic again taking hold. While he was desperate to run away, his body felt too weak, and his movements were slow and sluggish.

What did they do to me?

John managed to turn his head and search the area around him. It was empty again. He looked up the length of the lighthouse and saw nothing out of place, though he did feel a wind roll down towards him. He then summoned all the strength he had and started to crawl over to the door.

He thought of Benji, yet there was no sign of a body. John continued to inch closer and closer to the door, praying nothing would grab him before he was able to get clear. When he reached the threshold, more of his strength returning, John used the side of the opening to pull himself to his feet. He then stumbled outside into the welcoming daylight.

There were shards of broken glass on the ground, so he shuffled as quickly as he could toward the walkway while avoiding them, and eventually started to move down it. It was only when he reached the halfway point that he felt brave enough to turn and look back at the foreboding lighthouse. The glass of the head was missing.

A figure stood on the top story, looking out at him, skeletal and disgusting.

Benji.

The dead man didn't move. He simply stared, watching John.

John remembered the choice he'd made: the job he was now tasked with. As much as he hated himself for it, he knew he would have to be true to his word. He had to feed the beasts, for as long as he was able. Every soul offered up meant staving off his own ultimate, horrific fate.

But he knew that fate would come at some point. He took in as much of Benji's form as he was able to.

That will be you... eventually.

With tears in his eyes, John turned and ran.

NOTES FROM DR. BELLINGHAM

From the files of Dr. Antone Bellingham

NOT MANY PEOPLE WILL BELIEVE ME, I'M CERTAIN OF THAT. Getting people to acknowledge the existence of the supernatural isn't easy at the best of times, especially in my field. People scoff at ghosts and demons. So how do I get them to believe... *this?*

I don't have an answer to that. Not yet. But I do know the evidence I've collected points to something out there that is... new. At least, not commonly known. Not ghost, nor demon, nor monster.

These things are... something else.

2. CLOSER

16

2 - 1

Mia rolled off her husband and let her head drop onto the pillow, then released a long breath. Her legs were trembling.

'Wow,' Toby said with a laugh. 'Talk about a welcome-home present.'

Mia smiled and nuzzled closer to him, resting her head on his chest with the top of her head tucked in just below his stubble-lined chin. Her husband had been working away for two weeks and she'd missed him like hell.

'Glad you enjoyed yourself,' Mia replied, traced her fingernails down his chest, which was rising and falling deeply as he breathed heavily. Just like she was.

'I missed you,' Toby said and gave her an affectionate squeeze.

'I missed you too, babe,' she replied. It was the longest they'd ever been apart. However, Toby's recent promotion meant those trips might become a semi-regular occurrence. Neither of them was particularly thrilled with that, but the extra money was really helping, especially since they'd moved into a new house only three months ago. Technically,

Mia was well off, with a huge chunk of savings handed down by her wealthy parents, but she was adamant about making her own way as much as possible. So, after things with Toby had started to get serious, she'd told him she didn't want to use that pot of money unless they absolutely needed to. Thankfully, he had understood completely and agreed. She knew that was in part to his own pride: he wanted to show he could provide for them.

Mia felt Toby's hand gently glide up and down her arm, stroking her with the lightest of touches. 'How was it being here on your own?' Toby asked. Mia knew why he'd posed the question; she'd admitted to being nervous before he went away, being in the house all alone.

She'd gone from living with her parents and two brothers to moving straight in with Toby after they'd been together for three years. Mia had never lived alone.

'It was fine,' she said, though she knew she didn't sound convincing.

Mia felt him shuffle beneath her. She knew he was looking at her. 'That bad, huh?' he asked.

She chuckled. 'No, it really was fine,' she said. 'Just... a little scary at night.'

'But nothing happened, right?'

'No,' she confirmed. 'Nothing happened. You know me, though, I end up creeping myself out for no reason.'

'Yeah, I *do* know you.' Toby squeezed her again. 'You shouldn't watch so much horror. It doesn't help.'

'Oh, believe me, I didn't watch any while you were away,' the raven-haired girl replied, 'Nothing even remotely scary.'

'Well, that's something,' he said. 'And remember, this house is far too young to be haunted. It's, what, thirty years old at best? No ghosts are that young.' She could sense the sarcasm in his voice.

'That's *plenty* old enough for it to be haunted,' Mia playfully argued. 'But yeah, I think we're good here. There were no strange noises in the night, despite what my imagination tried to conjure up.'

While Mia was absolutely a believer in the paranormal, she knew Toby wasn't. Thankfully, he'd never been condescending with his strictly atheist views and had accepted her beliefs with little to no judgement. In fact, she'd never known him to be judgemental about anything.

The night air drifting in through the open window was starting to feel more than just cool on Mia's skin, so she reached for the sheets that had been thrown back in the heat of passion.

'Cold?' Toby asked.

'Getting that way,' she replied.

'Me too. Let me close the window.'

Toby stood and shuffled away from Mia. As he did, Mia kept her gaze firmly fixed on his rear, grinning. At six-two and with a broad build, Toby was *definitely* her type. Her husband had always been a bit of a gentle giant, which she loved, but she had also seen flashes of his protectiveness when it was needed.

Something else she loved.

He stretched and tilted his head to the side. Mia heard a small crack in his neck. Her husband gave a contented sigh and ran his hand through his short, brown hair, then drew the curtains back a little in order to close the window.

'Huh,' Toby uttered while pulling the window fully closed.

'What is it?' Mia asked. She could see her husband was peering out into the street, his head partly hidden by the thick curtain.

Toby was silent for a moment, so Mia sat up, waiting for him to respond.

'There's someone at the end of the street,' he eventually replied.

Mia furrowed her brow. She checked the digital clock on the nightstand, seeing it was a little after midnight. 'So?' she asked, not quite sure why her husband had found it strange. *It's probably just someone coming home.*

'He's just... standing there,' Toby said. 'Not moving. Like... at all.'

'Strange,' Mia replied.

'Yeah,' Toby said. 'He's kind of looking down the street. I can't make out too much, though. He's just outside the light from one of the streetlights.'

'Then how do you know it's a he?' Mia asked.

She saw her husband shrug. 'Just a guess. He's pretty big. Looks my height. Maybe bigger.'

Mia got out of bed. *Maybe he's just drunk and lost,* she thought. She shuffled herself beside Toby, pushing him aside a little to look out for herself.

There was a single-track road outside, and a grass verge beyond that, which ran for a few meters before hitting a high fenceline. That fenceline separated the rear garden of another street from their own.

There was a row of streetlights on the opposite side of the road, set into the verge, all spaced about ten meters apart. It gave just enough lighting for the most part, though there were pockets of dark between those illuminated cones.

Mia turned her head to the left and gazed up the street, where she instantly saw the figure standing just outside of the wash of the streetlights. She agreed with Toby's assessment that the person was male, judging by their build.

As Toby had said, the man was just standing in place, looking down the street, not moving at all. It was as if he was rooted to the spot. Mia frowned. Though she couldn't be certain—she was unable to make out exactly which way the man's head was facing—it felt to her like he was looking directly at their house.

'Weird,' she said, a shudder washing over her. 'Why is he just standing there?'

'No idea,' Toby said. He moved his head a little, obviously trying to get a better look. 'Is it one of the neighbours? Someone that lives in the street?'

'I don't think so,' Mia replied. Toby was the biggest person that lived on their street, by some distance, so no one matched the build of the stranger.

Eventually, Toby stepped away. 'Forget it,' he said. 'I'm tired. You've worn me out.' He wrapped an arm around Mia's waist and kissed her neck. 'We should get some sleep. Let the idiot stand out there all night.'

Mia turned to Toby with a frown. 'Just go to sleep with him out there?' she asked.

'Of course,' Toby replied. 'Why not? It's not like he's going to do anything. He's out in the street, we're in here. Forget it. He's probably just drunk, maybe lost as well.'

Mia had initially thought the exact same thing, but seeing the man, specifically the way he stood *so* still, unnerved her.

'Drunk people tend to sway when they're standing,' Mia replied, tilting her head to keep watch on the stranger.

'So maybe he's high. Or unhinged.'

Mia's eyes went wide as she snapped her head around to glare at Toby. 'Not helping,' she stated.

Toby laughed and pulled her towards him. 'I'm kidding,' he said. 'Look, it's nothing to worry about. The guy will be gone soon. Let's just get some sleep.'

'And if we're woken up by a crazy person standing in our bedroom and staring at us?' Mia asked with a cocked eyebrow.

Toby grinned. 'Then I'll throw you at him so I can escape.'

Mia hit him on the shoulder, making him laugh. 'No one is

going to break in, babe,' he said. 'If he does, I'll protect you. Now come on, I'm exhausted.'

Mia cast a worried glance back to the window, but climbed in next to Toby anyway. He then pulled her into him before grabbing the duvet and drawing it over them both. He then wrapped her up in his thick arms and kissed her on the cheek.

'I missed you,' he said again. She couldn't help but smile.

'Missed you too, big fella.'

Mia's eyes drifted open. She felt the warmth of Toby's body behind her, the weight of his arm draping over her. Mia was on her side, facing the outer wall, and she could hear Toby's light snores as he slept soundly. The side table was directly in her line of sight, and the digital clock atop it showed the time as a little after four in the morning. Her mind wanted to cling to a dream that had disappeared, and despite desperately trying, Mia could summon no memory of it.

Apart from the red glow from the clock, darkness enveloped the room.

Mia sighed, feeling her bladder making itself known. She wasn't absolutely desperate to go, but it had been enough to wake her, and she knew she likely wouldn't be able to sleep without dealing with it.

'Shit,' she whispered, annoyed. Mia snaked her way out from under Toby's arm, grabbed her phone, then walked quietly around the bed. Once on the dark landing, she used the phone screen to guide herself to the bathroom.

Then, after doing what she needed to, Mia quickly returned to the warmth of the bedroom, moving as silently as she could. It was probably unnecessary, though, as Toby always slept like the dead. It would take more than her just sneaking around to pull him from his sleep.

As she tiptoed around the bed, the curtain-covered window caught Mia's eye, and the memory of the stranger outside sprang up in her mind.

She paused. *I wonder.*

Mia carefully reached out her hand, pulled the curtain back, and pushed her head close to the glass.

The street was empty.

Relief washed over her. She suddenly felt a little silly for being so creeped out earlier, and even sillier for expecting the man to still be there.

After letting the curtain fall closed, she climbed back into bed again. *I'm so glad he's back home.*

17

2 - 2

THE COUPLE SPENT MOST OF THE NEXT DAY WALKING ROUND their local town, shopping, drinking coffee, and eating.

By the time they returned home, it was evening, and night had started to set in. Mia felt drained but content from a long, full day.

The only blemish on the day had been when Toby received a work call, despite having been promised he'd have a few days off. The call had happened when Mia had stepped away for a toilet break, and when she'd returned, she'd noticed Toby's long, apprehensive face.

'What's up?' she'd asked. It was then he'd told her that he needed to go away again—within the next few days.

'So soon?!'

'I'm sorry,' he'd said, looking glum. 'I don't want to, but it's a *really* important contract. I won't be going abroad again, but I will need to spend a few nights in London. There's a bonus involved, though. A good one. And the boss said I'm looking good for another promotion if I keep performing like I am. Are... are you okay with me going? I know it's so soon after the last time.'

Mia had felt a little deflated, but knew it couldn't be helped. She'd laid a hand on Toby's and smiled. 'It's fine,' she'd said. 'Do what you need to. I can't believe they are talking about a promotion already. That's amazing. Well done, babe, I'm proud of you.'

Toby had beamed with relief, then pulled Mia in for a hug. 'Thanks for being so understanding.'

But, as far as Mia was concerned, there wasn't much to be understanding about. Yes, it wasn't ideal for Toby to go away again so soon, but he was providing brilliantly for them during their early days of marriage, and in the grand scheme of things, she knew him being needed at work was a good problem to have.

As long as he didn't end up spending *too* much time away, of course.

That evening, the couple snuggled down together in front of the television to watch a movie. To her surprise, Toby suggested putting on a horror flick.

'You sure?' Mia asked.

'Why not?' he replied. 'Not my thing, but I know you've been starved of scary television since I've been away.'

'That's true,' she said as she leaned into him, resting her head on the crux of his shoulder and neck. 'Plus, I need to get my fix before you desert me again.'

Mia felt his body quickly tense. 'Mia, I'm not deser—'

But she quickly squeezed his leg. 'I'm joking,' she said. 'And you bit too easily.'

He laughed. 'I guess I did. I just feel bad running off again. I really do.'

'Like I said before,' she told him, 'it's fine, so don't worry. Besides, I have a few shifts at work myself, so it will give me time to push on with my assignments as well.'

Mia was five months into an online psychology degree,

and also had a part-time job, keen to ensure she was doing her part for their shared finances.

'Tell you what,' Toby said after kissing her on the top of her head. 'How about, when you get some free time, you look at a holiday for us to take sometime in the summer? Might as well put that bonus to use.'

She turned over to face him. 'Yeah?'

'Why not?' he said. 'We deserve it, and it's been a while since we've been away anywhere together. We'll spend a full week in the sun. Sound good?'

'Sounds amazing!' Mia confirmed and wrapped her arms around him. She kissed him, long and hard, snaking her tongue into his mouth. Things progressed, the movie was forgotten about, and the couple soon ended up in the bedroom.

'Don't look outside again,' Mia said from her position lying on the bed. '*He* might be there.' She did her best to keep a straight face, but wound up laughing at her words.

Toby had stood up and stretched, standing close to the window. The curtains were still open.

'There's no way,' Toby said with a light chuckle. He leaned closer to the window. 'See, the street is totally…' His body tensed up. 'Well shit,' he uttered.

'What?' Mia asked, sitting up in the bed. 'He isn't back, is he?'

Toby turned to look at her, a confused expression on his face. Mia tried to figure out if he was pranking her.

'Erm,' was all Toby said.

Mia quickly jumped up and moved to the window, half expecting to see an empty street and then Toby's grinning face. But the street wasn't empty.

The stranger was back.

'Holy shit,' Mia stated, bringing her hand to her mouth. The man was closer this time, standing roughly halfway down the street. He was again between the pockets of light and motionless, but Mia could make out a little more detail.

She guessed he was a little over six-and-a-half feet tall, and very broad. He was bald, and Mia could even see some kind of marks or lacerations on the top of his head. The man's face, however, was lost to the shadows. He wore a long overcoat that appeared grey, though the colour could have been distorted due to the orange hue of the nearby lights.

'It's so *weird*,' Mia said as she watched him, feeling her skin crawl. 'Why does he just stand there like that?' She remembered what Toby had said the previous night. 'Do you think he's really high?'

'He might be,' Toby said. He then grabbed some jogging bottoms and began to put them on.

'Where do you think you're going?' she asked him.

'To see what his problem is,' Toby replied flatly.

Mia's heart began to race. She grabbed Toby's thick arm. 'No,' she said. 'Don't go out and cause trouble.' What she really wanted to say was, *I don't want you to get hurt,* but she knew hearing that would only dent his pride.

'I'm not going to cause trouble,' Toby said. 'I just wanna know what his deal is. And then I'll *politely* ask him to leave.'

'Let's just call the police,' she suggested. 'Let them sort it out. No need for us to get involved.'

'He's on *our* street,' Toby replied. 'Plenty of reason for us to confront him.'

'Then let one of the neighbours do it.'

'Most people in this street are over fifty,' he said. 'It should be me.' Toby threw on a dark hoodie along with some trainers, then strode from the room with purpose. Mia followed. She grabbed him again as they reached the bottom of the stairs.

'Toby, please, just ignore it. For me.'

He turned to her, studied her face, then gave a reassuring smile. 'Babe, it'll be *fine*,' he said, and placed a kiss on her forehead. 'Just stay inside, okay?'

With that, he opened the door and walked outside into the street. Mia held out a hand and stopped the door from closing behind him so she could peer out as well. Toby, however, stopped midway down the drive. Mia could see why.

The man was gone.

Her husband then slowly moved farther into the street and looked left and right.

'Can you see him?' Mia called.

Toby turned to her and shook his head. 'Must have run off.' Arms wrapped around herself, Mia stepped fully outside, feeling the rough concrete of the driveway beneath her bare feet. She padded halfway down towards her husband while looking around herself. Other than the two of them, the street was clear. Mia was only in her night shorts and a tank top, so the night air bit at her skin.

'So odd,' she muttered to herself. 'Come on, then,' Mia then shouted over to Toby. 'Let's go back inside.'

'You go in,' Toby replied. 'I'm going to have a quick look around.'

He then started to walk farther down the street, towards the darkest area.

'No, Toby, please just—'

'I'll be fine,' Toby shouted back as he strode forwards, waving a dismissive hand. 'Just go back in, Mia. I'll only be a few minutes.'

Stop being so stubborn!

Mia sighed to herself, knowing he wouldn't be swayed.

She entered the house and ran quickly upstairs to get her phone, realising she should have grabbed it before leaving in case she needed to call the police. While in the bedroom again, she looked again out of the window, just able to make out Toby in the darkness. He soon walked back towards the house, passing through each pocket of light. Mia hoped he would come straight back inside, but instead he headed down to the other end of the street. She watched his every step, until he reached the very end of the road, which met another one running perpendicular. Toby looked around, then finally headed back. Mia breathed a sigh of relief.

She heard him come back inside a few minutes later, close the door, and ascend the stairs. He eventually reappeared in the bedroom.

'No sign of him?' she asked, already knowing the answer.

'No,' he said with a shake of his head. Mia detected a slight hint of disappointment.

'Wait, you *wanted* to find him?' she asked.

'Well… yeah,' he replied, getting undressed again. 'I want to put a stop to it. That's two nights in a row the freak has turned up.'

'Then let's hope tonight was the last time.'

'If he's back again tomorrow, I'm going straight out there. I don't know what his problem is, but he can go be a creep somewhere else.'

'Fair enough,' Mia said, closing the curtains. She dearly hoped the man wouldn't return, more so that Toby didn't go getting himself into trouble than anything. She took his hand and led him back to bed. 'For now, let's go back to bed. Hopefully we've seen the last of him.'

18

2 - 3

THE COUPLE SPENT ANOTHER GREAT DAY TOGETHER. DESPITE having fun, however, it remained in the back of Mia's mind that Toby would be leaving the following day. He'd be gone for three nights, and she was feeling apprehensive about it, despite not letting it show.

The guy in the street also added to her concern.

That evening, the couple settled on the couch, once again watching a movie. Mia was lost in her thoughts when she felt Toby kiss her on top of her head. 'Are you okay?' he asked.

'Fine,' she replied. They were snuggled together on the couch, her head resting on his chest. She looked up to see him watching her. 'Why do you ask?'

'You were just kinda... staring,' he said. 'Not watching the TV. Just kinda staring.'

'No, I was watching the movie,' she lied. Truth be told, she couldn't remember what had happened on the screen for at least the last ten minutes.

'You're lying,' he said and kissed her head again. 'Fess up.'

'I was just thinking,' she replied.

'About?'

Mia hesitated. 'About you going away.'

'Thought so,' Toby said. 'I'm really sorry, Mia. It's shitty needing to go so soon after just getting back. But if I get that promotion, I won't need to travel as much.'

'I know,' she said. 'And it's a good thing, it really is. I'm just gonna miss you.'

'I'll miss you too,' Toby replied, staring deep into her eyes. It seemed like he wanted to say something else.

'What is it?' she asked, poking him in the chest. 'Your turn. There's something you want to say, I know it.'

He shrugged. 'It's just… I feel doubly bad about leaving. Especially after… you know, the idiot out in the street the last couple of nights.'

'Look, if he keeps coming back, I'll just call the police,' she said, trying to ease his apprehension despite still feeling it herself. 'I mean, it's creepy, don't get me wrong, but it isn't like he's harassing us specifically. He's just… standing in the street, so he's as much of a nuisance to the neighbours as to us.'

'Yeah, I know,' Toby said. 'And I don't think it's anything to worry about, really. Still don't like it, though. Like you said, if you see him while I'm gone, I want you to call the police straight away. Don't hesitate, just call.'

'Don't worry, that's exactly what I intend to do. I won't mess around.'

'Good,' Toby said and gave her a squeeze. 'Are you *certain* you're okay with me going? If you want, I can call work and cancel. Say something urgent has come up.'

'No, it's fine,' Mia quickly replied. 'It's a great opportunity, especially if it leads to another promotion. If it does, you'll be around more *and* we'll have more money coming in. It's win-win.'

'True. Just sucks for now.'

'First-world problems,' Mia said. 'We're doing well, babe. If this is the worst we have to worry about, I'll take it in a heartbeat.'

He kissed her again, this time on the lips, strong and passionate. When he pulled away, he looked longingly into her eyes. 'Enough of the film,' he said. 'It's our last night together for a little bit, so let's make it count.'

Toby stood up, then effortlessly scooped her up in his arms, his left arm supporting her back and his right arm hooked under her dangling legs.

'How can I say no to that?' Mia said, grinning from ear to ear.

'All clear?' Toby asked from the bed.

Mia was gazing out the window into the dark, empty street.

'All clear,' she confirmed, pulling the curtains closed. 'Thank God.' As she moved back over to Toby, she checked the clock. 'Though it is a little earlier than when we saw him yesterday. Maybe he's on his way.'

'Don't tempt fate,' Toby said. As she approached him, he pulled her into the bed. 'I'll check a little later, if it makes you feel better. For now, why don't we go for round two?'

She cocked an eyebrow. 'Feeling pretty amorous, eh? You have enough in you to go again, stud?'

'You're about to find out,' he said, cupped her face, and kissed her.

Thirty minutes later, Mia was lying in Toby's arms, both sleepy and satisfied. They'd talked a little after sex, but the conversation had eventually lulled, so she was struggling to keep her eyes open.

'You've worn me out,' she said and playfully grabbed his nipple. He jolted.

'*I've* worn *you* out?' he asked with a laugh. 'I don't think I've ever felt this drained.'

Mia kissed him on the chest and slid out of bed.

'Where are you going?' he asked.

'To brush my teeth before I pass out,' she replied.

'Good idea,' he said, and got up to join her. Once the couple had finished in the bathroom and re-entered the bedroom, Toby got into bed. Mia, however, stood looking at the window. She saw Toby glance over at her, then to the window, and he finally nodded at her. 'I'll check,' he said.

Mia watched as her man slid out of bed and pulled back the curtains. She then saw his body tense.

'Mother*fucker,*' he uttered. Mia ran to the window and gazed out as well.

The man was back. And closer this time. He now stood at the end of the couple's driveway… facing their house.

Mia gasped.

She could make out a little more of the stranger, including the dirt and muck that lined his coat and more of the lacerations on his head. Some of the cuts looked old and partially healed, some even being nothing more than scars, though others looked relatively fresh.

One thing confused Mia, however: at such a close distance, and because of the nearby streetlight, she should have been able see his face. However, most of it was still inexplicably lost to shadow.

'I'm going to kill him,' Toby snapped. He turned and stomped over to the door, only wearing boxer shorts, not bothering to even throw on any jogging bottoms.

'Toby, wait,' Mia shouted and ran after him, grabbing his arm. 'Just wait. Let's call the police.' He didn't listen and continued on. Mia chased him down the stairs, now beginning to truly worry. 'Toby, stop,' she pleaded. 'Let's just get the police here, for God's sake!'

Toby threw the door open and marched outside. And just like the previous night... the man was gone.

But Toby kept going, fists clenched, striding down to the end of the drive. 'Wait!' Mia snapped at him from the doorway.

She couldn't understand how the man had disappeared so quickly, unless he had hopped a nearby fence. However, most of the fenceline was blocked by dense hedges, which should have slowed him down.

Toby was obviously thinking the same thing, and he trotted over the road, marched across the grass, and fought his way through the hedges to the fence. Mia knew his exposed skin would likely get scratched to high hell from the thin branches, yet he seemed not to care.

She saw him grab the top of the head-height fence and pull himself up, looking over into what was someone's rear garden. He turned his head left and right multiple times before finally letting himself drop down again. He then fought back through the hedge and made his way over to her, face filled with anger.

'He's gone,' Toby seethed. 'But I'm gonna call the police. I won't accept some freak messing with us like this.' He ushered Mia into the house and closed the door behind them, before heading upstairs to grab his phone.

It took the police a half hour to turn up, and the two officers spent less than fifteen minutes with the couple going over everything. The officers also checked the area outside, but with nothing else to go on, they left the couple while offering some final advice: call again if the guy showed back up, and consider getting some security cameras.

However, after they'd left, Mia was left with the feeling that the call had been pointless.

'Fat lot of good that did,' Toby said as the pair retreated back upstairs. He took a seat on the edge of the bed and Mia could feel anger radiating from him. She sat next to him and rubbed his shoulder. He leaned sideways into her. 'I'm gonna call work first thing tomorrow and explain things. Tell them I can't go.'

Mia immediately felt guilt rush through her. She knew her reaction was foolish—it wasn't *her* fault the psychopath had shown up, after all—yet she didn't want Toby being worried about her to be a reason they missed out on a better future.

'No,' she said. 'Just go. Please. I *want* you to, really.'

'Not a chance,' he said with a shake of his head. 'Not when this keeps happening. Short notice or not, work will just have to deal with it. He wasn't just on the street this time, Mia, he was at the end of our drive. *Facing* our house. He's getting closer every night.'

'I know,' Mia said, rubbing his shoulder. 'But... I won't be here.'

He turned to look at her, confused. 'Huh?'

'I'll go to my parents. They have plenty of space.'

He studied her face. 'You sure?' he asked. 'It isn't fair you having to leave your house.'

But Mia shrugged. 'I know. But it's only for a few days. I'll also go out tomorrow and get some cameras for the house, set them up on a feed. I want to know if he tries to break in.'

Toby hesitated for a moment, still studying her. 'Don't go and fall off the ladder and get yourself hurt,' he said and playfully. 'Ask your dad to help you.'

'I'm perfectly capable, Toby,' Mia said with a frown.

He held his hands up. 'I know you are,' he quickly replied. 'You're certainly better at DIY than I am. But I also know what you're like—you wouldn't think twice about scrambling up the ladder just to get something done, without anyone at the bottom holding it for you. You're rather bull-headed when you set your mind to something. So... make sure your dad helps.'

'Fair enough,' she told him.

They sat in silence for a couple of minutes. 'You sure?' Toby asked her.

She nodded. 'I am. I really am. I'm not letting some idiot that likes spooking people ruin our future.'

'Thanks,' he said, and kissed her temple. 'You tired?'

'Not really,' Mia said. 'But I know you need sleep for your drive tomorrow. That's going to be a slog.'

Toby nodded. 'Yeah, it will be, but I'm not sleepy either. Too wired.'

'Come on,' Mia said, pushing him down to the bed. 'Let's snuggle for a bit, see if we can drop off.'

The couple lay in each other's arms for several hours before they were both asleep, with Mia drifting away last.

She awoke in the middle of the night, eyes snapping open. Something lingered in her mind: a dream she couldn't quite remember. It had scared her, she knew that much, but... she couldn't remember why.

Mia let out a sigh, annoyed at having her sleep broken a second night in a row. She'd rolled away from Toby in the night, and was now close to the edge of the bed. Her eyes moved over to the window. She kept thinking of that man.

It was obvious to her there was something wrong with him: no normal person would stalk a street like that, night after night. She wondered if it was drugs, as Toby had suggested. *If he's high, he might not be in control.*

But then another thought struck her: *He keeps coming back to this street specifically. That seems like he knows what he's doing.*

Then there was the way the man didn't move at all, just stood stock-still like a statue.

What if he's out there now? she wondered. The thought caused a creeping sensation to work its way up her spine.

She knew she wouldn't be able to sleep again until she'd checked. After taking a breath, Mia quietly lifted herself from the bed, leaned over, and pulled the curtain back so she could look out into the street.

Thankfully, the coast was clear. *Thank God.*

Mia got back into bed and snuggled down. She thought about what the next day would bring. She'd have to explain to her parents what had been going on; they would no doubt worry, so she wasn't looking forward to that.

But at least you'll be out of the house and away from that creep.

It was a comforting thought, so Mia held on to it until she eventually drifted back to sleep.

19

2 - 4

'IS IT WORKING?' MIA'S FATHER ASKED AS BOTH OF THEM stood outside her house. She had just set up cameras on the front corners of the dwelling, unreachable unless someone had a ladder. Mia checked the app on her phone, which was hooked up to the cameras, and saw the streams were live. The images on-screen showed herself and her dad looking up.

'It is,' Mia eventually replied, satisfied with her work.

After a moment, her father turned to her. 'I still can't believe the police didn't do anything,' he said.

'I know,' Mia replied.

'You have a bloody *stalker* and they're just shrugging it off. If I ever get my hands on the shit-bag that's doing this...'

Mia smiled at him. Her father was in his late sixties, short, balding, and walked with a limp due to a bad hip he refused to go to get fixed. In truth, she knew there wasn't much her father could do, but she loved him for thinking that way.

'Well,' she said, 'we don't know that it *is* a stalker. Plus, the police didn't really have anything to go on, as frustrating as it is. They can't just magic up leads to follow.'

'They could leave a car outside your house.'

Mia laughed. 'For how long?' she asked. 'I don't think the police have the manpower for that. Besides, if he comes back tonight, we'll see him on the stream.' She wiggled her phone.

'I guess that's true,' her dad said. 'But now there's no-one to stop him if he tries to break in.'

'Yeah, but at least we'll get him on video,' Mia replied. 'And hopefully it would help the police catch him.' She wanted to add that she didn't think the man's intention *was* to break in. Him doing that just didn't make sense to her. Why just stand there on show for night after night if it was his intention?

Of course, that made his true motives, whatever they may be, seem more nefarious.

The two then returned to Mia's parents' house. She took with her a case she'd packed with clothes, toiletries, and other necessities, plus some nonessentials, such as her tablet, laptop, earphones, and an e-reader. She loved her parents, but felt weird returning home after so long and knew she would need plenty of time to herself.

Upon entering the house, Mia's mother came straight over to her, demanding to know more. Her mother was full of concern, just as Mia's father had been.

Eventually, Mia was able to appease them both to some extent, telling them she and Toby would get things sorted out and that this was only a temporary issue. Mia also stressed that, technically, the man hadn't done anything wrong yet. He had only been standing on a street at night, creepy as it was. Her mother dismissed that notion, saying he was obviously leading up to something... which Mia found hard to argue. Her mother also made a cutting remark about Toby going away, implying he should have stayed, but Mia ignored it.

The rest of the day was relatively pleasant, and Mia enjoyed spending time back with her parents, who waited on her hand and foot. That evening, they all watched a movie her mother picked out, though Mia didn't pay much attention to it. She instead spent most of the time scrolling on her phone and checking the feed. At about eight-thirty, she received a video call from Toby—she felt her mood soar.

'It's Toby,' she announced to her parents. 'I'm just gonna take this upstairs.'

'Tell him hello from us,' her dad said.

'And tell him to come home sooner,' her mother added. Mia just rolled her eyes and left the room, heading upstairs to the spare bedroom she was using, and answered the call en route.

'Hey!' she said as she climbed onto the landing. 'How's it going, babe?' It felt good to see his smiling face, even though she'd seen him that morning before he'd left.

'Good,' Toby replied. 'Drive was okay and work was productive. A good day. Well, as far as work goes. Still hate that I had to leave you.'

'I'm fine,' Mia said with a grin. 'Mum and Dad have been doting on me all day and treating me like a queen.'

'I'm sure your mother just *loves* that I've gone away and left you to deal with what's happening.'

'She hasn't mentioned it,' Mia lied.

Toby just laughed and shook his head, clearly not believing her. 'Did everything go okay with the camera installation?' he asked.

'It did,' Mia said. 'I'll send you the link for the app, as well as the login details. Then you can check the stream on your phone as well, if you want to.'

'Yeah, do that,' he said. 'Are the cameras visible from the

street? Like, is someone going to know they're being watched?'

'Yeah,' Mia confirmed. 'But they're high up, so no one can get to them, unless they climb up there as well.'

'Perfect,' Toby said. 'The sight of them might be enough to deter the guy.'

'Gimme a sec,' Mia said. She minimised his picture on the phone, and with a few clicks sent him the information he needed for the feed. She then brought him back to fullscreen. 'You should get a message soon, then you'll have everything you need.'

She heard a *ping* through her phone. 'Yup, got it,' he confirmed. 'Thank you. I'll get everything set up on my end once we finish here.'

'I bet we're both going to check it all night long,' she said with a laugh.

'Probably,' Toby said. 'There's nothing else to do in the hotel here, to be honest.'

'Have you eaten yet?'

'Yeah,' Toby replied, 'Had something as soon as I finished work, just before I called you.'

The couple continued to chat for another half-hour, filling each other in with more detail about their respective days, about whether they thought the stranger would show up again, and about what they would do if they saw him on the feed. They both agreed: call the police.

Finally, it came time for the call to end.

'I'll speak to you tomorrow,' Mia said, blowing Toby a kiss.

'Yeah, speak tomorrow, babe,' he replied. 'Unless I spot something on the feed. Then I'll be on the phone straight away.'

'Ha, then this is the one time I don't want you calling back,' Mia said. 'No offence.'

'None taken,' he replied with a grin. 'Hopefully he gets bored and goes to harass someone else.'

'Or, you know, he just stops harassing people altogether.'

'Probably a better option,' Toby conceded.

The couple then said their final goodbyes and Mia went back downstairs. Her dad asked how Toby's trip was going, and she told him it was going well, then they started to watch television again. Thankfully, there were no further snide comments from Mia's mother. As the evening wore on, Mia found herself constantly checking her phone and looking at the feed, which came as no surprise. It was odd to see the outside of her house in the grey tones of the night-vision footage. It was like something out of one of the horror films Mia watched, and she kept expecting something creepy to shamble into view.

Thankfully, every time she checked—each time with a tingle of apprehension—the coast was clear.

The lack of sleep from the previous nights was starting to catch up with her, so at ten-thirty Mia announced that she would be turning in for the night. She gave each of her parents a quick hug, then headed up to her room, which overlooked the considerable rear garden.

After going through her nightly routine, Mia climbed into bed and sent a goodnight text to Toby. After that, she checked the stream on her phone again. The stranger still wasn't there. A reply came from Toby, wishing her a good night and telling Mia he loved her.

Satisfied, Mia set her phone to charge, placed it on the nightstand, rolled over in the bed, and closed her eyes.

Mia awoke in the dead of night. Yet again, she had the impression of strange dreams that were now lost to time.

I should go back to sleep.

Her bladder again had other ideas. She sighed, then crawled out of bed and tiptoed over to the bathroom door in the dark. Once done, she came back... then noticed a white light coming in around the edges of the curtains.

Strange, she thought, and realised it was the security light from the back of the house. After a few moments, the light went off. Mia padded over to the window, moved the curtain aside, and peered out to the long garden.

She gasped.

2 - 5

THE MAN WAS CLOSE TO THE HOUSE.

No!

Terror seized Mia. Her heart hammered in her chest. Her breathing came in short, sharp breaths. She couldn't believe what she was seeing.

He... he's followed me here!

The realisation terrified Mia. She couldn't remember fear as extreme as the sensation currently gripping her. It had her frozen and rooted to the spot, as motionless as the man outside.

While Mia could see more of his dirty, ragged clothing, the man's face was still frustratingly obscured by unnatural shadows.

Mia didn't know what to do. She thought of her mum and dad, who she realised were now in danger as well—all because of her.

Because I brought this freak out here.

Mia couldn't wrap her head around *how* the psychopath had been able to find her. *How long has be been watching me?*

The thought that she might have been a target for a while caused her to shudder.

The stranger continued to just stand perfectly still. Mia was tempted to open the window and scream at him, maybe scare him away. There was an anger mixed in with her fear, and she wanted to unleash it. *Who the fuck does he think he is?* However, she refrained, knowing angering the man might be dangerous, since she had no clue how he would react.

She dearly wished Toby was there by her side.

Call Toby! She knew she should call the police first, but wanted to hear her husband's voice. So, Mia moved swiftly to her nightstand, grabbed her phone, and called him, praying Toby's phone wasn't on silent and that ringing would wake him. Upon pulling back the curtain again, however, her eyes widened in surprise.

The man was gone. *No, not again!* In that moment, she realised she'd never actually seen the man move. He always disappeared when out of view. *That can't be a coincidence.*

Mia looked around the garden as best she could from her vantage point, but couldn't see any sign of him. The phone in her hand continued to ring.

How could he have gotten away so quickly?

The only thing she could think was that he'd moved farther back into the darkness—there simply hadn't been enough time for him to have moved anywhere else. *But if he'd moved, the security light would have gone off again.*

'Mia, is everything okay?' Toby's voice came through, groggy, but full of concern.

'He's here!' Mia quickly said. She tried to keep her voice low, so as not to wake her parents, but couldn't keep the fear out of her tone.

There was a moment's silence. 'He... *What?*' Toby asked, obviously shocked.

'I just saw him in the back garden, Toby. He was standing

there, just like he was before. I ran to get my phone to call you, but when I came back to the window… he was gone.'

Another brief silence. 'And you're still at your parents' house, right?'

'Yeah.'

'So… he followed you out there?'

'I think so.'

'Jesus Christ,' Toby uttered. He sounded panicked. 'Okay, I'm gonna jump in the car and get back there now.'

Mia couldn't help the flush of happiness at his words, however… 'It'll take you hours to drive back,' she said.

'I know,' he replied. 'Have you called the police?'

'Not yet,' Mia admitted. 'I wanted to call you first.'

'Call the police as well. Do that now. Please. I'll get packed and leave straight away.'

'What about work?'

'Screw work,' he replied. 'They'll understand. And if they don't… fuck them. I shouldn't have left in the first place. I'm such a fucking idiot.'

'Don't blame yourself,' Mia replied, unable to stop the feeling of guilt. 'We didn't know he would go this far.'

'Do your parents know he's out there?'

'No,' Mia said. Hearing Toby say 'he's out there' just reinforced the fact that it wasn't over. The man *was* still out there, prowling around in the dark. She knew it, and immediately shivered. 'They're still sleeping,' she added.

'Okay,' Toby replied. She heard him moving around. 'Call the police straight away, babe. They'll send someone out. Just make sure you're all safe. I'll get to you as quickly as I can. Keep me updated and ring when you can.'

'I will,' Mia replied. She felt her chest tighten at the thought of having to hang up.

'I love you,' he said. 'I'll be there soon. Stay inside and call the police,' he reiterated.

'I love you too,' Mia replied. 'And I will.'

With that, she hung up, took a steady breath, then called the police. Just as the phone started to ring, the bedroom door opened and light flooded in from the corridor, causing Mia to let out a yelp of surprise. She turned to see both her parents standing in the doorway.

'You scared me!' she snapped.

'What's going on?' her mother asked with a frown. She flicked on the bedroom light as well. Mia's mother then pointed to the phone in Mia's hand. 'Who are you talking to?'

'The police,' Mia quickly replied. 'That man... he's... he's out in the garden.'

Her mother's face dropped, and her dad's eyes shot open wide. 'Jesus,' her father muttered, then hurriedly moved over to the window.

'He's hiding somewhere,' Mia said. 'But I know he's still here. I saw him when I woke up.'

'Hello, what is the nature of your emergency?' a male voice came through on the other end of the phone.

'Hello?' Mia said. 'Someone is outside my house. No, sorry, it's my parents' house. This man has been following me for days now, and I—I think he's still outside.' She also quickly gave the address, then continued on, getting more and more panicked: 'I know he's still there. I just know it. Please send someone quickly. I think we're in danger.'

'Okay,' the male voice said, 'Please remain calm. Can you—'

A piercing scream from Mia's mother forced Mia to spin around, and then she started to scream as well.

The man stood in the open doorway.

21

2 - 6

'MA'AM?' PETE PHELAN SAID INTO THE PHONE AFTER HEARING screams from the other end. The woman he'd been speaking to had already sounded frightened, but something had obviously happened to escalate things.

Given the commotion he was hearing, Pete's gut told him the stalker had gotten inside. The screaming continued. 'Ma'am, can you hear me? A car is en route,' he said, trying to keep his tone level and calm. 'Are you able to get somewhere safe?'

'His eyes!' the woman on the line screeched. 'Oh my God, his *eyes!*'

'Ma'am?' Pete said again.

The screaming increased, coming from multiple people, and getting so intense he almost wanted to throw off his headphones. *Good God, what's happening?*

Pete noticed another sound mixed in with the shrieking, though he couldn't quite make sense of it. It was a kind of whispering, which was impossible, since the screams should have drowned that out. Regardless, he was *certain* he could hear it, yet he couldn't understand the words being said.

The blood-curdling screams continued, getting higher and higher, until finally… everything was silent.

'Hello?' Pete said desperately into the phone. 'Hello? Ma'am? Are you there? Hello?'

22

2 - 7

Though Toby's face was set like stone, tears ran down his face as he watched Mia's coffin slide slowly into the furnace. Once it was completely inside, two velvet curtains fell across the opening, shielding the coffin from view.

Toby bowed his head. His body shook. Unable to hold it back any longer, he started to sob uncontrollably. Toby then felt his mother's hand on his shoulder. She had attended Mia's funeral as well, both because she'd known and liked Mia, but also to lend emotional support to her son.

The crematorium was packed. Toby could have only imagined how full it would have been had all the funerals taken place at the same time—Mia's, her mother's, and her father's. But in the end, Mia's brothers had decided to hold her funeral separately. Mia's was first.

Toby still hadn't come to terms with what had happened. While losing the love of your life was obviously traumatic and would take a long time for him to get over, it was the circumstance of the death that was making things that much harder.

All three of them, murdered, in the most savage of ways.

Whoever that stranger was, there had been no sign of him since the fateful night. The police had nothing to go on as far as Toby could tell, and if they had, they weren't sharing the info.

The moment he'd arrived at Mia's parents' in the early hours of that morning, Toby had known straight away the worst had happened. En route, he hadn't been able to reach her by phone, and upon pulling into the estate, Toby saw a cluster of police squad cars in front of the house, lights flashing. Men and women in white suits had been marching in and out of the house, which itself had been cordoned off with tape.

At first, when Toby had run towards the house, a police officer had stopped him and demanded to know who he was. Toby had explained frantically he was Mia's husband, but anger had overtaken him, so he'd struggled to keep calm and explain himself rationally, resulting in three officers having to restrain him.

After more questions, the police divulged what had happened and Toby learned the terrible truth: his wife and her parents had had their eyes messily pulled out and their craniums savagely caved in.

Three weeks later, Toby still couldn't understand the why. Killing a person was bad enough, but murdering an entire family in such a sick fashion...

People started to file out of the crematorium. Many were crying. A few cast sympathetic glances over to Toby.

Initially, Toby himself had been taken into custody, and he was sure he was being treated as a suspect. However, phone records, his hotel booking, and footage from the hotel's security cameras had all cleared him of any involvement. But with him out of the picture, it seemed the police had no more leads to follow, and their updates to him on how the case was progressing dried up.

The police did believe Toby's story about the stalker; they had the incident report where police had visited Toby and Mia's house earlier that week. But they had nothing else to go on. Toby was aware of a call made to the police by Mia before she was killed, though he hadn't been allowed to hear it.

A wake was scheduled for straight after the cremation, held in a local pub. People had asked if it was going to be at Toby and Mia's house, but Toby didn't have the strength to host something like that. It was too painful to be there, in their house, knowing Mia would never come home. In truth, he'd avoided their home as much as he could over the past three weeks.

While at the wake, Toby spoke to people only as much as he needed to, then made his excuses and left. He didn't go home.

Instead, he went to a nearby hotel, where he'd been staying for the last several days. Toby didn't want to be around people and at the same time didn't want to be anywhere familiar. He felt an overwhelming desire to just escape.

After entering his room, Toby just collapsed onto the bed and began to cry.

Only a few weeks ago, he'd had the perfect life, shared with the woman he loved. That had all changed in an instant.

While on the bed, Toby turned his head and gazed at the window in the room, which looked out over the car park. For reasons Toby couldn't explain, he felt a draw, a kind of morbid longing to pull back the curtain and look outside.

Will I see him if I do? Will he get closer and closer to me every night, like he did to Mia?

The thought it hadn't *really* been a man at all—but something *else*—crept again into Toby's mind. He'd admonished himself every time he'd thought it, but each time it seemed

161

more and more plausible to him. *Stupid,* he told himself. *Mia was the one who believed in that kind of stuff.*

Unable to resist any longer, he sat up, swung his legs off the bed, and stood. He felt tension gripping him, scared of what he might see. *There's nothing there,* he told himself. *Nothing at all.*

Regardless, he slowly walked to the window. Then, just as he'd done every day for the last two weeks, he reached out a hand, steeled his nerves, and pulled back the curtain.

3. THE ATTIC

3 - 1

'Looks good,' Marc said as he and the owner of the home moved back to the main living space. 'You sure you can commit to the full six months?'

'Absolutely,' replied the owner—a stocky man in his late fifties named Dave. 'I normally do shorter-term leases, but I'm happy to block it out for the full duration, provided you're happy to pay fifty percent up front.'

Marc nodded. 'That's okay with me. I just need a place for my job, and this is a perfect location.' He held out his hand. 'Shake on it?'

Dave chuckled and shook, his grip firm. 'Excellent,' he said. 'A gentleman's agreement can't be broken, though.' He raised a finger while saying this. 'No changing your mind before I get the paperwork updated.'

'Don't worry,' Marc said, 'no way I'll find anything more convenient than this. How soon can you get the approval information over?'

'Later today. I'll email it to you, and if you get it signed and returned straight away, that'll lock the house in.'

'Sounds great,' Marc said.

Just then, Dave's mobile phone rang, but when the man pulled the device from his pocket and looked at the screen, a frown crossed his face. 'Not sure who this is,' he said and looked back to Marc. 'Mind if I take it?'

'Go ahead,' Marc replied.

The other man stepped away and answered the call. As he did, Marc glanced around again at his surroundings.

The house was modern, built within the last six years, and sat at the end of a terrace. What had surprised Marc most about it was the height of the ceilings. He knew with most newer houses, the ceiling heights tended to be around two and a half meters, yet not so with these. Marc estimated the ceilings here to be closer to three and a half metres, with that extra meter giving the two-bedroom dwelling a spacious feel not normally present in terraced houses.

The decor was simple but worked: light white walls, a light brown carpet, and flat ceilings. The colours used were basic and inoffensive colours for the most part, which made sense considering the owner was aiming for broad appeal. Dave had mentioned that he'd purchased the house right after construction with the sole intention of leasing it out.

Given the milquetoast setup in most of the dwelling then, it was the kitchen that stood out most to Marc; it was in stark contrast to the rest, and the one room he really didn't like. It had all the required amenities, but the many, many cupboard doors running from floor to ceiling were a bold red gloss, which was overpowering and striking upon entering the space. The colour reminded Marc of those seats in American diners—not that he'd ever visited any in person —and was completely at odds with the unobtrusiveness of the rest of the decor. To him, it almost seemed like the owner had made sure to keep things sensible through the rest of the house, and then finally broke and just cut loose in the kitchen.

Shame, Marc had thought, but he knew it was inconsequential in the scheme of things. The house was clean and well maintained, which were far more important. Odd colour choices weren't a deal breaker for him.

The kitchen had a circular dining table with gaudy red-backed chairs around it, though it wasn't large enough for him to work from. However, the living area had ample space for him to move in a small desk, which he could use when he needed to do extra hours at home. The living room also had a sliding glazed door that looked out to the rear garden and allowed a lot of natural light to come through. Though the term 'garden' was stretching things a little: high brick walls enclosed a small space with some artificial grass, a shed, and a two-person metal seat.

The kitchen was situated at the front of the house, overlooking some parking spaces and more housing beyond, with the entrance hallway adjacent to the kitchen that led to the living room. There was also a small downstairs toilet just off the corridor.

The stairs were accessed from the living room, with no separating door to them, just an opening.

Upstairs, there was a landing that ran both left and right, and Marc had earlier noticed a loft hatch in the ceiling there. To the left was the master bedroom and its en-suite. A large bathroom was straight ahead, and the second bedroom, which was still spacious and offered even more storage space, was to the right. As with the ground floor, the high ceilings were a benefit, though Marc had a feeling they would be a pain to clean—not that it would matter during his residency.

'Sorry, it's just gone,' Marc heard Dave say into the

phone. 'I'm literally standing with someone right now who has booked the house for the near future. Sorry, I can't meet those dates. I do have another property nearby which might work for you, though.' Dave moved from the room as he spoke, walking off into the kitchen.

The place seems popular, Marc thought to himself. *Figures, it's in a good location.* While the surrounding estate was fairly run of the mill, it *was* close to a major motorway, giving good access to surrounding areas. One such area was an industrial estate only a ten-minute drive away, and the company Marc worked for had a production plant there. Marc had been assigned to oversee some operations at the industrial unit for the next half year, hence his need for temporary accommodation.

Dave soon came back, wearing a smile. 'Looks like you were just in time snapping this place up,' he said, holding his phone in front of him and wiggling it as if to emphasise his point. 'Luckily I think I have something else for them, so all good.'

Marc gave a polite smile in return. 'Guess so. Do you need anything else from me?'

Dave shook his head. 'Nope. Just sign the documents and get them back to me as soon as you can.' He hesitated. 'I will say, though, if I don't get the signed documents back in a day or so, I'll consider advertising the place again. I've had people mess me around with leases before.'

'I'll get them back today,' Marc stated.

'Great,' Dave replied with a big smile. 'Then, unless you want another look around or have any questions, we're all set.'

'I'm good,' Marc told the other man. Marc had seen everything he'd needed to, and asked all the questions he could think of. In truth, he did think the rate was a little high, but since his company was footing the bill, he saw no point in trying to haggle. He also knew places offering short-term leases were generally more expensive. That was just how it worked. Marc knew he could have gotten a six-month lease with a more traditional landlord, but it would also mean he couldn't break the lease early if needed. Dave only required a single weeks' notice, and there was no cancellation fee. The company would pay more in the long run, but there was nothing else as well situated. Plus, the house was fully furnished.

'Excellent,' Dave said. 'I'm sure you'll love staying here. Where are you originally from, if you don't mind me asking?'

'Farther down south,' was all Marc offered in reply. 'And thanks, I'm sure I'll be fine here.'

With that, both men headed outside, and Dave locked up behind them.

Though the property Marc was renting was at the end of a terrace, there was a pair of semi-detached units just to his right, laid out ninety-degrees to the longer terrace. The ground outside was one big mass of pastel-orange block paving, with no front gardens to break up the space.

There was, however, a walkway not too far away leading to a small, grassed children's play area. A group of kids were currently running around there laughing and playing tag, weaving in and out of a climbing frame.

Marc noticed all the dwellings on the estate had similar designs, with mainly brick outer walls mixed with sections of horizontal shiplap timber cladding to break up the elevations. The metal-framed windows were long, with most being full height and running down to floor level.

'Right then,' Dave said, offering his hand again. 'I gotta hit the road. Pleasure meeting you, Marc. Get the forms back to me and we're in business.'

Marc shook again. 'Will do, Dave. Nice meeting you as well.'

Dave jumped into his large, black SUV, and Marc ambled back to his car. After he did, he turned to look at the house once more.

Yeah, he thought, *this will do nicely.*

24

---

3 - 2

NOT TWO WEEKS LATER, MARC HAD FINISHED MOVING IN. THE only furniture he'd needed to bring with him was a desk, which had been a pain to get into the living room on his own. However, he'd eventually managed to wedge it in place and set up his laptop there with an external monitor.

It had just turned six in the evening when Marc entered the house after a particularly hectic day. He hung up his coat, kicked off his shoes, and strolled through to the living room with his laptop bag slung over his shoulder and a bag of takeout food also in hand. He connected his computer to the monitor, then started working again while eating the burger he'd brought home.

Marc checked his watch while cycling through his emails. *Another hour, then I'll call it,* he thought. His first couple of days had the standard teething problems he'd expected, especially relating to the existing management, who resented his presence. Over the past week, however, he'd bulldozed through that and made sure everyone knew their place. They could dislike it all they wanted, but the fact was that if things had been going well at the plant, Marc wouldn't have been needed in the first place. Even so, upon first impressions, Marc felt six months would be more than enough time, and he hoped he might actually get things wrapped up with a month or so to spare, provided the quarterly financial review showed enough improvement.

Something to aim for.

As he worked, Marc began to think again about how much time he was spending away from his home, something he had been doing more and more of lately. The truth was, he was getting tired of it. Which was unfortunate, because that was his job. He was a fixer, and for the longest time, he'd had no issues with it—he'd even enjoyed it. Lately, though, that had started to change.

It was time to have a word with the higher-ups, go for a promotion and hopefully get settled in one location. Marc knew if he pushed hard enough, it would happen, as the company dearly didn't want to lose him. He wasn't one to hold his employers hostage, since he had plenty to be thankful for, but he also knew his worth.

Marc continued to work while munching on his burger, using wet wipes to keep from getting grease all over his keyboard. Eventually, he called it a day, closed his laptop, and carried his rubbish to the bin in the gaudy kitchen. As Marc dumped the greasy brown bag into the rubbish, he caught sight of his stomach straining the bottom buttons of his shirt. While Marc wouldn't classify himself as obese, he knew he had been putting on more weight than he should have. Maintaining a gym routine with his current lifestyle had proven difficult over the last few years.

You're approaching forty, Marky-boy, gotta start taking more care of yourself. Otherwise, you'll go out early with a heart attack like the old man did.

Marc used to take pride in his appearance: at six-two, with a square jaw and full head of dark hair, he always thought he'd been dealt a good hand in that department, so he'd tried to make the most of it by maintaining a good physique. Now, however, his hair had started to thin and was peppered with grey, and he'd noticed the glances from women had become quite a bit less frequent.

As he stared down into the bin, he had a pang of regret over his decision to stay single. It had always been his contention that a wife and kids would be nothing more than an anchor around his neck—he valued his freedom too much—but over the last couple of years, doubt had started to creep in. He closed the bin and walked back to the living room.

Get a grip, Marc told himself. *You're fine.* He made a decision to get up early the next day and go for a run. The path through the play area outside led to a walkway along a river, which would make for a nice route.

For the remainder of the evening, he intended to settle down on the sofa in front of the television, then get an early night. After flicking through the channels, he decided on a documentary on the drug trade coming into London and the effect it was having on the local communities. Not exactly the most uplifting of things to watch, but it certainly held Marc's interest. As the programme went on, Marc heard intermittent noises from outside: cars pulling up as people came home, chatter from teens as they walked by, and even the shrill laughter of young kids, who he thought were up way past their bedtime. Marc also heard the door of the next door property slam, someone either coming home or leaving. The sound absorption in the house wasn't great, and noise travelled over from the neighbouring dwelling; over the last few days, he had often heard the family there talking, the television playing, and the doors slamming at all hours.

The noise wasn't so bad as to be a major problem, but it was an unforeseen annoyance.

When the credits started to roll on the show, Marc switched off the television, stood up, stretched, then checked the front door to make sure it was locked. That done, he turned the lights off downstairs, switching the landing light on upstairs at the same time, then headed up.

When upstairs, he glanced at the switch that controlled the hallway lighting. There were two switches on the wall plate, and he hesitated for a second, wondering again what the second one was for. It was something he'd noticed after moving in, though even after flicking the second one a few times previously he hadn't figured it out yet. He switched it again. Once, twice, then a few more times.

Nothing.

Marc shrugged and moved to the main bathroom to shower and brush his teeth. He had always been one to shower in the mornings and evenings, and also preferred to use the main bathroom of a house rather than an en-suite, not liking the idea of steam from a shower, or smells and shit particles from the toilet, drifting through to where he slept. In truth, Marc had never understood the appeal of en-suites, but people seemed to love them.

Once he was done, Marc exited the bathroom and padded over to the master bedroom, switching the light off to the hallway when he reached the bedroom door. As he did, he paused, then turned, realising there was light coming from somewhere. He looked up at the attic hatch above him. Warm orange light seeped through around the edges of the hatch, and it suddenly dawned on Marc what that extra switch was for: a light in the attic.

He felt a small amount of satisfaction at having solved the mystery, and it made sense why he hadn't noticed it before.

He flicked the switch again—and sure enough, the light above him disappeared.

Marc did wonder how anyone was supposed to gain access up there. The ceilings were so damn high that he'd need a ladder to reach it. Marc had a feeling there was a ladder attached to the lid, which was common, but someone would also need a bloody long pole or something to unlatch it in the first place—and he'd seen neither hide nor hair of such an implement since moving in.

Maybe something to email Dave about, he thought to himself. Marc really didn't see a reason why he'd need to get up to the attic in the first place, but still, it would be good to have the option should he need it.

He settled down into bed with the nightlight on and picked up the book he was halfway through, allowing himself thirty minutes of reading time to help his mind unwind before sleep. The book was a thriller—the newest in one of Marc's favourite series. The latest offering was one of the best so far. While things had begun getting a bit repetitive, as tended to happen with a longer series, Marc still found it enjoyable. There was comfort to returning to familiar characters and their thrilling adventures.

As he read, Marc's eyes moved over to the other side of the king-sized bed. He imagined someone lying there with him. Not a one-night stand, but someone he could talk to, maybe about the book he was reading, or about his day at work. He felt that yearning again, as well as a certain fear.

I'm thirty-nine. Is it too late to find someone? Too late to start a family?

The sound of a *thump* above him drew Marc's attention back to the present. He looked up, confused. While he knew it *couldn't* have come from the attic above him—that space was empty—the sound had seemed close. However, knowing how easily noise travelled in that house, he just assumed it was his neighbour busy in their own attic. *That has to be it.*

As Marc stared through the darkness up towards the ceiling, he waited, expecting another thump to come. Nothing did. So, after five minutes, he shrugged to himself, turned off his light, and shifted over to his side, allowing sleep to take him.

---

25

3 - 3

THE RUN WAS HARD GOING, WITH MARC WINDING UP OUT OF breath much sooner than he'd anticipated. *I really have let myself go.* Still, dawn was just breaking, and as he ran alongside the river, the view of the rising sun certainly made the effort worthwhile. He passed a few dog walkers and gave each one a warm smile, not having the energy to actually say anything.

Marc's only saving grace was that he *was* at least pushing himself. This wasn't a breezy early-morning stroll; it was hard work, and Marc didn't let himself ease up one bit. *Rest when you're done. If you're gonna do it, do it right.*

When he finally reached his front door again, panting and sweating profusely, Marc checked his watch. He'd set himself a goal of completing the route in a half hour, and he was pleased to see he'd finished with four minutes to spare. When he went for his shower, he felt a good bit better about himself.

The workday passed without any real incident—sure, management was still proving prickly, but nothing he couldn't handle—and he realised he had a certain spring in his step thanks to that morning's efforts. He did consider going again the next morning, but knew recovery was equally important, so decided on the day after. On his way home, Marc stopped at a supermarket to grab a salad and plenty of bottled water. As per the previous night, he did a few more hours of work on the laptop, but then decided to go for an evening walk rather than watch television so he could keep his body moving. He smiled to himself as he left the house: *you're really taking this seriously*. He just hoped he could keep the motivation going beyond this initial spurt.

He again followed the route alongside the river, with a rail to one side of him and trees rising up an embankment on the other. Again, there were plenty of dog walkers and joggers, more than the morning, but this time Marc felt energised enough to give a pleasant, 'Hello,' along with the friendly smile. There was even a lady walking her dog alone who had caught his eye, and her smile had lingered. He hoped to bump into her again in the future, maybe try to strike up a conversation.

But if it went somewhere, would you be willing to settle here?

Marc surprised himself with the question. Thinking long-term had never really been his thing with relationships. With career goals? Sure. But not when it came to dating.

When he got back home, it was pushing nine in the evening, so Marc decided to take a shower then read in bed before having an early night. Even if he wasn't going to be up running, the idea of another stroll was appealing. He locked up downstairs, then headed up. After a quick shower, he moved across the landing and switched off the hallway light, turning to glance up at the attic hatch.

He paused. The light there was on again.

Marc was *certain* he'd switched it off the previous night. He quickly hit the second switch and saw the light around the edges of the hatch blink out.

That's... odd.

He searched his memory, wanting to be absolutely sure; indeed, he clearly remembered looking up to see the light around the hatch's edges blink out, as it just had then.

Then, the only logical explanation came to mind: *I bumped it by accident this morning and didn't notice.* It was feasible. More than feasible, in fact—it was the only thing that could have happened, and it was a good-enough explanation for him, so Marc went into the bedroom and closed the door behind him. He then settled into bed and began to read. However, Marc was having difficulty focusing on the words on the page, and he kept listening out for another *thump* from above.

He quickly grew frustrated with himself. He'd lived alone all of his adult life and had never been one to creep himself out over nothing, so he couldn't understand why something so mundane had begun playing on his mind. *The sounds from last night were just the neighbours, and you accidentally flicked on the attic light this morning. That's all there is to it.*

While he knew that to be true, a kind of creeping dread slowly fell over him, like an invisible blanket fluttering down from above. Annoyed, Marc set his book down, turned off the nightlight, and rolled over. It took him over an hour to eventually drift off. He slept soundly for a few hours, until...

Thump.

Marc slowly opened his eyes, pulled from sleep, though his mind and body were still exhausted. He blinked and looked around in the darkness, unsure why he'd woken. There was a fading impression of a weird dream, but the images dissipated quickly—Marc couldn't remember anything about the dream despite trying. It was like his mind was trying to grab smoke. He lifted his head from the pillow and reached over to his phone to check the time: two-thirty-five in the morning. He groaned, set the device down, then rested his head again, hoping he'd drift off quickly.

Thump.

Marc's head snapped up and his eyes flicked up to the ceiling. *What the hell?*

He held his breath, body tense, and continued to stare through the dark. The ceiling was so high that he couldn't even make out its colour. He waited, his mind arguing with itself, part of it telling him it was just the neighbours again, the other insisting the sound had come from *directly* above him.

Besides, why the hell would the neighbours be rummaging around at two-thirty in the morning?

Marc continued to wait, breath caught in his throat.

Thump.

He jolted at the noise. It had sounded like a heavy, deliberate footstep, and definitely sounded like it was coming overhead. After a few more moments, it came again.

Thump.

Marc threw his covers off and moved to the hallway, where he saw the light was on again in the attic.

What the fuck? He remained motionless, looking up. *There can't be anyone up there. There just can't be.*

'Hello?' he called, voice stern, feeling anger overtake his fear. Silence was his only response. His anger grew.

Thump.

Marc jumped. *That came from near the hatch.* 'Hello!' he shouted. Silence.

He *had* to believe someone was there. But why? He wondered if there were holes in the ceiling a person could use to look down. It creeped him out to think someone might have been watching him. *Maybe there's a hole in the adjoining wall where someone could get through. It's the neighbours, has to be!*

He turned and moved towards the stairs, intending to march next door and give them a piece of his mind. But then, just as he was halfway downstairs, he stopped, doubt clouding his mind. If it wasn't them, he would be causing a scene for nothing.

He also wondered if there was a way someone could get across the terrace using the attic spaces. While he would have expected the shared walls between properties to go right up to the roof, he supposed it *was* possible they weren't constructed that way. There would need to be some kind of fire barrier, of course, to stop any spread, but the material used might have been easily breakable. Regardless, Marc was left in limbo.

So he went back to his bedroom and grabbed his phone, brought it back out to the hallway, and began to film. Given it was quite dark, the image on the screen was grainy, but it still picked up the square-shaped line of light around the hatch—and it would also pick up the next thump that happened. *I want proof of this.*

That way, if he found out *who* was doing this, Marc could at least confront them with tangible evidence. However, though he waited and waited, nothing happened. He gave it another ten minutes, constantly stopping the recording to start afresh, yet there was nothing. *Maybe they left,* he considered. *Crept back to their own house now that they know I'm onto them.*

Though even if the person had tried to sneak away, Marc thought he would have heard *some* kind of movement. *Surely no-one could be* that *quiet.* Alternatively, Marc realised he might be in some kind of stand-off, with the stranger above waiting for Marc to move away. *Maybe they're watching me right now?*

The thought made him shudder.

In that moment, Marc resolved to call Dave first thing in the morning to find out how to get up into the attic.

Maybe there's a ladder or hook out in the shed? Marc considered. He was tempted to go check, but wasn't comfortable leaving the house with a stranger up there.

Another thought suddenly popped into his head. *What if it's Dave?*

The notion gave Marc pause. Dave was the one person that would have access to the house, and Marc had been out most of the day, giving the owner plenty of opportunity. *But why would he do that?* The only thing Marc could think was that Dave could be a perv who got off on voyeurism, watching his tenants when they weren't aware. Another shudder worked its way up Marc's spine.

He knew he had to keep his mind in check—he'd gone from blaming the neighbour, to suspecting someone down the street, and finally to the owner of the house. The truth was, Marc didn't know *who* was up in the attic.

Or if they were still there.

Eventually, he sat down on the floor. The adrenaline in his system had started to wane, and he was exhausted. Marc checked the time on his phone to see it was three-fifteen.

Shit.

He knew the next day at work was going to be hell. Marc didn't operate well without a full night's sleep.

But, for the time being, he knew he couldn't just stand around on the landing for the rest of the night. At the same time, he knew he couldn't just go back to bed. He again considered going to check the shed. While it didn't feel right giving the stranger a full run of the house, Marc knew it was no different from when he was out at work. Plus, it wouldn't take him long to look.

Screw it, he said to himself.

He flew down the stairs and opened the sliding doors to the back garden before sprinting over to the shed. Once inside, he used the flashlight on his phone to look around. He was confused when he saw rakes, hoes, and a watering can, considering the grass was artificial. There was also a length of old, frayed rope, some tools, and a short set of stepladders, which would be no use. There was nothing that could reach the hatch.

Waste of time.

Annoyed, Marc quickly ran back upstairs. The hatch was still shut, and he could still see the light around the lid. Then, something occurred to him that he should have thought of much sooner.

Call the police!

He felt stupid for not having considered it before... but at the same time, the idea of calling them brought with it a kind of shame. *What if they get up there and it's all clear? What if it really was just the sound travelling from the neighbours?*

The idea of the police gazing at Marc in judgment after finding nothing was enough to make his face flush.

Regardless, he dialled and was soon put through to a call handler, who went through a few preliminary questions before finally asking about the nature of the call.

'I heard someone in the house I'm staying at. Up in the attic. I'm still inside, but the ceilings are too high for me to go up and check.'

'Okay, can you get out of the house?' the man on the other end of the line asked.

'I mean, I can, yeah, but I'm not going to.'

'Sir?'

'I'm not worried, exactly,' Marc said. 'Whoever is up there either has access to a neighbouring property or is trapped there now. But if they're stuck, I don't want them getting away. Can you send someone?'

After a little more back and forth about Marc leaving, the

handler finally informed him: 'Armed response has been dispatched.'

'Wha... *armed response?*' Marc asked, shocked. 'Isn't that a little... extreme?'

'Not for a potential break in. Also, regular officers don't carry ladders. Armed response will have the capability to get up there if you don't have any other means.'

'Oh... okay,' Marc said. He suddenly had visions of armoured trucks pulling up to the house and SWAT teams piling out. While it probably wouldn't be that bad, Marc still felt embarrassed, and knew the neighbours might see.

Shit.

But he couldn't back down and change his story now. Plus, he *had* heard someone. Calling was the correct move, regardless of what his pride was telling him. So, Marc waited with the other man still on the line. All the while, no further sounds came from above him.

Eventually, after no more than ten minutes, there was a firm knock on the front door.

Marc ended his call and ran down to answer. When he opened the door, he was met by two tall, burly men, each in black with protective vests around their torsos. One had an automatic weapon, and the other held a folded-up metal ladder, with a sidearm strapped to his thigh. Marc looked at the automatic weapon of the first officer. He'd never seen a gun like that in real life, and it made him uneasy.

'Sir,' the man with the ladders began, 'apparently there is an intruder up in your attic?'

Marc was still staring at the gun, but eventually nodded. 'Erm, yeah,' he said. 'I woke up and heard them walking around. The light's on up there, and it wasn't when I went to sleep. No one has come out, so unless there's another way for them to escape, they should still be there.'

'When was the last time you heard the person moving?' the man with the larger gun asked.

'A while ago,' Marc replied. 'It's been quiet for about an hour or so.'

'An *hour?*' the first man asked, eyes widening. 'Why did you wait so long to call us?'

Marc hesitated for a minute, then admitted, 'I wasn't even going to at first. I thought I could deal with it myself, but the bloody ceilings are too high—I don't have any way to get up there. This is a rental property, so there aren't any ladders.' He nodded at the one the officer was carrying. 'As I'm sure you were informed.'

'You should have called sooner,' the man with the gun said, making Marc feel like a schoolboy being chastised. Marc then stepped aside as both men entered.

After he'd pointed the way to the stairs, the two policemen ascended and ordered Marc to wait below. He felt a pang of frustration.

Once at the top, the armed officer spoke loudly while looking up at the hatch. 'This is the police. We are an armed response unit. Whoever is up there, come out now and make sure we can see your hands. If you don't come out, we're coming up.' He gave it a few moments. 'It's better for everyone if you just come out. Give us a knock or something so we know you can hear us, and then slowly open the hatch.' Still nothing. The man shook his head in annoyance. 'We're coming up,' he called. 'As I said, we are armed, so keep back and don't try anything.'

The other officer then quickly unfolded the ladder, leaning it against the wall directly below the hatch. 'Keep back!' he then shouted, before slowly climbing up. The first man kept his foot on the ladder, weapon still in hand.

When at the top, the policeman on the ladder gently unhooked the latch and let it fall open, keeping his head down. From his position at the bottom of the stairs, Marc could still see the hole was clear, with no one looking back down.

'Watch yourself,' the man on the landing whispered up to his colleague, and the officer on the ladder nodded in response, then slowly peeked over the lip of the hole. Marc watched on, heart in his mouth, and he could see the officer's head slowly turn as he looked around. Interestingly, the man hadn't drawn his own weapon. Marc assumed it was so he didn't escalate things. The officer continued to look back and forth, and after a few moments Marc saw his body visibly relax. The policeman then looked down at his colleague and shook his head. 'I'll go up and have a proper check, but pretty sure we're all clear.'

Marc didn't know what to think. *They must have gotten out somehow. There* has *to be a hole in the adjoining wall.*

'Want me to come up?' the man at the bottom asked.

'Nah, I got it,' the other said, then disappeared into the space above. Marc heard him walking around, the footsteps giving the exact same *thump, thump, thump* Marc had heard before. After a few minutes, the officer reappeared and started to climb down again. 'Yup, all clear,' he confirmed.

'Was there a place they could have gotten out?' Marc called up. 'Like a hole or something?' But the man just shook his head in response.

'No,' he said flatly. 'Not that I saw. Sir, would you like to come upstairs, please?'

Marc frowned in confusion, but ascended the stairs as requested. 'There has to be,' he said. 'I heard someone. I'm not making it up.'

'I'm sure you heard something,' the officer replied, quickly glancing at his colleague before turning his eyes back to Marc. 'But it might have just been from next door.

Feel free to use our ladder so you can go up, check yourself, and set your mind to rest.'

'Are we allowed to let the public use our stuff?' the other man asked.

The first officer waved a dismissive hand. 'It'll be fine.' He then turned to Marc. 'Just don't fall, don't want a lawsuit on our hands.'

Marc nodded, then carefully climbed up the ladder himself, poking his head into the hole at the top.

A single bulb hung in the centre of the attic, but its light was enough that Marc he could see pretty much everything: the ridge line at the top of the triangular space, the walkable boarding on top of the joists, the yellow wool insulation poking out from between, cardboard boxes and even a Christmas tree that had been stored up there, and also the end wall that separated it from the neighbouring property.

That wall was whole, with no gaps and no way through. The entire area was completely enclosed.

And there was no one up there.

Impossible, Marc said to himself. *I know what I heard.*

'Feel free to walk around up there if it'll help,' the officer at the bottom of the ladder shouted, so Marc did just that. Other than behind the boxes, there was nowhere to hide, and his search came up empty.

On the one hand, that was good, as it meant no one had been lurking around while he slept, but on the other, it didn't help explain the noises at all. Marc saw a switch plate fixed to one of the vertical roof timbers. He clicked it and the surrounding light went out; hitting it again turned the bulb back on.

As much as he thought someone up here had to have turned it on, he couldn't deny what his eyes were showing him. No one was there.

Maybe they got away when I went to the shed? he thought,

then quickly dismissed it. He'd been too quick. There was no way someone could have gotten down, closed the hatch, and gotten out the front door—which had still been locked from the inside—before he'd gotten back.

Eventually, Marc climbed back down the ladder and sheepishly faced the two policemen. The one that had been in the attic smirked. 'Don't worry about it,' he said. 'You aren't the first person to get unnerved over nothing. It happens. Especially if this place is a rental, you're just not used to it.'

Marc shook his head. 'I heard something. I *know* I did.'

'We believe you,' the second man said. 'But it might have just *sounded* like it came from up there'—he pointed to the ceiling—'but it was probably from next door. I've seen this kind of thing a lot, you're not alone.'

Marc considered it. As much as he didn't want to admit he'd been so wrong, he knew it was possible. Hell, now that he'd seen the attic, it really was the only explanation.

'But the light was on,' he said, feeling his prior certainty slip away.

'Are you sure that wasn't you?' the officer asked. 'You could have just forgotten you'd hit the switch. Or maybe just bumped it by accident.'

Marc wanted to shake his head again but refrained. Again, he had to admit it... was possible.

'I guess I've wasted your time,' he eventually said.

'It's fine,' the first man said. 'But if that's everything you need from us, we'll be going. That okay?'

Marc gave a solemn nod, then led the men back downstairs. After they'd left, he sat on the sofa and rested his head in his hands, feeling tired and utterly embarrassed.

---

3 - 4

THE FOLLOWING DAY AT WORK WAS A LONG ONE. AFTER THE incident the previous night, Marc had forced himself to try to get more sleep, but only got a couple of hours at best and didn't make his planned morning walk. At lunch, he made a point of heading over to a local store to buy an extendable ladder. While he had considered messaging Dave to ask if the landlord had anything to use, Marc decided he didn't want to wait. *Better to just get the ladder and be done with it.*

As soon as he arrived home, Marc decided to go upstairs and check the attic again.

The ladder he'd picked out was a self-supporting one, with an adjustable, sliding head to give extra reach. After setting it up on the landing, and making sure it was sturdy, he flicked the attic light on from below, then climbed up. He felt a little unsteady at the top, but was able to easily drop the hatch. He then climbed a little higher and pushed his head inside the opening.

All was exactly as it had been the previous night: completely enclosed and completely empty.

Marc heaved himself fully inside and started to inspect

the triangular separating wall more closely, taking his time, pushing against the exposed blocks to see if any were loose and able to be removed. None were. In addition, there weren't even any gaps in the roofing that seemed like someone could have climbed in through—not that Marc thought it likely someone would scale a roof just to get inside.

That meant he was forced to face the facts: no one had ever been there while he'd been in the house, and the footsteps must have just been travelling noise. And the light... well, he *must* have accidentally bumped it without realising.

There was no other explanation.

He remembered the looks on the faces of the police. While they hadn't been rude, he knew they'd been quietly judging him. Fresh shame overcame him. He felt like an idiot.

With nothing else to see, Marc went back down to the storey below, folded away the ladder, and stored them in the second bedroom. It was only eight in the evening, though he didn't feel like watching television or reading. In fact, all he wanted to do was sleep, but decided instead to push himself and go for a walk, hoping the fresh night air would help clear some cobwebs.

The evening air was pleasantly crisp, and the sound of the running river beside him was soothing. Marc still felt unsettled because of the last twenty-four hours, and definitely still embarrassed, but getting outside helped put things into perspective: he'd made a mistake and this was all just a blip. After an early night and plenty of sleep, he could get back on track tomorrow.

And if he did hear more noises, he now knew they were nothing to worry about.

Eventually Marc got home, locked up, and went upstairs to shower. He enjoyed letting the hot water cascade down over him. Just as he was finishing washing himself, Marc suddenly paused. He cocked his head to the side and looked up, moving his face away from the stream of water.

He'd heard a *creak* in the ceiling overhead.

Easy, he told himself, *that could have been anything. All houses creak from time to time.*

Marc kept looking up. The sound didn't persist, so he quickly put it out of his mind, finished his shower, and dried off. After that, he moved over to the master bedroom, checking the attic hatch on his way to make sure the light was off. With everything clear, he switched off the landing light, checked the attic one final time, then went into the bedroom. He finally got into bed, feeling far more relaxed, and absolutely exhausted. Marc looked over to his book, trying to decide whether or not it was worth reading tonight. Eventually, he decided against it and simply rolled over. It didn't take him long to fall asleep.

He slept uninterrupted for a while. Then, a sound pulled him from his slumber.

Thump.

3 - 5

MARC ROLLED TO HIS BACK AND FORCED HIS EYES OPEN. HIS head hurt. Yet again, smoky remnants of a dream dissipated just beyond his mind's reach.

He remembered the sound of a thud above him. *Did I dream it?*

He sat up, feeling groggy, and vigorously ran his hands over his face. Marc then tilted his head to stare up into the darkness. He waited. And waited. And w—

Thump.

Though his body tensed immediately, Marc forced himself to keep calm. While the *thump* sounded like it came from *right* above him, he knew that couldn't be true, not after yesterday.

Thump. Thump. Thump.

Three footsteps came in quick succession, sounding like they were moving across the ceiling. Marc quickly grabbed his phone and switched on the flashlight, aiming it up so he could make out the plasterboard of the ceiling. If there *was* someone walking, maybe he'd see movement on the ceiling's surface.

To his frustration, the sound didn't return.

Go up there and look again, he told himself. It was late—or early, depending on how you looked at it—and all Marc wanted to do was to fall asleep, but he knew the uncertainty would keep playing on his mind. Despite having checked only a few hours ago, he knew he'd need to go up again to put any lingering doubts to rest. Marc dragged himself out of bed and moved out to the hallway.

The light was on again.

I switched it off! I know I did!

But rather than letting himself panic, Marc tried to look for a logical explanation. *Faulty wiring?* It was all he could come up with. After entering the second bedroom to get the ladder, Marc again heard a *thump*, this time sounding like it was right next to the attic hatch.

There's no way that's coming from next door.

He grabbed the ladder and moved quickly back to the landing, setting it up just beneath the hatch; he let the light from above wash down over him to guide him. Once he was ready, he stared up at the hatch, holding for a moment in case another footstep came. When it didn't, he started to climb, phone in hand, just in case he needed to get a photo or a video. After nearing the top, Marc steadied himself. The ladder was strong, but he wasn't exactly used to it, and felt like he was going to topple off the side. Still, he reached up, unlatched the attic door, and allowed the lid to drop. Stale air drifted out of the opening along with more light. After climbing a little higher, Marc was able to fully see inside, using his free hand on the top of the ladder to keep himself steady.

The attic was empty. As he'd expected. Whatever was making the noises *wasn't* coming from up there, despite how it sounded. He could be certain of that now. Whatever the explanation, it wasn't an intruder. *Well, at least that's something*. He felt a small wave of relief.

Then, with a *click*, the light in the attic blinked out.

Marc dropped the phone out onto the attic floor in shock. He instinctively took firm hold of the top of the ladder to keep from falling. The steps beneath him wobbled for a moment after his jolt of fear, and Marc thought he was going to tip over to the side. Eventually, he managed to right himself. Once steady, he looked into the yawning darkness of the attic, no longer able to see much.

What the hell?

He couldn't understand how the light had switched off on its own. His instincts told him to climb down quickly and get away, but Marc forced himself to stay put. He picked up the phone again before him and activated the flashlight, then aimed the device ahead so the spotlight could push back the darkness. While holding his breath, Marc slowly swept the beam around to his left, finally settling it on the switch. Again, no one was around. He then continued his sweep around the rest of the space, turning on top of the ladder as he rotated before eventually coming full-circle.

After another moment, Marc climbed back down, and flicked on both the landing light below and also the attic one once again. He then looked up to the hatch and watched, waiting to see if the light would go out again.

Could still be the wiring, he told himself. *Don't panic.*

The warm hue from the attic light stayed steady. Eventually, Marc ascended the ladder again, feeling apprehensive but trying to keep control of his emotions. He'd seen with his own eyes there was no one there fucking with him, and he certainly didn't believe in ghosts or any of that shit.

So there's no need to be scared, he told himself, more than once.

He looked into the now-lit attic again, using his phone once more, but this time to record rather than illuminate. If the attic light switched itself off again, he wanted to get it on camera. At least then he could contact Dave with proof of faulty wiring.

If it is an electrical fault, I don't want it affecting the rest of the house.

He waited, still staring ahead.

A forceful breath came from directly behind him, and an ice-cold breeze drifted over his neck.

Marc froze—the light clicked out.

'Fuck!' he yelled in fright and instinctively ducked down. In doing so, he lost his grip on the ladder and toppled off. His other hand released the phone, and he felt his left leg slip between the rungs of the ladder mid-fall. Marc felt the horizontal metal step press into the back of his thigh as he flipped upside down, dangling for a moment and wrenching his leg to the side. His phone hit the floor. Marc let out a cry of pain, then his leg slipped free, allowing him to fall the rest of the way down to the landing, where he slammed painfully against the base of the ladder and rolled off to the floor. He groaned in pain but forced himself to his back to look up to the hatch in panic.

The void inside the attic hatch was pitch black. Nothing came into view.

What the fuck was that? Was that... was that a breath?

His left leg throbbed in pain, especially the back of his thigh and also his knee, which had been twisted almost out of the joint. After forcing himself to a sitting position, Marc quickly retrieved his phone, then grabbed both the ladder and the bannister to pull himself up.

Pain began shooting through the knee the moment Marc tried to put some weight on it. He then hobbled for a moment until he gained his balance, keeping his weight off his left leg. He looked up again, unable to make sense of what had happened and trying desperately to remain calm.

He couldn't see anyone through the hatch and he *knew* the attic was empty. *There's no one there. There isn't.*

Then, he remembered he'd been recording before he fell, so Marc played back the video he'd just taken. It showed the lit attic. Then, sure enough, the phone picked up the sound of someone loudly exhaling. After that, the light cut out, and the footage shook wildly when Marc fell.

On the screen, he saw his body hit the floor, and he reflexively winced. The footage only stopped after Marc's hand eventually came into view to retrieve the phone.

Marc then watched it again. The sound was unmistakably a breath.

He gazed up to the darkness of the attic hatch, squinting. It felt to him like someone was staring back, even though he could see nothing—a cold chill ran up his spine.

I saw it myself. There's no one there. There was nowhere to hide! He kept telling himself that, yet struggled to believe it.

Marc then reached out and hit the light switch, driving back the darkness above. He considered his options. Ultimately, he knew he wouldn't be able to just go back to sleep now, not without checking up in the attic once more. He *did* consider phoning the police again, but was too conflicted, especially after how they'd judged him the last time.

He took a breath, put his phone in his pocket, and placed his bad leg on the bottom rung. He put the slightest bit of pressure on it and immediately groaned—it hurt like hell.

Still, Marc was sure if he bore most of his weight on his other leg, he would be able to climb. So, he grabbed the ladder, lifted his other foot—using his grip to hold most of his weight—then settled his second foot on the ladder. He looked up again.

There's no one up there, Marc told himself. *No one.* Marc knew he couldn't live in fear for the next six months—he had to figure this out *now*.

He began to climb, favouring his right leg, and going as easy on his left as he could. Just before the top, Marc stopped. He realised he was too scared to actually push his head up into the attic again.

Coward!

Instead, he drew out his phone, hit record, then lifted his hand through the opening while aiming the device forward. After a moment, Marc lowered it and played the footage back.

At first, nothing stood out, but towards the end of the video, just before the camera lowered again, something caught his eye. Marc replayed the footage once more and hit pause towards the end. He felt a look of confusion cross his face.

The still image was grainy, frozen in motion, but Marc could see something coming out from behind one of the boxes that was deep in the attic.

Can't be.

It looked like… an arm: long, thin, and pale, with spindly fingers that were outstretched. Marc continued to stare, struggling to make sense of what he was seeing. *Can't be,* he told himself again. And then again.

The image wasn't completely clear, so Marc knew he couldn't be one-hundred-percent certain. Even so, growing dread curled up from his gut. He looked to the hatch, knowing he should climb higher and see with his own eyes… but he couldn't. Instead, he set his phone to record again, started to raise his phone back into the air, then glanced up —and froze.

A face was looking back down at him.

All the lights blinked out.

Marc screamed, pushing himself off the ladder in desperation to get away, phone still aimed ahead as he dropped backwards and fell. His left leg hit the floor first, twisting as it did, and he felt an explosion of pain, followed by a pop in his knee. His back slammed into the floor a second later, forcing the wind from his lungs. To his surprise, Marc had managed to keep hold of the phone. He gazed up, dazed, and saw that face again, staring back from the dark hatch: it was long and gaunt, with its mouth hanging open, skin alabaster white and eyes so wide they seemed to pop from the sockets. Both eyes were completely black and glassy, like obsidian marbles.

Another scream erupted from Marc as an unnaturally long arm reached out of the hatch, down towards him. Though the hand wasn't quite able to grab him, Marc was still shocked at how far the arm was able to come down from the hatch.

Ignoring the agony throbbing from his knee—which he knew was dislocated—Marc flipped to his stomach and pulled himself along the floor towards the stairs. At the same time, desperation rising, he called the police. Fear and panic flooded through him.

This can't be happening. This can't be happening.

Marc clawed at the floor with his free hand and used his good leg to kick off, constantly pushing himself forward. He managed to pull himself around the corner stair post to the top step. The phone rang, waiting to connect, so Marc allowed himself a panicked look back. Though it was dark everywhere, he could still make out the face hovering over the opening of the hatch… staring at him.

'Hello, what is the nature of your emergency?' a voice came through the phone. Marc started to slide forwards down the stairs, controlling his descent as much as he could as his heart hammered in his chest.

'Someone is in my house!' he shouted. 'You have to send

help!' He then blurted out his address and begged for someone to save him. As he babbled, he heard a loud sliding sound against the ladders, followed by a huge *thump*.

'It's coming for me!' Marc shouted. He turned and looked back to the top of the stairs. A figure crawled into view, slowly moving on long arms and legs, like some kind of human spider-hybrid. It paused at the very top, gazing down at him, expressionless.

Then, it gave an unholy shriek and shot forward down the stairs. One long arm reached out before it.

Marc let out his final scream as an ice-cold hand grabbed his throat.

28

---

3 - 6

'SOMEBODY BETTER BE INSIDE THIS TIME,' OFFICER KIERAN Allison said to his partner, Paul Sloan. They had both just gotten out of their car and were approaching the house.

'The call cut off apparently,' Paul said. 'But the guy was panicked.'

'But we searched the place last time we were here,' Kieran stated as they trotted closer to the door. 'It was nothing.'

'I know, but just stay alert,' Paul said.

Paul was carrying the 'big red key,' which was a standard-issue, small, red battering ram. They already had clearance to use it to gain entry immediately. He did the honours, with his partner shouting instructions for anyone inside to stay back and make their hands visible. It took only three hard strikes from the ram before the door popped open.

It was dark inside, and both officers shouldered their weapons before entering.

Each again shouted for whoever was inside to show themselves. There was no answer, and everything remained quiet.

After a sweep of the ground floor, both men moved up

the stairs, but stopped midway up. The light from Kieran's torch illuminated a dark patch on the carpeted stairs.

'Blood,' he whispered, feeling a sense of dread building.

The quick search of the next floor revealed nothing. A ladder sat beneath the open attic hatch.

'I'll go first,' Kieran whispered. Paul nodded his agreement.

Kieran climbed as his partner footed the ladder, keeping it steady. Once at the top, Kieran carefully lifted both his head and weapon through the hole. He aimed his flashlight into the darkness of the attic.

His voice caught in his throat, cutting off a shout.

The beam of light showed the man from earlier. He was strung up to the roof rafters, stomach and throat both pulled open.

It took Kieran a moment to realise the man's own intestines were what was holding him up, with the fleshly organs wrapped around the timbers and the man's limbs like rope.

'Jesus Christ,' Kieran uttered in shock. He swept his weapon and light both left and right quickly.

'What is it?' Paul shouted up.

'We have a problem,' Kieran replied.

Two hours later, the house was a hive of activity. Kieran had made the call for backup straight away, and more cars had arrived soon after. The house had then been thoroughly searched.

Once it was given the all clear, a forensic team headed over and began doing their thing. Kieran was outside, leaning against his car. Despite it being the dead of night, neighbours had still come out into the street to find out what was going on. However, the police weren't saying anything.

How the hell would you even explain *that to them?*

His partner approached him, head hanging low. 'Not sure we'll be needed for much longer,' Paul said and leaned against the car next to Kieran. 'You ever see anything like that before?'

'Fuck no,' Kieran replied with a shake of his head. 'And I never want to again.'

As grotesque as the scene had been, what had stood out most to Kieran was the look on the poor guy's face: like a scream frozen in time.

'Been speaking to some of the forensics people,' Paul went on. 'Early days, but one of them said they couldn't find any evidence so far. Not a shred to show anyone else has been in the house.'

'Strange,' Kieran said. 'There's usually *something* obvious. Then again, we searched the place thoroughly when we were here before. No one was there then.'

'I know,' Paul said. 'But that doesn't mean they didn't come back to finish what they started. Maybe the guy was right and someone *had* been there before we arrived.'

'I suppose,' Kieran stated. 'Seems like they knew what they were doing, if they didn't leave any trace behind.'

Paul patted him on the shoulder. 'Just put it out of your head. We did our job. The rest is someone else's problem.'

Kieran knew Paul was technically right... but it wasn't that easy for him to switch it off.

Just then, a senior officer approached.

'You two look like you've seen better days,' the man said.

'We're fine,' Kieran replied, though didn't mean it.

The other officer shook his head. 'You don't look it. Both of you go home. Get some rest. We'll take it from here.'

Kieran didn't argue.

The next day, before his shift started in earnest, Kieran went in to the office to see the leading detective on the murder case. Detective Gibson was someone Kieran knew fairly well.

He had already heard the rumours of the footage that had been found on the victim's phone. It had sent a buzz through the local constabulary, and Kieran—who still wasn't able to shake the image he'd been greeted with in the attic—wanted to see it for himself.

'Come on, you can show me,' he said to Gibson after initially being refused. 'Everyone else has seen it.'

'Not everyone,' Gibson said, who was sitting in his office, Kieran perched on the desk just before him. 'But too many bloody people have—it stops now. It's evidence, Kieran, not a meme to be shared around.'

Kieran raised an eyebrow. 'You know what a meme is? I thought you'd be too old for that.'

'You're a funny shit, ain't ya?'

'Come on, Gibs, I... I need to see it,' Kieran said. 'I'm not interested in spreading gossip or anything like that, you know me. It's just... seeing how that bloke was left, all strung up... I can't get it out of my head. I need to see the fucker that did it. People say he looks weird. *Really* fucking weird.'

Gibs nodded. 'That's true. He does, aye.' The detective studied Kieran for a moment, then sighed. 'Fuck it,' he eventually said and leaned forward, tapping on his computer. Gibs spun the screen around to face Kieran. 'We took this from the phone,' he said. 'There was another video before this one, where the guy seems to be filming around the attic while he's on the ladder. You can actually see an arm in that footage. At least, we think that's what it is. The recording you're gonna watch now was taken just after. It shows... well, see for yourself.'

Kieran watched. His mouth dropped in horror as he saw the pale, gaunt face on the screen look down from the attic hatch. Then the victim obviously fell. The footage aimed up again and the person in the attic reached out. The camera shook, spun, and the footage cut out a second later.

'Bloody hell, what *was* that?' Kieran asked. He took control of the computer without asking permission and scrolled the video until the image showed the face. 'It looks like a fucking—'

'Don't say it!' Gibson warned with a raised finger. 'The black eyes could be contacts, and there are plenty of pale people around. I've already heard some people saying it's a bloody ghost—I won't have coppers spreading that rubbish around the constabulary. We'll be a laughingstock.'

'I know... but Gibs,' Kieran said, pointing to the screen. '*Look* at it.'

'I *have* been looking at it,' Gibson replied. '*All* bloody day. Anyway, you've seen it, now bugger off and start your shift.' Kieran just continued looking at the image. 'Did you hear me?' Gibs asked, clicking his fingers.

Kieran shook his head. 'Yeah, I hear you. Thanks for showing me.'

'Feel better for seeing it?' Gibson asked with a knowing grin.

'Not really, no.'

'Didn't think you would. I'll be honest, it makes me uneasy. But we'll catch the fucker. He's human and we'll get him.'

'Forensics come back with anything yet?'

Kieran saw the confidence falter on Gibson's face. 'Not yet, but it's early.'

'But they haven't given you *anything* to go on?'

Gibson hesitated. 'As I said, it's early days. *Literally* only the next day, in fact. They'll turn up something.' The man didn't sound confident.

Kieran took one last look at the screen. The haunting face stared back at him. He didn't know how to explain it, but Kieran knew in his gut that they weren't going to catch... whoever the hell that was. He thanked the detective, stood up, and left.

The image of that face stayed with Kieran for the remaining twenty-three years of his career, and then throughout his retirement. They fervently investigated the case for three months, then tapered off and kept it on the back burner.

Even now, thirty-eight years later, the case has not been solved.

4. THE RETREAT

ANNIE WAS WIPED.

She switched off her computer and sunk farther down into her chair, pinching the bridge of her nose and letting out a long sigh.

Finished. Thank God!

It had been a hell of a day at work—always the same on the last day before a well-earned break. It was because people knew she would be away for a week, so they felt the need to overload her with everything in a desperate attempt to make sure things were done before she left.

Annie worked as a freelance designer. Often, she didn't hear from clients for weeks at a time—until they realised she was going to be away. Then everyone contacted her at once, all seemingly in a panic at the thought of her briefly disappearing.

It's only a week, she'd thought repeatedly, after each frantic email. Annie would never say that to her clients, of course, and acted professional and courteous at all times, but deep down she knew her absence wouldn't affect their business in any real way. She'd planned the time off meticulously, ensuring all deadlines were met, but that didn't stop some of her higher-paying clientele from ushering in new deadlines.

Unfortunately, it was normal for her business, especially as she was self-employed. There was just no patience with people anymore, no time for planning. Everything was a reaction.

It seemed like she had no time to look after her personal well-being.

So Annie had to force the time. She knew she had been close to burnout. Her working hours had become ridiculous, especially with overseas clients who cared little for time zones or her need for sleep.

At her friends' and parents' behest, Annie had reluctantly booked time away to a cabin out in the countryside. It had cost a pretty penny, but the reviews for the place were great. The best thing: no connectivity. There apparently wasn't much in the way of a phone signal, and there was absolutely no Wi-Fi. At first, that thought had terrified her, and she'd almost dismissed the location out of hand. But after she'd pondered it more... it had grown in appeal, and she'd eventually realised it was *exactly* what she needed. In fact, that was how the rental company sold it: highlighting the lack of Wi-Fi as a feature. So, once Annie had gotten over her fear of being so disconnected—and managed to somewhat convince her largest clients her temporary absence was nothing to panic about—she'd booked it.

Annie stood up from her desk and stretched, feeling her vertebrae pop from her shoulders down to the middle of her spine. It felt good.

Being hunched at her computer for twelve-hour stretches was hell on her body.

Annie then checked her watch. Nine-thirty in the evening. She knew some of her friends were meeting up in a pub nearby, but Annie didn't have the energy to tag along. *I never have the energy,* she told herself. She thought again of what her father had told her, about working herself into an early grave. At the time she had dismissed his concerns, telling him she was too proud of the six-figure income she'd built to ease up. But now, his words had been replaying more and more in her mind, and she was starting to pay them more heed.

Perhaps there is more to life.

After letting out a yawn and rubbing her eyes—which felt like they had sand coating the surface—Annie headed to the kitchen of her apartment to fix herself a late dinner. It wouldn't be long before she was tucked up in bed and passed out, but despite her fatigue, she was excited about the next day, which would start with a four-hour first class train journey. That would be followed by a week of forced relaxation with, hopefully, no stress. It was then she realised, for the first time in a long while, that she felt good. She was excited about something other than the next paid invoice hitting her bank account.

After eating, she showered, brushed her teeth, and settled into bed, deciding to read a little on her tablet. Annie didn't even finish the first page before letting the e-reader drop gently to her chest and falling asleep.

Don't check it, don't check it, don't check it, Annie kept telling herself. She hadn't brought her laptop, but did have her phone, which was connected to every facet of her business. It was a Saturday morning, but she'd learned long ago weekends meant nothing in business. People expected you to be contactable all day *every* day.

She pushed the thought of waiting emails from her mind

and concentrated on the green countryside that flashed by the window of the train. It brought to mind her childhood, when she'd visited the farm of her grandparents and had her grandfather take her out into the fields. *How long has it been since I've been in a bloody field?* Most of her adult life had been confined to a concrete jungle.

Annie felt a pang of guilt and longing for the past. She thought of her grandfather again. She hadn't been able to attend his funeral seven years ago because she'd been too busy with a deadline. While she'd felt bad at the time, her father and grandmother had said it was fine and that they understood. They'd also told her that her grandfather, a workaholic in his own right, would have fully respected her decision. But now, it made her think of her own funeral. *Would anyone come? Will people even remember me a few years after I've gone?*

'Tea or coffee, my dear?'

The voice interrupted Annie's thoughts. However, she welcomed being pulled from the depressing place her mind had been heading towards. She looked up to see a middle-aged blonde woman in a red apron with a black metal cart in front of her. The cart was filled with cups and dispensers.

'Coffee please,' Annie replied with a smile.

The lady filled up a cup of steaming black coffee and placed it down on Annie's small table. 'Milk or sugar?'

'Both,' Annie said.

Sachets of sugar and condensed milk were placed down before Annie as well. 'You heading anywhere nice?' the lady asked.

Annie nodded enthusiastically. 'A cabin in the middle of nowhere, if you can believe it,' she said with a laugh.

The service attendant's eyes went wide. 'Oh! That sounds like heaven! Just getting away from everything, eh?'

'That's the plan,' Annie said.

'I'm jealous,' the lady added. She then kicked the brakes off her cart and started to push it forward. 'Enjoy, dear,' she said, moving away.

Annie added the milk and sugar to her coffee and took a long drink. It wasn't fantastic by any measure, but she'd been craving a caffeine kick, and it did hit the spot. Annie even had to fight from letting out a long, contented 'ahhhhhh.'

She let her head fall back into the seat and looked out the window again, keeping the mug grasped in her hands while enjoying the warmth that seeped through into her palms. It was early autumn, so the leaves on the trees that zipped past were a glorious mix of greens, yellows, oranges, and browns. The sky had a few dark clouds, but was mostly crystal blue, and the still-rising sun cast its warm glow over everything. The scene was certainly picturesque.

A small town whizzed by the window by in an instant. The streets had been empty, and the settlement had consisted mostly of stone cottages with lots of front gardens. Annie got the impression it was a place with a slower pace of life.

That sounded appealing. It was clear her subconscious was trying to give her a very specific message: *Don't work yourself into an early grave.*

Annie realised that she had a decision to make. She was at a crossroads—keep going down the same path and build her bank account so she could afford the finer things in life, or concentrate on herself and enjoy the simpler things. After all, what good were the finer things if you never really had time to appreciate them?

After taking another sip, Annie set down her coffee and pulled out her phone. However, she avoided her emails and went straight to the booking information, wanting to again read the description of the cabin. She'd already gone through the information about four times, but found comfort in doing it again. It stoked her excitement. It had two bedrooms, a fully stocked kitchen, an open living and dining area, a study, a library, and on top of that, everything was on a single storey. There was also a deck outside. The dwelling sat in a clearing of trees, with forest around as far as the eye could see.

The website had plenty of photos as well. Though the place was marketed as a cabin, to Annie it was more than that, looking like a single-storey home, though the walls were clad in horizontal shiplap boarding as opposed to the more common brick and mortar throughout the U.K. The footprint of the building was roughly 'L' shaped, with a bedroom at each end. The roof of the cabin had a low pitch, and was covered in slate tiles. The windows were timber-framed and the main door a solid oak.

The interior looked well decorated, with thick carpets to the living room and bedrooms and light wood flooring to the kitchen. The walls were a mix of white paint and dark oak wooden panels. Most importantly, the beds looked big and extremely comfy, as did the sofas and chairs in the living area. The whole place screamed 'relaxation.'

Annie realised she was smiling as her eyes scanned the screen of her smartphone. An email alert popped up on the screen, but she quickly swiped it away, focusing instead on the photos of the clearing around the cabin. The description detailed some nice long hiking routes, which was something else Annie was looking forward to. The only slight concern she had was that her walking boots were new and not yet broken in, since she'd bought them specifically for the trip. Still, she hoped two pairs of thick socks would prevent any blisters.

Still smiling, Annie set her phone down and took another drink. *This is going to be great,* she told herself, feeling more and more excited with every passing second.

---

4 - 2

'YEAH, I KNOW WHERE YOU MEAN,' THE TAXI DRIVER SAID through the open window. 'Hop in. I warn you, though, it's about a fifty-minute drive.'

Annie was outside a small train station in one of the nearest towns to the cabin.

'That's fine,' Annie said. 'Can you open the boot?' she asked, pointing down to her case.

'Oh bloody hell, sorry, love,' the burly man replied. He hopped out of the car and strode around to the back. He was tall and well built, with thick forearms jutting out from three-quarter-length sleeves. He had brushed back hair and, despite the crisp weather, he wasn't wearing a coat. He opened the boot and grabbed Annie's case, lifting it easily and slipping it inside. 'Should have seen your case. Honestly, my wife thinks I'm blind. She might be right.'

Annie smiled. 'That doesn't fill me with confidence.'

The man waved a dismissive hand. 'Ah, don't worry. Most people scream loud enough before we hit them, so I usually wind up avoiding them.' Annie froze in place and her eyes widened. 'It was a joke,' the man added.

'Ah,' Annie replied. She was usually quick-witted, at least she thought so, but his delivery had been so deadpan it had thrown her. 'Then I'll make sure to shout if I need to.'

The driver gave her a thumbs up, then got back inside. Annie initially started to move to the rear doors to get in behind him, but hesitated for a moment before climbing into the passenger seat. 'Don't mind if I sit up front, do you?'

'Not at all,' the driver replied. 'This is your carriage, love. You sit where you're most comfortable. I wouldn't be offended if you felt better sitting in the back. I know some-times people feel safer that way. Especially when sharing a car with a big lump like me.'

In truth, Annie normally *would* have sat in the back and stayed silent the whole journey, but she was in an uncharac-teristically chatty mood. She buckled up, and they set off.

'Do you take many people up to that lodge?' she asked when they were en route.

'A few times a month,' the driver replied. 'Seems like a nice place. Everyone always says how quiet and relaxing it is. Helps being out in the middle of nowhere, so they can switch off, you know?'

'That's exactly what I need,' Annie said. 'Just to decom-press for a little while.'

'Stressed out at the minute, eh?'

Annie laughed. 'You could say that.'

'Is there a reason for that? Work? Partner? Family?'

'Work,' Annie replied.

Now it was the driver's turn to chuckle. 'That's the most common answer I get, unsurprisingly. Seems to be a lot of professionals that favour this place. The world isn't slowing down, is it? Everyone's getting busier and busier, always hunched over computers and phones. Not good for a long life, if you ask me. Course, I sit on my arse all day cramped in this car, so I'm not one to talk.'

'I've been thinking about that more and more, actually,' Annie said. 'Not about you sitting on your arse all day,' she added with a smirk, which drew a laugh, 'but that life is just passing me by.'

'Well, good that you realise it,' the man said. 'At least you can make a change.'

'Maybe,' Annie said. 'It... isn't always that easy, though.'

'Sure it is,' the driver stated. 'I'm going to go out on a limb and say you make good money, which is great, but... do you need it? Some of the happiest people I know don't earn much and they are perfectly content. They just make sure they live within their means.'

'Again, not that easy,' Annie replied. 'An illness, accident, or something else outside your control could derail all that. It's a nice thought, not chasing money, but life isn't that simple a lot of the time. It's normally a struggle.'

The driver was quiet for a moment. 'I suppose you're right,' he finally said. 'Which is a shame. I thought I was sounding all sagely and wise there for a second.'

Annie giggled. 'It was a good effort.'

There was another brief pause before the driver started talking again, seeming keen to keep the conversation going. 'A lot of the time I bring groups up here. Couples, at the very least. You going to be okay on your own? Won't it be a little—'

Annie turned to him with a raised eyebrow. 'What, scary? You think I'll be frightened up there on my own just because I'm a woman?'

The man grinned but shook his head. 'I was going to say *boring*. But thank you for jumping to the wrong conclusion.'

'Ah,' Annie replied. 'Erm, actually I don't think so. I'm used to my own company, so I'll just read and relax, go hiking, that kind of thing.'

'Sounds nice. Quite like the idea of having time to yourself.'

'You not get much?'

The man shook his head. 'Spend most of my time chatting to people in this car, and then I have a wife and three kids at home. Wouldn't change it, of course, but it doesn't leave much time for just me. What are you doing for food while you're out here?'

'The owner has the fridge and cupboards all stocked, so I can cook. Can't imagine there will be any restaurants nearby.'

'Not really. You're looking at another taxi ride back here to town if you want anything. But some people do that. There's a few places that are really nice and worth the trip. I'll give you one of my cards, so if you want to nip back, you just call me.'

He shuffled in his seat, keeping one large hand on the wheel while his other fished around in his side pocket. Eventually, the man pulled out a business card with frayed edges. He passed it over. Annie looked at the name on the front.

'Tim Pile.'

'That's me,' he said, flashing a smile, and she noticed one of his side teeth was missing.

'I might take you up on that, Tim,' she said. 'It would be nice to get out to eat for at least one night. I'm Annie, by the way.'

'Pleased to meet you, Annie,' Tim said. 'You know how to reach me if you need me.' He pointed to the card. 'My number is on there. As you said, might be good to get out of the cabin at least once. Plus...' He trailed off. Annie noticed a dark expression fall over his face.

'What?' Annie asked.

He took another beat. 'Well, you can ring me any hour, is all I'm saying. If you need to, that is.'

He still looked troubled, which confused Annie. 'Why would I need to, Tim?'

The man shuffled in his seat. 'Well... let's put it this way: you see anything... strange... up there, you just call me, understand? I'll come get you straight away.'

Annie frowned. 'Strange? What do you mean by that?'

'I mean... alright, I don't want to worry you, but though most people enjoy their stay, some people have told me... stories.'

'What kind of stories?' Annie asked with a cocked eyebrow.

'You know. About hearing strange noises, *seeing* strange things. Things they can't explain. A few of the punters were really shook up.'

Annie stared hard at Tim, trying to work out if this was another deadpan joke, but his face gave nothing away. 'Define... *strange* for me, Tim,' she said.

'You probably wouldn't believe me,' Tim replied.

'Probably not,' Annie stated. 'I mean, if you're going to tell me the house is haunted, then no, I won't believe it. I have no time for that kind of thing.' She actually felt a small pang of relief. For a moment, she'd worried other guests had had trouble with strangers coming to the lodge to mess with them or something like that. Ghosts she could handle.

Simply because there was no such thing.

'Well, then you'll be okay,' Tim replied. 'Though I'll always remember the story one woman told me. She didn't believe either, of course. But when I picked her up after her stay, she swears blind that on the last night she woke up during the dead of night. And she said—and I swear this is true—that she heard a baby crying outside the cabin. But it was just her and her husband there, no one else. Certainly no kids. At first she thought she was still dreaming, but then she got up and went to the window. She looked out…' His voice lowered to a whisper as he said, 'And that's where she saw it. It was just standing there, looking back at her.'

'Go on,' Annie said, leaning forward.

'A woman in white,' Tim went on, voice still low. 'Holding a child. Just standing out there in the woods.'

That was when Annie saw it—the slightest crack of a smile at the corner of Tim's mouth. A smile the man was clearly trying to repress.

She grinned. 'Nice try,' she said with a laugh and shook her head.

'Damn it,' Tim said, and playfully slapped the wheel. 'I was keeping such a straight face the whole time. Thought I had you.'

'Sorry to disappoint,' Annie said. Tim certainly seemed something of an oddball, but she liked him. 'Like I told you, ghosts don't scare me.'

'Me either,' Tim said. 'All a bunch of rubbish, you'll be perfectly safe up there. In truth, I've never heard of *anything* strange happening. Even with it being so far out, every single person I've spoken to has had no trouble at all. I think you're all good for a relaxing trip.'

The drive took around fifty minutes, as Tim had promised, and Annie noted that at around the thirty-five-minute mark, much of the built-up areas around them began to slip away, with stretches of green fields and dense trees taking over. Eventually, the road became a single track where it entered a section of woodland. This area of trees, however, wasn't quite as dense as most Annie had seen thus far, with plenty of light getting through between the canopy of branches. Thankfully, the road itself was still asphalt and in good condition, so it was a smooth ride all the way up to the house, which soon came into view.

'There it is,' Tim said, pointing ahead. 'Nice, eh?'

'It sure is,' Annie replied, leaning forward in her seat as she gazed out of the front window.

The cabin was situated in a spacious clearing surrounded by pine trees, ash ones, and even a smattering of oak. The dwelling looked elegant, with the timber boarding a light ash colour and the frames of the window a darker stain. Both roof slopes of the L-shaped building were mono-pitch, sloping up and away from the entrance, which sat at the inner point of that 'L.'

'So, do the people that own the cabin own the woodland as well?' Annie asked.

Tim shrugged. 'Maybe. I'd guess so. There's actually another cluster of cabins on the other side of the trees, but that's quite a distance away. They charge less to stay over there, so this one is a little more upmarket. It's supposed to be real nice inside.'

Annie nodded. 'I love it.'

The car pulled to a stop close to the cabin. Tim left the engine running but started to get out. 'Let me get your bag,' he said.

'Oh, you don't have to—' But he was already out and walking around the back before she could finish.

By the time Annie got out and moved to join him, her bag had already been set on the asphalt.

'There you go, m'lady,' he said with a wide grin.

Annie laughed. 'Thank you, Tim. You made the trip thoroughly enjoyable.'

'I'm glad. And remember, if you need me just call.'

Annie paid the fee, making sure to tip generously, and waved to Tim as he drove off back down the narrow road.

Once the hum of the engine started to fade, she turned to look at her home for the next week.

She noticed a small key-safe lockbox fitted to the wall just next to the entrance door. After moving to it, Annie punched the code she had been sent and it clicked open, revealing a set of keys on a small keychain. Annie retrieved the keys, found the one for the front door, and opened up the cabin.

A smell of old incense and polish wafted over her as soon as Annie stepped into the entrance area. The flooring there was of marble tile, which was an off-white colour with streaks and swirls of dark-grey. Turning her head to the left, Annie saw the lobby opened straight into the large living and dining area, where the flooring changed to a plush, light-brown carpet in the living space and stained wooden boards to the dining room. There was a large, dark leather sofa that looked like it would swallow her whole should she drop into it. Before that, a massive television was mounted to the wall. There were plenty of windows around the perimeter, most of which ran down to ground level, with a horizontal transom midway up that allowed the top sections to open. Two armchairs and a small table were clustered around one such window, giving a gorgeous view of the woodland outside.

In addition, Annie could see an assortment of small side tables, cabinets, and a large, solid oak dining room table that completed the decor. A classical-style landline telephone sat on one of the waist-high circular tables, which was pressed against one of the walls. That was her primary method of contacting the outside world, given how spotty she knew her cellphone signal would be.

To Annie's immediate left was a door, which she knew led to the main bedroom. The door straight ahead gave access to the bathroom. She checked the bedroom first and was pleased with what she found—the bed was *huge*. Easily a super king-size, and topped by a thick, white duvet with flowery teal patterns adorning it. An elegant, silver pendant light hung down from the sloping ceiling. Annie was also pleased to see a large, built-in wardrobe, which was more than enough for her needs, despite having a chest of drawers and nightstands as well.

The bathroom was also spacious, with a large tub that sat on clawed metallic feet. There was a large walk-in shower close by, and the room even had vanity units fixed to the far wall, with tall mirrors just above.

Annie wheeled her case through to the main living area; there, she saw two more doors just off the dining space. The right-hand one gave access to the second bedroom, which was much like the first but smaller. The left-hand door opened into the small study, with an ornate writing desk pushed against one wall. There was another door on the far side. After pushing it open, Annie found herself in a small library with full-height bookcases on two walls, filled with leather-and-fabric-bound tomes. She guessed the books were just for show and had never once been read. Still, they served to enhance the feel of the cabin. She then moved back to the living room, unable to help the smile that played on her lips.

Perfect, she said to herself, and started to unpack.

4 - 3

ANNIE TOOK THE FIRST SIP OF HER AFTERNOON COFFEE. SHE'D found ground coffee beans and a cafetière when nosing through the kitchen and promptly fixed herself a steaming mug before moving over to one of the armchairs facing a window. There, she'd sunk down into the plush seat and taken a drink.

It was delicious.

She couldn't help but smile as she stared out the window, enjoying the view of nature beyond it. All thoughts of work drifted away, and she felt immediately at peace. A small goldfinch flittered into view and landed on a nearby branch. It was so close Annie could see its black eyes as the bird's head darted left and right. It chirped a few times, then took off.

After a few minutes of taking in the scenery, Annie debated going to get one of the books she'd brought with her, but instead decided to remain where she was, simply enjoying her coffee and letting her mind go where it wished. Thankfully, the caffeine kicked in just as her eyes were beginning to feel heavy. She drained the last of her drink and checked her watch. Four in the afternoon. That meant she had another couple of hours of sunlight before it started to get too dark to go out. Though she was beginning to get hungry, Annie had a desire to do a little exploring outside. She'd keep close to the house, but it would be good to get out in the sun, and she could prepare plenty of food afterwards. Annie had already spied enough ingredients in the kitchen to prepare a lasagne, one of her favourite dishes.

The idea of just staying in her comfy chair was still appealing, and pulled to Annie somewhat, but she heaved herself up and got ready, slipping on her hiking boots, a thick coat, gloves, and a wool hat. She threw the keys into her pocket and stepped outside, breathing in the crisp air and savouring the strong scent of pine.

The idea of becoming a hermit and living out in the middle of nowhere suddenly became appealing to her—such was her level of tranquillity. Though in truth, Annie knew she needed her creature comforts far too much for that.

Just outside of the main door was a large, circular asphalt area that Tim had used to drop her off. Then the road ran off ahead through the tree line. Instead of following the road, however, Annie wandered around the back of the cabin, and while she saw the expected rear deck, there was also a smaller decked area about a hundred yards farther into the trees. It had seating and a covered canopy, and was not something Annie had seen on the website. She smiled as she imagined herself sitting out there, all wrapped up, with a book and a glass of wine. She approached the decking, her feet stomping through the moss- and pine-covered ground, and inspected the seats, pleased to find they were clean and dry.

There was a trail just beyond the area that snaked off into the trees, so Annie decided to follow it. After she'd walked for about five minutes and dropped down a steady incline, the cabin disappeared from view.

Now that Annie had lost sight of her home base, however, her feeling of tranquillity diminished slightly. A certain sense of... unease... crept in. Annie realised it was a natural reaction to being out in the woods alone away from safety. Regardless, it still took her by surprise. She knew she *was* ultimately safe, but also knew human evolution had embedded a caution of the unknown into our psyche for a reason.

Annie pressed on, ignoring that hint of worry. Even so, she remembered the conversation with Tim, where he'd asked if she would be okay on her own. For the first time, she wondered if that uneasy feeling in her gut would grow when darkness set in.

Stop scaring yourself.

She pushed all those thoughts from her mind and focused solely on the beauty around her, as well as the sounds of the woodland. The song of chirping birds was soothing.

Crack.

Annie stopped. Her head snapped up and she looked straight ahead. The residual sound of snapping wood continued to echo faintly through the trees.

What the...

Though she couldn't be certain, the noise had seemed to come from quite a way off, and Annie guessed a large branch that had been broken, given how loud the sound was.

She continued to listen intently, trying to stop her mind from running away with itself. While she hadn't seen any larger animals nearby, she knew there would be a natural explanation.

Crack.

Annie took half a step back, her sense of unease growing.

Crack. Thwack. Crack.

It now sounded like someone was hitting a length of wood against the trunk of a tree, over and over.

That doesn't mean it's anything to worry about, Annie told herself. *Tim said there were other cabins out here.*

As rational as she was trying to be, Annie found the appeal of hiking had waned completely. She decided to turn back and head home, maybe try again the next day when it wasn't as close to nightfall. Hopefully by then, Annie would be more used to her surroundings and not as easily spooked. Slightly disappointed in herself, Annie was soon back to the warmth and safety of the cabin.

The skies outside darkened just as Annie was finishing her meal.

When done, she cleaned up, and while she did, she looked through one of the windows to watch the pretty sky, which was ablaze with burning reds and oranges.

The cabin didn't have a sound system, but she'd brought a speaker with her, which was hooked up to her phone via Bluetooth. Annie currently had one of her favourite albums playing in the background: rock straight out of the eighties. People were always surprised when they found out she was a rocker, given she didn't dress that way. Not that she didn't *want* to, but her work, which was her life, demanded a professional appearance whenever others could see her.

Once the dishes were loaded into the washer and the table wiped down, Annie poured herself another glass of red wine. The wine rack in the kitchen had an impressive display, and the bottles were included in the price of the stay. She was, however, limited to three bottles for the week, unless she wanted to pay extra.

With her glass in hand, Annie drew most of the curtains, then settled herself into the armchair in front of the window again. She'd left that curtain open so she could gaze out. Annie then cracked open the book she'd left on the table, curled her legs up, and sipped her wine while reading. Every so often, she would glance out of the window and watch the dark of the night completely take over. It was a pleasant sight to see stars in the sky between the trees, aided by the lack of light pollution in the woodland.

Annie had always loved reading, and often lamented the fact her work meant her favourite pastime was becoming a rarity. So, she intended to make the most of it while out at the cabin. The book she was currently working through had her utterly gripped—it was about a woman in a dystopian future, who had found a djinn willing to lend her its wishes. There would be a price, of course, but with anything she desired at her fingertips, the protagonist set out to seek revenge on a society that had wronged her.

As Annie was reading, a white light suddenly bloomed from outside, startling her. She snapped her head up in shock. Then... she relaxed—it was just a security light flicking on. Annie hadn't even realised the property *had* a security light. And she also spotted the reason for the light: a large badger had wandered close to the house, sniffing along the grass. The animal seemed unfazed by the bright light flooding the area. Annie slowly set her book down, reached for her phone, and lowered herself down to her knees.

I want a picture of this.

She'd never seen a badger before in real life, and for some reason, she'd always thought they were smaller. Using the camera on her phone, Annie managed to snap some shots as the creature went about its business.

Soon, the security light faded out, but it came on again a few seconds later as the badger moved once more. Annie got several additional pictures before the animal eventually wandered off completely—including one final photo just before it was out of sight. However, just as she did, movement on the edge of the light caused her to narrow her eyes.

Whatever was out there had quickly ducked out of the light splash, so Annie hadn't been able to make out what it had been. Initially, she'd assumed it might have been another animal, but from the brief flash she'd gotten, it had seemed far too tall. Eventually, the light faded out again, leaving Annie staring out into the blackness that swallowed up the scenery.

It's nothing to worry about, she told herself sternly, trying to stop her mind from getting carried away again. Especially after cutting her walk short earlier, Annie refused to ruin the trip by freaking herself out. *It could have been anything. Even a deer.*

She then had the idea of checking the last picture she had taken. *Maybe it shows something.*

Annie opened the picture and studied it. There was something in the distance, but it was little more than a blur in the shot. She zoomed in, but was still confused.

Is that a person?

No, Annie quickly admonished herself. That was a leap. In reality, she couldn't tell what it was, given it was mostly cloaked in darkness. The only reason she could make it out at all was because of the slightly lighter tones of its form.

Faces in the fire, she said to herself. *You don't know* what *you're looking at. But it isn't a person.*

Annie put her phone down and pulled the thick curtain closed. While she was adamant she would not get creeped out, the idea of the curtain staying open didn't sit well.

She then grabbed her wine and moved over to the main sofa, which she dropped into. After setting her wine onto a side table, Annie kicked her feet up across the couch and grabbed the television remote, hoping to find something good to watch. After flicking through some channels, she found nothing of interest, but then remembered seeing a drawer full of DVDs when looking around. She heaved herself back up and opened that drawer, looking through the collection. There looked to be some good thrillers, but Annie was hoping to calm herself, so eventually chose a comedy that she had seen before, a good comfort watch.

Once the DVD was set up, she took her seat again and made herself comfortable, finally pressing play on the remote.

About an hour later, Annie got up to pour herself another glass of wine, but resolved to make it the last one. She wanted to get an early night, sleep well, then rise early for a healthy breakfast. After that, she could go out for another hike. A proper one this time.

Just as the film drew close to finishing, Annie noticed something from the window she'd been looking through earlier—a sliver of white light was coming in through the crack in the curtains. She had quite a lot of the living room lights on, so it was difficult to distinguish, but when she focused, she could see it.

It was the security light again.

Wonder if my badger friend is back?

While part of Annie wanted to go and look, part of her didn't, worried about what she might see.

Eventually, Annie decided to ignore the light, knowing any kind of woodland wildlife might have set the sensors off. She couldn't allow herself to get frightened every time the damn light clicked on.

So, Annie finished the film, downed the rest of her drink, and set the glass in the dishwasher. She then took a quick shower, enjoying the hot water blasting away the aches in her bones from a long day. Once that was done, she got herself ready for bed, leaving the nightlight on and curling up once more with her book.

As she read, Annie began to realise she now didn't like the bedroom being on the ground floor. It felt somehow… exposed. She kept glancing at the curtains covering the window. It was hard not to imagine someone being right outside, staring straight in through the window. The notion caused a small chill to work its way up Annie's spine.

Annie closed the book and switched off her light, annoyed with herself. She hadn't even been at the cabin for a full day and was already getting worried about nothing.

Get some sleep and start again tomorrow with a fresh mind.

She also decided to take Tim's advice and go into town the next evening. A nice meal and some drinks would be welcome, even alone.

Annie rolled over to her side, tucked the thick duvet up to her chin, and closed her eyes. She took a deep breath to relax herself.

Crack.

Annie's eyes snapped open. She pushed herself up on her elbow. The sound outside repeated itself.

Thwack. Snap. Crack.

They seemed to come from somewhere in the distance, the exact same ones she'd heard earlier. Now, in the dead of night, however, she started to get *seriously* creeped out.

Thwack. Crack. Crack.

It was getting harder and harder for Annie to keep her mind in check. She desperately tried to search for a rational explanation. It certainly didn't seem like an animal could make the sounds; it wasn't like there were bears roaming around the UK's forests, pulling branches from trees.

So it has *to be a human.*

But who? And why?

What possible reason could there be for someone to be out there in the middle of the night?

The only thing she could think of was youths causing trouble. But then... given the sounds had come earlier as well, it meant they would have been in the woodlands all day as well as the night. *What about food?* she thought. *Unless they left and came back. Could be they have a meeting spot and hangout close by.*

But then, none of the online reviews Annie had read made mention of any troublesome youths or strange noises. Suddenly, the image of the spectral woman holding a child from Tim's story popped into her head, even though she knew he'd made the whole thing up.

Crack. Crack.

Ignore it, she told herself—because there was nothing else to do. She remembered again about the other cabins. Could be that one family over there just had a particularly annoying teen with them who was creating the noise?

Regardless, going out to investigate certainly wasn't an option.

After a few minutes, the noises stopped completely. A few minutes later, Annie began to feel a little embarrassed at getting so worked up. *Does it matter who was making the noise? They aren't going to do anything to you.*

She settled herself back down, eyes still wide. Over an hour later, she finally drifted off into a restless sleep.

It was still dark when Annie's eyes opened again.

Her bladder pressed against her, shouting to be emptied, her heart was beating quickly, and the last remnants of the dream still echoed—the specifics were lost, however, just a faded memory.

Before getting out of bed, she listened carefully, half expecting to hear that sound again.

There was nothing.

Relieved at the silence, Annie flicked on the nightlight, swung her legs out of bed, and padded over to the bathroom, switching on the lights as she went. Within five minutes, she was back into bed and pulling the duvet over herself once more. However, she paused in place just as her head settled back on the pillow.

The sound of movement came from *just* outside.

Annie sat upright immediately, looking over toward the curtained window. A definite shuffling sound came from beyond it.

Someone's out there!

The sound came again. Annie's first thought was that they were footfalls on the fallen pines. *An animal? Maybe my badger friend again?* She hoped so. With her body tense and teeth clenched, Annie forced herself back out of bed and approached the window. She held out her hand and slowly pulled the curtain back a little, moving her head close to peer out. Though darkness covered almost everything, she was able to tell there was nothing in the immediate vicinity. Annie narrowed her eyes to try and break through the dark, yet couldn't see any movement. She waited there in front of the window for another ten minutes before finally relaxing, eventually satisfied all was clear.

She returned to bed feeling utterly exhausted. This time, sleep was quicker to claim her.

---

4 - 4

THIS IS BETTER, ANNIE TOLD HERSELF MID-STRIDE. THE CABIN was out of view, but she still felt fine. The autumn air was dry, and though there was a chill, the layers Annie wore offered ample protection.

During breakfast that morning, she had given serious consideration to cancelling the trip early. After the previous night, part of her just wanted to call Tim and head home, despite the money she would have lost. However, she was embarrassed as to what Tim—or anyone else, for that matter—might think about her.

Leaving over nothing.

So, she'd forced herself to get ready and take a hike to help clear her head, tired though she was. And now, as she clomped through the woodland, she was glad she'd stayed.

The air had indeed helped—her thinking was clearer. Yes, the sounds from the previous night had been odd, but odd didn't mean dangerous. There was nothing inherently worrying about noises she couldn't explain. The same with the sound outside her window. That could have been anything. *I'm in a damn woodland full of wildlife, not a city.*

The scenery around her was lovely and helped put her back in that state of Zen she'd felt after first arriving.

Annie had followed the trail out back of the cabin and stuck to that route. There hadn't been any branching paths, so finding her way back would be easy. That was good, because there were very few landmarks of note—everything looked the same. A few fallen trees stood out here and there, and there was an area that took her up a small hill, but other than that it was like those cartoons that used the same background over and over.

More of the same.

Which, on the one hand, wasn't a bad thing at all. Annie, being a city girl, had never really appreciated the beauty of nature. She'd seen plenty of pretty pictures online of places she'd like to visit, but physically getting out and experiencing them was something different entirely. She decided there and then it was something she wanted to do more of.

That being said, Annie could never see herself *actually* camping out in the wilds. There were limits to everything.

As she walked, she thought more about work—not about deadlines or the stress of what was waiting for her, but about how her life was currently balanced. Or *un*balanced, as the case may be.

I need a change.

Making that change wouldn't be easy, she knew, because she *did* need to work, but Annie also understood she had to find a way to pull back a lot. Or even change careers, if that was what it took. The notion hit her with such certainty and finality that it seemed like a revelation. *Change careers*. It wasn't a question anymore; it was something that needed to be done.

The decision made her feel lighter. Though she was tired, renewed energy coursed through her. She continued her hike with a smile, deciding to call Tim when she returned to the cabin—not to go home, but to head into town for a slap-up meal and some drinks. A nice way to toast the change she had committed to.

'You seem to have a spring in your step today,' Tim said as they set off. It was still light outside, but the first hints of darkness were beginning to show. The taxi ambled its way back down the road between the trees, leaving the cabin behind.

'Really?' Annie asked from the passenger seat. 'How so?'

Tim shrugged. 'Dunno. You're really smiley, I guess.'

'I wasn't smiley yesterday?' she asked with an accusing but playful look. 'You're saying I was a grump?'

'Well, I wouldn't go that far at all,' Tim said. 'But it looks like the wilderness air agrees with you. Enjoying your time out here?'

'I am, actually,' she replied. 'It's helped me put things into perspective.'

'Glad to hear that. And now you get to have a night out on the town. What could be better? Though… don't go calling me to pick you up if you're too drunk. I'm *not* cleaning vomit out of my car. Done that before and it takes a week for the bloody smell to go away.'

Annie laughed. 'Oh, I'm not one for getting drunk like that. Don't worry. A few glasses of wine will be enough.'

'Any idea where you wanna go to eat?' Tim asked.

'No clue. I'm just kind of winging it. Anywhere good? Somewhere I don't need to book, obviously.'

'You should be fine most places,' Tim said. 'The town doesn't usually get busy enough to need to reserve a table. Don't get me wrong, it isn't a graveyard, but you'll be fine pretty much wherever. What kind of food are you partial to?'

'Italian,' Annie stated immediately. 'Though I'm in the mood for something with a little more kick.'

'Ah, feeling adventurous, eh?' Tim asked. 'There is a fantastic Thai place I'd recommend. I go there all the time. Not too expensive, but the food is bloody brilliant.'

Annie thought about it for a moment. 'Thai it is,' she replied.

'Alright, sounds like we have a plan. I'll head there and drop you at the door. The staff are great, they'll take care of you.' After a beat, he added, 'So, how's the cabin? Everything you hoped?'

'It is,' Annie confirmed. 'Lovely decor, and the area is so peaceful and quiet. Well... mostly.' The moment the words had left her mouth, Annie regretted it.

'Mostly?' Tim asked. He turned his eyes to her and raised an inquisitive eyebrow. 'Something bothering you?'

'No,' Annie quickly said, 'not really. Just...' She trailed off. She *really* didn't want to tell him about what she'd heard, and especially how it had made her feel. *He's going to think I'm nuts. Or worse, a coward.*

'Go on,' Tim prodded. 'What is it? You have me curious.'

Annie sighed. She knew she couldn't exactly avoid the issue now. 'It's nothing, really. I just heard some... odd sounds, that's all.'

Tim waited a moment. 'Define 'odd.' '

'It sounded like someone was beating a branch against a tree or something. I don't know, it's hard to explain.'

'Hitting a tree?'

'Yeah,' Annie said. 'But I've heard it quite a few times now. During the day, and also in the middle of the night. Could be anything, I suppose. It's just annoying.'

'And it creeped you out?' Tim asked.

'No,' Annie was quick to say, turning to him with a frown. 'What makes you think that?'

Tim just shrugged. 'It's written all over your face. Plus, hearing things you can't explain would unnerve me as well. Especially out there. No shame in that at all.'

'Really?' Annie asked, slightly surprised. She'd half-expected Tim to tease her a little.

'Of course,' he replied. 'Thing is, unless you're used to the wilderness, you're always going to hear things you can't explain. It's a lot different from urban areas.'

'Yeah, but... this *had* to be a person,' Annie said. 'Animals don't go around beating the hell out of trees, do they.' It was a statement, not a question.

'Well, maybe not, but there will be a rational explanation, I'm sure.'

'I actually agree,' Annie replied. 'It freaked me out a little, but I've got a few ideas.'

'Like what?'

'Someone from the other cabins,' she said. 'Maybe a couple of teens, bored and just messing around in the woods.'

'There you go,' Tim said with a smile. 'That sounds plausible.'

Annie appreciated his warm attitude. However, she quickly remembered him trying to trick her on the ride out to the cabin. A subsequent idea formed, and she had to fight to stop a smile. *Time for a little payback.*

'You know,' she went on. 'There was something else as well.'

'Go on.'

'I heard... something outside my window in the middle of the night. Thought it was a person at first.'

'Really?' Tim asked quickly, now starting to frown.

'Oh yeah,' Annie said. 'So... I went to check. Opened the window and looked out. And I—I saw someone, Tim.'

'You... *saw* someone?' Tim asked, shocked. He even took

235

his eyes off the road for a moment to stare at her. 'Outside the window? Did you get a good look at them?'

'Oh yeah,' Annie stated with a nod. 'A *real* good look.'

'So… who was it?' he replied, looking genuinely worried.

He's totally falling for it.

'It was a fucking *ghost,* Tim!' Annie exclaimed. 'A woman, just standing there. Holding a child. Can you believe it?'

Tim paused for a second, then burst into laughter and slapped the wheel. 'You had me there for a second,' he said, sounding a little relieved.

'Yeah, I could tell. You were really drawn in.'

'Bloody idiot,' Tim teased. 'I thought someone was stalking you.' He laughed again.

Annie chuckled along with him. 'Actually, joking aside, there *was* something outside my window during the night. I wasn't lying about that part. It could have been anything, though. A badger wandered up to the house at one point, so I'm thinking it came back.'

'Yeah, lots of wildlife out there, like I said. But nothing that can harm you, as long as you keep your distance. Badgers can have a nasty bite. Don't go trying to feed them.'

'Wasn't planning on it, but I'll remember that,' Annie said.

The drive with Tim was again pleasant, and the pair chatted and laughed during the whole ride.

'And here we are,' Tim eventually announced as he pulled up close to the building. The restaurant was situated on a terrace of buildings, all a mix of shops—most of which were closed—bars, and restaurants. That street seemed to be the centre of activity for the town, as far as Annie could tell, but it wasn't exactly swarming with people.

'How much do I owe you?' Annie asked. 'Same again?'

'Well, if you need a trip back, we'll just settle it then.'

'You sure?' Annie asked.

'Of course. It's actually a bit of a trick. This way, you *have* to use me. You'll feel guilty if you don't, and I lock in an extra fare.' He was grinning again, and Annie found the smile contagious.

'Sounds good,' she said. 'See you in, say, three hours?'

'No problem.' Tim replied. 'Here,' he gave her another card. 'In case you need to change the time. Phone signal should be fine here in town, not like the cabin, so just call if you need to. If not, I'll see you here in three hours. And when you finish your food'—he turned and pointed over the road—'there are three bars over there that I recommend. Low key, but upmarket. I think you'd like them.'

'Thanks,' Annie said. 'I'll probably give them a try. Shame you aren't on hand to be my tour guide.'

'Sorry, working tonight,' Tim said. 'Besides, I don't think my wife would be too thrilled to find out I'd been showing a pretty young lady around town.'

'Pretty? *Young?*' Annie said with a smirk. 'How very nice of you to say.'

'Don't let it go to your head,' Tim shot back. 'Most people are pretty and young when compared to *this*.' He pointed to his own face. 'Now, go and fill your belly and have some drinks. I have another fare to get to.'

'I will. Enjoy your night, Tim.'

Annie got out and waved goodbye to the driver as he set off.

The night was similar to the previous one—a little cold, but crisp and dry.

Annie then did as Tim ordered: she filled her stomach with some fantastic Thai food—which had *just* the right amount of kick—and indulged in some cocktails, deciding to forgo wine. She didn't get completely drunk, but certainly had a light buzz.

Despite Annie only having herself for company, she still enjoyed the night immensely. The bars weren't very busy, and she noticed quite a few people who were out on their own as well, either with their heads buried in their phones, or even working on laptops or tablets. Annie had no desire to strike up a conversation with any of them, but it did make her feel better knowing she wasn't the only one flying solo.

After finishing a fairly strong drink in one of the trendy, dimly lit bars Tim had recommended, she checked the time. *He'll be here soon.* She debated calling Tim to push back their pick-up slot. However, given it was only ten minutes until the allotted time, it would have been unfair to him and his scheduling. Plus, in truth, Annie had had her fill—the buzz would last her until she was asleep. Thankfully, she hadn't drunk enough that she would feel sick the next day. *Going back now is the right call.*

After stepping outside, Annie looked around the street. There were some shops that piqued her interest, though they were currently closed. A quaint little bookshop looked particularly enticing. *Maybe I'll come back tomorrow,* she told herself.

Annie had about three minutes remaining when she got to the pick-up spot, but even so, she saw that Tim's car was already there. She smiled to herself as she walked over, pleased that she'd made an acquaintance who was so helpful. A brief thought of caution sprang up in her mind, which made her ask herself *why* he was being so helpful.

But she quickly pushed the warning away. *All he's done is drive me around, which I've paid for. Get a grip.* He was chatty and friendly, sure, but that wasn't a crime. In fact, it was almost a required skill for his line of work.

She got in the passenger seat.

'Good night?' Tim asked.

'Yes, it was great, thank you,' she said. 'Just what I needed.'

'Good stuff,' he replied. 'And you don't look too squiffy.'

'Squiffy?' Annie asked.

'You know, plastered. Hammered. Drunk.'

'Ah.'

'Means I don't need to worry about you puking your guts up. Now, let's get you back. You're not going to fall asleep on me, are you?'

'Depends how boring your conversation is,' she replied with a smirk.

Thankfully, the resulting conversation was fun. However, she couldn't help but be a little unnerved when they finally broke onto the woodland road. *It's so dark.* Annie imagined the headlights picking something up eerie in the trees ahead. She forced herself to continue talking, to keep her mind sane, desperate not to go backwards to paranoia again.

Soon enough, the car pulled up just outside the cabin.

'There you are, Annie. All safe and sound,' Tim said. 'Will you be venturing back into town again during your stay?'

'Actually,' Annie replied, 'I think I'd like to have a wander around during the day. Are you free tomorrow for me?'

'Of course,' Tim replied. 'What time were you thinking?'

Annie considered it. 'Early. I'd like to get breakfast somewhere. Say… eight-thirty?'

'I can do that,' Tim replied. 'I'll be back then. Now, you get inside and have a big glass of water. It'll help prevent a headache tomorrow.'

Annie laughed. 'I'm fine, but will do.' She opened her door. 'Good night, Tim.'

'G'night,' the man replied. Annie got out and trotted over to the entrance, activating the security light as she did. That light, plus those from the taxi, bathed her in a strong white glow. Once she opened the front door, she turned back to wave, shielding her eyes from the glare of the headlights.

Tim didn't pull away until she was inside, which she appreciated, and she watched the vehicle move off into the distance, then closed the door. The sound of the vehicle grew faint. Then, oddly, it remained constant for a moment, as if it was standing still, before finally cutting out—she found it strange, but shrugged and ignored it. *Sound behaves strangely out here,* Annie reasoned.

She debated reading or watching television for a little while, given it wasn't particularly late. Her heavy eyes disagreed with her, however, so she decided to turn in. One of her goals during the trip was to get as much sleep and rest as possible.

As she was getting herself cleaned up, a loud *thump* on the front door caused her to draw in a breath.

She stood in the bathroom, soap on her face, body locked, head tilted towards the bathroom door.

What the hell?

She waited for the sound to repeat itself. It didn't.

Annie quickly rinsed her face, dried off, and then carefully approached the main entrance. She could tell through the small frosted glazed panel that the security light was on outside. Her breathing quickened.

Stop it, she told herself. *It's nothing to worry about.* She suddenly realised she'd been trying to calm herself down *a lot* on this trip. *Stop being such a coward!*

Annie tried to think of a logical explanation for the sound: *A bat flying into the door, maybe?* But she knew its senses would have kept it away from the cabin. *An owl?* That seemed similarly unlikely. *It'd have to be a particularly stupid owl to fly into the house.*

'H… Hello?' Annie called, hoping she was talking to no one. Thankfully, she didn't receive a response. Soon, the security light faded out. She tiptoed over to the closest window and pulled the curtain aside.

Darkness engulfed everything, meaning she could only see a few feet beyond the window. However, the area outside remained still.

At first.

It was only after staring for a while that she noticed something right on the edge of her vision. It was little more than an *impression* of a shape, possibly human, but not definite, standing out against the dark only slightly. Whatever it was pulled back a second later, getting completely swallowed up by the night. Annie waited by the window for a long while, body tense the whole time, waiting for it to re-emerge. After fifteen minutes, she started to relax somewhat. Her mystery caller showed no signs of reappearing. She again considered calling Tim and high-tailing it out of there.

However, if Tim was even able to come get her... then what? She had no accommodation booked, so would have to hope she could find something in town tonight and catch a train the next morning.

Then there was the shame she knew she'd feel once she was back home. Annie had no doubt logic would then take over—she'd start to chastise herself for being a coward, for running away over nothing. She also imagined how the conversation with her parents would go when they asked how her trip had been.

I could lie, she thought, hating the idea of it.

Yet again, she decided to wait until the morning and take a view on it, hoping she would feel less paranoid.

I really don't want to cut the trip short.

The thought of going back to work again so soon, even if a change was coming for her, felt like a lead weight in her gut. And Annie knew if she did go home, she'd check her emails, and would quickly slip back into the old habit of work, rather than taking the days she already had scheduled off. Back home, she was too connected.

Never able to switch off.

Annie knew she needed the few extra days to try to disconnect more and get used to not being eternally on call.

It was the first step in making a meaningful difference in her life.

Annie then let the curtain fall closed and began to walk back to her bedroom. The security light clicked on once again outside.

There was a knock on the door.

33

---

4 - 5

ANNIE'S HEART WAS IN HER THROAT. SHE STARED AT THE DOOR, trying to see through the small, obscured, glazed section at the top. There *was* someone out there—she spotted a shape moving around.

The outline of a head moved close to the glass, as if trying to see inside.

Annie couldn't breathe. Terror clamped around her heart, making the organ feel like it was going to burst.

Oh fuck, oh fuck, oh fuck. Why would anyone knock on my door at this time of night?

She couldn't think of a single sane reason.

Wait, maybe it's someone from another cabin that just needs help.

'Who is it?' she asked weakly, voice shaking with fear. 'What do you want?'

There was no answer besides another knock—Annie's heart seized again. 'Go away!' she snapped, surprising herself with the anger she summoned. 'Go away now or I'm calling the police.'

There was a slight pause, followed by more light knocking: *tap, tap, tap.*

With her fists clenched, she drew in a breath and bellowed: 'Get the fuck out of here! Now!'

Annie waited, staring forward, eyes wide in panic. The figure outside the glass didn't move for a few moments, though eventually it did back away. Annie remained rooted to the spot, terrified to go and look. However, part of her *needed* to know who was out there, and why. She summoned all her courage and ran to the closest window. After pulling back the curtain, she moved her face closer to the glass.

Breath fogging up the window, Annie was terrified at what she might see.

Nothing.

That just made things worse. Her mind ran riot, imagining what kind of psychopath was out in the darkness, tormenting her.

She now knew it couldn't be someone from the other lodges—they would have answered, not run off.

No matter *who* it was, Annie was certain they weren't friendly. Her hands were trembling.

What do I do?

Her mind raced for ideas. *Call the police!* It seemed the most appropriate course of action. She was alone and being harassed, so there was no reason not to. She briefly considered calling Tim, but quickly expunged the idea. *What can he do that the police can't?*

What Annie was certain of was that her trip was now done. After calling the police, she intended to pack up her case. When they arrived, she would get them to drive her away from the lodge and she'd figure out where to stay later.

Annie instinctively drew out her mobile phone, but cursed when she saw there was no signal. So, she ran over to the landline and lifted the receiver.

The line was dead.

What the hell? Annie's stomach dropped. *There's no way.* After she'd first arrived, Annie had lifted the handset to check and had heard the dial tone then.

It's been cut.

The realisation terrified her further.

The security light clicked back on outside. Annie drew in a sharp breath, still clutching the phone. She could just make out the sound of movement and involuntarily took half a step back. A second later, she saw a blurred form move across the frosted glass.

Someone was running. They were moving around the house.

Annie dropped the receiver. Her head turned, following the sounds as it moved towards the back of the property.

To her bedroom.

Annie sprinted over to the kitchen, where she pulled out one of the large, sharp cutting knives. Then, she inched towards the bedroom door, listening intently, terrified that the stranger would try and get in through the window. When she heard a tapping on the glass a few seconds later, Annie almost cried.

'Go away!' she screamed. Despite her mind begging for her not to, Annie forced herself to slowly open the bedroom door. She flicked on the light. The curtain to the window was drawn, but the tapping continued.

Tap, tap, tap.

'Who's there?!' Annie demanded, though she knew she would get no answer. Her visitor seemed intent only on scaring her.

I have to go pull the curtain back. Regardless of how scared she was, she *had* to find out who was terrorising her. It was hard to force her body into action, but she crept forward.

The tapping stopped, replaced by a sudden and violent

banging on the wall next to it. The sounds caused Annie to jump, and she almost dropped the knife. The thudding continued, moving away, as if someone was running down the length of the wall and hitting it as they went. Annie started to sob, pulling in desperate, ragged breaths.

Keep calm. You aren't helpless. You have a knife. But... can you use it?

Even as a desperate measure, the thought of actually sinking the blade into someone's flesh filled Annie with repulsion.

Eventually, the stranger outside ended up back at the main entrance, where they started to savagely bang on the front door. It sounded as if they were kicking and punching it. Annie heard the heavy door vibrate in its hinges, though she knew it was far too strong to give.

Still, that knowledge didn't stop her from crying out in terror while she inched out of the bedroom.

'What do you want?' she cried out.

The banging suddenly stopped. However, a moment later there was the sound of rapid footsteps running away from the house, off into the distance. The sounds eventually died out completely.

Standing in the centre of the room, gripping the knife, Annie listened intently. Then, an indiscernible amount of time later, she started to sob. She prayed it had just been some sick fuck who got their kicks scaring people and had finally had their fill.

Seconds passed. Then minutes. Annie's grip on the handle of the knife didn't ease up. Her fingers and knuckles were white.

Eventually, she felt brave enough to move towards one of the front windows. She drew in—and held—a deep breath, and moved the curtain back.

As before, she could only see a few feet outside the dwelling, but the coast was clear.

What do I do?

Annie knew her options were extremely limited. She didn't have a car, and she also had no way to contact the outside world. She knew from her previous walks that there were pockets of phone signal, but wandering around hoping to find one was far too risky. That meant all she could do was to wait inside and hope her tormentor didn't force their way in.

But how long do I wait? Annie asked herself. Help wasn't coming, because no one knew she was in trouble. That meant waiting for the morning. If she could hold out until daybreak, perhaps the stranger would leave her be. Plus, Tim would be there at eight-thirty. That was still *hours* away, but... it was hope.

Realising she couldn't just stay rooted in place for hours on end, and satisfied she couldn't hear anyone approaching, Annie set about checking every window in the house, just to make sure they were bolted shut.

During that process, Annie continued to listen. It would be easy for someone to sneak up to the cabin, though, and she knew she'd heard her visitor only because they'd wanted her to. Once satisfied that all windows were as secure as they could be, she returned to the front room.

All the windows there were covered by the thick fabric of curtains, and while it stopped anyone from looking in at her, it also blocked her view of anyone approaching.

Annie contemplated making another lap of the house to open all the curtains. Having them closed did bring a kind of comfort and helped her feel less exposed, but if she had a clear view out, then she would be able to see the stranger return. She would also find out exactly *who* it was. However, before Annie could move, her body froze up.

She heard something approaching.

They're coming back.

However, the sounds she heard outside were different now. Soon, it made more sense: something was being *dragged.*

Annie held her breath. The light out front came on again, and a breath later, Annie heard a muffled groan of pain only a few feet in front of the cabin.

Close enough to see, she knew. *Maybe the fucker hurt himself? Good! I hope a branch went through his leg.*

However, she again heard running, then more smacking on the walls as the stranger circled the house once more. Annie closed her eyes and held her breath, trying to bring her erratic breathing under control.

Please go away, please go away, please go away.

Then there was a particularly violent smack against her bedroom window.

They're trying to get inside!

The strikes there continued, over and over.

Annie wanted to curl up into a ball on the floor. She wanted to be with her parents. She wanted to be *anywhere* but that fucking cabin.

However, after allowing herself a moment of fear, Annie gritted her teeth and forced herself to move to her bedroom, trying to focus on the anger that was mixed in with the fear. At least it was something she could use. Annie yanked the door open and screamed at the top of her lungs: 'Leave me the fuck alone or I'll kill you! I will fucking kill you!'

The hitting against the window suddenly stopped, though the glass reverberated for a few moments more. Annie sprinted to the window and flung open the curtain. As she'd expected, the assailant had vanished. She then smacked the window herself with her free hand.

'What the fuck do you *want?!*'

Annie backed away, glaring out into the darkness, waiting for someone to appear. She didn't know how much more she could take.

Her mind again tried to think of who it could be. All that made sense was it was someone lodging in the site across the woodland. The whole area was too remote for it to be anyone else. Unless someone had seen her in town and had followed her and Tim back, but they would have surely noticed a car trailing them, especially along the single-track road through the trees.

Then... her focus settled on Tim.

A sinking feeling came over her. Things started to knit together in her mind.

Tim knew Annie was out there alone. He'd known from the beginning. He knew *exactly* where the cabin was, and how to get there. She then remembered how his car had cut out for a moment in the distance, rather than its engine simply fading away. *Because he stopped the car and shut off the engine.*

Her eyes widened. *He didn't actually leave!*

Annie felt sick. Everything suddenly made sense. Her friendly taxi driver was actually the one terrorising her. And Tim was a *big* man. Much bigger than she was. She knew he could hurt her.

Annie gripped the knife tighter.

'Tim!' she yelled. 'I know it's you. Stop this now! Just go. Go away and I won't tell the police. I give you my word. But just fucking *go!*'

There was no response. Regardless, she went on: 'Think it through. If you *do* try anything stupid, you'll be the first person the police look at. There are cameras in town, so I was filmed getting into your car more than once. There's no way you can get away with anything. So... please... just see reason. Whatever kicks you're getting from this, just be done with it and fucking leave.'

By that point, she was panting. Her throat was raw from prolonged shouting. There was no response from the person outside, and no further movement.

Annie waited. Maybe silence was its own response. *Maybe I got through to him.*

Putting a face on the stranger did make Annie think there was hope. It humanised her harasser, crazy though Tim clearly was. She just hoped she'd humanised herself to him as well.

Maybe that was a stretch, given how far the taxi driver had gone already to scare her, but the more time that passed, the more Annie allowed herself to believe it. *Maybe he's gone.* After checking the window in the bedroom again, Annie crept back into the main living area. Once there, she checked the side windows first, ensuring the curtains were all left open as she moved.

Nothing.

Finally, she moved to the front of the house and approached the window closest to the main door. As soon as she yanked the curtain back, however, Annie gasped. Her body locked. A scream built up within her.

---

4 - 6

ALL HOPE OF ANNIE BEING LEFT ALONE EVAPORATED IN A single, terrible moment. The horrible image she was staring at meant the situation was far worse than she'd imagined.

I'm going to die.

The harassment wasn't just about scaring her. Annie knew that with finality now. She also knew that Tim *wasn't* the one stalking her.

Because Tim was dead. She was currently staring at his body. Annie started to howl and shriek.

The ghastly sight was given awful illumination by the security light, bathing Tim in a brilliant white light that made the crimson blood coating his naked form glisten.

The taxi driver's body was covered in deep cuts and gashes, all still leaking with blood. His stump of his neck was a bloody mess, with much of the insides poking out.

Tim's head lay a few feet in front of his body, carefully positioned on the ground, looking back at Annie. *No, not looking back,* she realised. His eyes were missing, leaving only messy black pits where they had been gouged out.

Annie instinctively knew the display had been for her to see.

She backed away, still screaming hysterically. She had never seen a dead body before, much less one in *that* state. It was too much to process. There was a quick, loud bang on one of the windows to her side. She spun around with a gasp, just in time to see something slip from view.

'Leave me alone! Please!' she managed to shout, though she knew it was futile. The person out there had cut the phone lines and also killed a man—there was no chance this was going to stop now. Whoever it was, they were in too deep. They were going to kill her. Annie knew that.

There was nowhere for her to go, and no way to call for help. *I'm already dead.*

It was still hard for her mind to accept what was unfolding. Things like this didn't happen in real life, they were confined to books and movies.

No, Annie told herself, still shrieking aloud. *This is happening and you have to come to terms with it.* She knew being rooted to the spot and screaming her throat raw wasn't going to get her through the night. So, she forced herself to stop yelling, though she couldn't stop from shaking.

I still have the knife.

She looked down at the large blade. The edge was razor-sharp. It was something.

It could kill.

Any doubts she had about using it vanished. A survival instinct kicked in. Annie desperately tried to formulate a plan as she continued to gaze at the window, making sure no one came back into view. As Annie had feared the previous night, she now felt exposed having some of the curtains open.

She contemplated trying to flee. If she could get out of

the house, maybe she could outrun her attacker. Then she could just keep going until she hit civilisation.

But if not... going outside was a death sentence.

And what if there's more than one of them? The thought hadn't occurred to her before, but it was a terrifying possibility. *There's no way I can outrun two of them.*

Everything was an unknown.

Remaining inside was the only other option. That notion seemed slightly less terrifying, but at the same time, it just meant she was trapped. Whoever was outside wouldn't stay out there forever—she knew they would eventually force their way inside. She looked at the windows. They were double glazed, thick, and secure... but not unbreakable. And there were so damn *many* of them lining the walls. The amount of windows had been a selling point to the cabin, now Annie felt like they were a death sentence.

Plus, she didn't know how long she'd have to wait before someone came out there to check on her. It would be *days*. Tim was the only person who would have known something was wrong, and now...

Annie knew she couldn't hold out for that long.

Images of an assailant smashing a window and crawling inside sprang up in her mind. Then, however, her imagination went to the idea of running over and stabbing the fucker.

She realised that would actually be the perfect opportunity to strike—they'd be vulnerable. A quick plunge of the knife into their neck was all it would take.

Maybe that's my best shot, Annie thought, *just wait for them to make a move.* But to do that, she had to know *where* they would come from.

So Annie quickly got to work, making sure all internal doors were open, as well as every curtain in the house. The library was an inner room, accessed off the study and impossible to see from the living room. Thankfully, it didn't have a window, so it wasn't a concern.

Annie then chose a spot roughly in the centre of the living room where she had a view of almost all the entry points.

However, no spot was perfect.

The best she found still didn't let her see one of the windows in the second bedroom. To do that, she had to walk closer to the room—which then made her lose sight of the windows in the master bedroom on the other side of the cabin. The imperfect location led to her quickly pacing between two points, marching the route over and over, her frightened eyes flicking over to every single pane of glass, waiting for someone to show themselves.

Come on, you fucker.

Several minutes into her patrol, Annie saw movement at the front of the house as something swooped past one of the windows. She instinctively tensed up and raised the knife. Whoever it had been had disappeared *just* before she'd managed to get a look. Annie waited, teeth clenched.

A hand slowly came into view. It snaked from the side of the window and its palm then pressed against the glass.

Annie gasped.

The hand looked… odd. Elongated, with fingers that seemed abnormally long. The skin was off colour and appeared grey, though she realised that could be a trick of the light.

'Go away!' Annie shrieked. The palm moved away for a moment, however it only inched back so that it could smack down onto the glass again with a *thud*. It slapped again, and again.

He's teasing me, Annie realised, though she didn't know for certain it was a 'he.'

Slap, slap, slap.

Finally, a head tilted into view. Annie screamed.

Oh my God!

She instinctively backed up, moving away from the terrifying face with bulging eyes. Eventually, she collided with a wall behind her. At that distance, she was able to see less of the face's detail, which was a mercy.

Even so, she could see how much the eyes popped from the skull, as if they were ready to fall out completely. The stranger wore a grin so wide it stretched up to the cheek bones.

The person looked male, and had thin, scraggly black hair that came down past his shoulders. The skin on his face seemed... wrong: too tight, with odd wrinkles in the wrong places, like it was a mask of thin flesh.

Annie held the knife higher, hoping to scare the man off.

Instead, he leaned forward and opened his mouth, which revealed short, stubby teeth. A fat purple tongue slopped free, and he licked the window, leaving streaks of saliva behind. The man then stepped to the side, completely disappearing from view again.

Annie couldn't believe what was happening. She drew in a breath and screamed as loud as she could: 'Somebody help me! Please! Somebody help me!'

She kept yelling, desperately hoping it was loud enough for other cabins in the woodland to hear. Deep down, however, she knew it wasn't. She was too far away.

I'm on my own.

Annie continued to glare at the window, waiting, gripping the handle of the knife tightly. There was a *thud* on a window to her left. She jumped in fright and spun her head, seeing the man now standing before a full-height window on the side wall, then cried out again.

The stranger was tall, the top of his head higher than the window head, and he was completely naked. She saw his small genitals hanging below a tuft of black, matted hair. Intermittent clumps of hair clung to his chest. The chest itself was so thin it was like he had no pectorals at all.

What's wrong with him? Annie thought to herself. He looked too tall, too stretched out. *What does it matter? Just run!*

However, Annie knew she couldn't 'just run.' She couldn't be certain of outrunning him, and with how tall he was, it was unlikely. All she could do was hold her ground, despite desperately wanting to flee.

Tim's car! she suddenly thought. It would likely be still out there on the road, and maybe still usable. *It could be my way out.* Unless, of course, the stranger had cut the brakes or something.

Still, the car represented a chance, a glimmer of hope. Getting to it, however, could be suicide.

Her disgusting visitor leaned forward and licked the window again, dragging his fat tongue up the glass. She realised he was trying to disgust her, to freak her out—to intimidate and scare her.

It's fucking working.

Annie was terrified. She'd never felt fear like this in her life, yet through the fear a resolve to fight came through. Annie knew she couldn't just curl up and cry. She had to *act*, to do something.

To fight.

The first thing she needed to do was to overcome the panic currently gripping her and force herself to move. It was easier said than done, but Annie managed to take a step forward, blade held up before her.

'Come on, then,' she shouted. 'Come inside. Break through and see what happens!'

Since begging the man to leave hadn't worked, she hoped showing some fight and aggression would instead.

The man stared at her, unmoving... then his head cocked to the side, like a dog trying to figure something out. *Is he trying to work out if I'm bluffing?* Annie thought.

'Try me!' she shouted.

As if in answer, the man raised his hands, balled them into fists, and smashed them against the glass. The top pane of the window exploded inwards.

Annie cried in shock and scampered backwards. She heard excited laughter coming from the stranger, who started to slowly crawl in through the opening, with his body hanging over the transom and skin dragging over broken shards of glass.

Fear gripped Annie again, but her mind screamed at her to act. *Now! Do it now!*

She clenched her teeth and ran forward with a roar. The man looked up, shock on his face for the first time since coming into view, and Annie thrust the knife forward. The blade found his neck. *What did I do?* Annie felt some initial resistance, then the knife slid inside with a *squelch*.

Annie gasped in horror, then backed away, leaving the weapon embedded in the man's neck. She stared in shock, eyes wide, hands over her mouth.

I've... killed someone.

The stranger looked back at her, motionless. His look of shock was gone, and wore an empty, soulless grin. Annie waited for him to drop.

After a moment, she noticed no blood was spilling from around the knife. The man continued to stare, continued to grin, but he didn't flop down. He didn't even look in pain.

Then, the stranger brought his hand up, grabbed the handle, and slowly pulled the knife from his flesh. Annie watched on in horror, seeing the steel was coated in some kind of black liquid that certainly wasn't blood. The man held the knife up to her and wiggled it, as if taunting her.

Annie couldn't believe what she was seeing. *He... he isn't human!* It made no sense to her. Her mind reeled in confusion.

Run! it eventually shouted.

Annie bolted, sprinting to the main door and leaving everything behind. She could see no other option. Staying inside was a death sentence. And while the same might be true of fleeing, at least there she had something to run towards.

The car.

At the door, she fumbled with the thumb turn, glancing back to see the man continue to slide his way inside before hitting the floor with a *thump*.

Annie was crying and sobbing hysterically, but managed to fling the door open. She lunged through, yanking the door closed behind her just to buy herself a tiny bit more time. She turned and ran, shrieking again upon seeing Tim's decapitated body.

Then she was off, sprinting down the road as fast as she could. The lack of available light was a hindrance, but the road was straight and flat, meaning she just had to push on forward and forget everything else. Annie considered pulling out her phone from her pocket and using the flashlight, but that meant slowing down.

And slowing up even a little wasn't an option.

Thankfully, she had *just* enough moonlight to see a few feet ahead of her. That was all she needed.

Annie continued to sprint, pushing her legs as much as she could, trying to ignore the fire in her chest and how much she was struggling for breath.

Keep going.

She didn't look back once—mainly because she didn't feel brave enough. But she also knew it would slow her and increase her risk of tripping. So she listened, trying to make out any sound beyond her slapping feet and ragged breaths.

Annie fully expected to be tackled to the ground with every step, for that horrific stranger to fly out from the darkness and grab her. She kept going. Her legs burned along with her chest, and her vision became hazy—her pants and gasps had become desperate.

Eventually, Annie saw something up ahead. *The car!* It was parked in the middle of the road and her heart leapt at the sight of it.

It looked intact. No slashed wheels, no smashed windows, and no actual damage that she could see. The driver's side door was open, but other than that, nothing out of the ordinary. As she sprinted towards it, Annie wondered if Tim had been forced to stop and gotten out of the car of his own accord.

She ran towards the open door, pushing herself on that extra few feet. As she reached it, Annie looked inside to see the keys still in the ignition. Her heart soared further.

I can get away!

She jumped into the seat. As she did, her foot caught the clutch pedal. The car came to life.

Annie was confused. Then, she realised the car had a start-stop system, making it automatically shut off if not active. She'd once had a rental that did the same. Pushing down the clutch pedal was enough to restart everything.

That meant Tim *had* likely gotten out of his own volition. *And then he was killed,* Annie thought. She reached out her arm to close the door, casting her eyes over to it.

The man was standing directly outside.

4 - 7

ANNIE SCRAMBLED ACROSS THE SEATS TO THE PASSENGER SIDE, crying and screaming and kicking. Cold hands kept grabbing at her as her assailant reached in, laughing manically and sounding like an overexcited child.

'No! Get away!' she shouted in absolute panic. Long fingers grabbed the jumper she was wearing. Annie managed to take hold of the door behind her and force it open, but she was quickly yanked away from it, towards her attacker. She kicked out at him.

'No,' she said again, desperate. Thinking quickly, she managed to lean the top half of her body forward as the man pulled at her top. At the same time, she ducked her upper body and raised her arms, allowing herself to slip out of her top completely. The attacker pulled the garment away, but Annie was able to scramble back over to the passenger side and out of the car, where she fell to the ground.

She quickly got to her feet and spun, planting her hands on the roof of the car and staring wide-eyed at the man. He loomed over the vehicle, standing a good two feet above the roof.

He was still grinning.

The man then lifted up his hand, clutching Annie's jumper, and brought it to his face. With his bulging eyes trained on her, Annie heard the man inhale deeply and then let out a pleasurable moan.

Annie felt a fresh revulsion surge through her. It only increased when she saw him lick the jumper, lapping at the material like a dog with a bone. He continued his excited grunting, always keeping his eyes on Annie.

Though there was a car between them, Annie still felt trapped. The man had survived a knife to the neck, so she knew he wasn't human, hard as that was to believe. And, given he'd popped up from nowhere next to the car, Annie knew she had no chance of outrunning him.

Which meant... she had nowhere to go. All she could do was wait for him to act.

And wait for the end.

The car was still an option, but climbing inside meant getting closer to the stranger. And the driver-side door was still wide open.

The man pushed his face deeper into the jumper, taking longer, heavier breaths. In doing so, he covered his face completely, letting out more excited moaning. He was getting louder and louder, each breath becoming deeper, until he was huffing at the material. Then he dropped his head back, the sweater still pressed over it, and moaned even more.

Annie saw an opportunity.

Taking her life in her hands, she carefully lowered herself down. Then, being as silent as she could, Annie leaned forward, putting a hand on the passenger seat to steady herself. She slowly started to crawl forward, always watching her assailant, who seemed lost in ecstasy.

Just as Annie worked her way over the centre console,

the seats creaked. She froze in panic, eyes locked on the man. He didn't move, however, still sniffing the garment in his long hands.

Annie started to move again. She was close to him now. Horrifyingly close. Enough to feel the coldness emanating from his body. The cold was accompanied by a sour smell completely unrecognisable to her.

Annie then tried to angle her body so she was in a sitting position, still watching the freak right next to her, his chest rising and falling with each deep breath. She was also head height to his groin, but refused to look at it, despite her periphery vision indicating just how excited he was.

Just as Annie was hooking her legs over the console, the man suddenly stopped.

She watched in horror as he started to lower the sweater. Finally, his eyes made contact with her.

'No!' she cried, slamming the car into gear and flooring the accelerator in a single motion. Her attacker let out an excited laugh just as the car shot forward. When it did, she felt his fingers grab her hair, but the car moved with such speed a chunk was ripped clean from her scalp. Annie screamed in pain but kept a firm hold of the wheel, fighting to stop the car from veering off the road. She swerved left and right, attempting to keep control, and at one point thought she was going to flip the car completely. To her utter relief, she managed to right the vehicle, and eventually held it steady, keeping a straight line as she shot down the road, leaving the stranger behind.

Her head throbbed, she felt blood trickle from her scalp, and her gasping was still out of control.

While driving, Annie checked her rear-view mirror, but saw only darkness. Both car doors were still open, and the drag against them was making it difficult to control the vehicle.

Eventually, as Annie sped up, the driver's door drifted farther closed, so she was able to lean over, grab the handle and force it completely shut. There was nothing she could do about the other one, however, so Annie ignored it and kept going. She did, however, manage to reach across with one hand and click her seatbelt into place.

The road was mostly straight, and the only bends were very gentle ones. The headlights revealed the road ahead, where she kept expecting to see the man come into view, standing motionless. If he did, Annie resolved to run the fucker down. She had no idea if it would kill him, slow him down, or even hurt him at all, but she didn't care.

However, the next thing that did come into view was the exit out onto the main road.

Annie was elated but had a decision to make. She didn't want to slow down at the junction for fear of what might catch her, but flying straight out could mean running into a passing car.

There weren't any nearby lights from oncoming traffic, and she listened through the whipping wind for any sign of another vehicle.

After a moment, Annie *did* hear something. It was obviously something big, like a truck, but it was off in the distance to her right. Annie took a breath as the junction rushed closer. *Go for it!*

She took the corner without slowing. The car screeched out into the main road, sliding round to the left, with the back end drifting away from her. Annie thought she was going to spin off into the trees, so she steered hard into the skid.

The back end of the car crossed the centre line of the road, and if something *had* been coming the other way, the accident likely would have killed her. Thankfully, the road was clear, and Annie was soon able to regain control of her vehicle again. She accelerated down the road, adrenaline rushing through her, hope rising with every second.

I'm going to make it!

Then, the headlights showed something standing in the centre of the road.

It was the stranger, still holding her jumper. And still wearing that monstrous grin.

4 - 8

Fuck you! Annie thought. Teeth clenched, and she gripped the wheel tight. She remembered what she'd said before—she'd promised herself she'd run the fucker down if he was standing in the road.

And there he was.

Now protected in a vehicle doing close to seventy miles an hour, Annie felt the first pangs of control she'd experienced since the ordeal had started. The anger she had for that... thing... for what he he'd done to her, for what he'd done to Tim, enveloped Annie.

Once again, she didn't know if hitting him would do anything, but she was seeking some modicum of revenge. It was only after she moved the vehicle into the middle of the road and it was too late to turn away that she realised hitting someone at such speeds wouldn't be good for her either. She held her breath as the vehicle ploughed straight into her tormentor.

It was like hitting a wall.

Annie's body jolted forward. The car's bonnet crumbled, and the vehicle pitched to the side. She screamed, but the airbag deployed in her face, cutting off the sound. She felt the car tip. There was a squealing and crunching of metal, so loud it was almost deafening. The car started rolling, and while the seatbelt held her in place, she hit her head on the side of the car. Pain exploded in her temple as gravity spun.

She clamped her eyes shut and screamed as her world was savagely thrown around.

Eventually, things settled. By the time Annie's mind came back into focus, she realised the car was on its roof and she was dangling upside down in the seat, still restrained by the belt. She looked around in panic, breathing rapidly, trying to figure out if she was injured. Through the windscreen ahead, now a mess of spiderweb cracks, she saw the stranger again.

He was stationary, still holding her top, showing no signs that a car had just rammed into him at full speed.

Annie began to scream again. She noticed her vision was blurry—her mind started spinning and her strength ebbed away.

I'm... I'm about to faint, she realised. If that happened, she knew she was dead: a sitting duck for the man to rip apart just as he'd done to Tim. She fought against grogginess. *No! Stay awake!*

Then, Annie saw the man start to move closer. His walk was odd, as if he wasn't used to his own body, like the act of moving itself was alien to him. Annie fought against her belt but could barely move her arms. Darkness swam around the edges of her vision.

No!

The man drew closer. Annie also picked up on another noise—loud rumbling drew ever closer. It took a moment for her to realise it was the engine she'd heard earlier.

Headlights soon came into view behind the approaching man. Annie realised her car must have spun completely around, now facing back the way of the cabin.

As the engine rumbled louder, the man stopped and slowly turned. The lights of the vehicle grew brighter. They were higher than that of a car, and Annie soon realised it was indeed a truck, as she'd first guessed.

Her assailant continued to stare away from her towards the oncoming headlights. Then... a strange thing happened. The lights actually started to go *through* his form.

The truck started to slow down. *He saw the wreck,* she realised. She wondered if the driver had also seen the man, but even now, looking for herself, she realised that *she* couldn't even see him anymore. It was like his body had been swallowed up by the light and completely disappeared.

Eventually, the truck stopped, and a moment later she heard the door open. Annie screamed for help. Unconsciousness still threatened to take her, yet she continued to fight desperately against it, screaming her throat raw. She eventually heard a voice.

'It's okay,' a man said. 'You're okay. Just hold tight. I'm gonna call for help. I don't wanna move you, but I'll wait right here by your side.'

'No, he's here!' she shouted. 'Help! We have to go!'

Annie didn't stop screaming until she saw the blue lights of an ambulance approach. When the paramedics were telling her to stay calm, she finally passed out.

37

4-9

ANNIE WAS CUT OUT OF THE CAR THAT NIGHT AND TAKEN TO hospital, somehow having avoided serious injury.

The police paid her a visit in short order. Not just because of the crash, but because of the body they'd found in a nearby cabin. Apparently, Annie had been babbling about 'Tim' at the lodge while unconscious.

Despite knowing they wouldn't believe her, she told them *everything*. About the sounds she'd heard during her stay, about finding Tim, and about the man with the bulging eyes that she'd stabbed and hit with a car.

They looked at her like she was crazy.

Unfortunately, the truck driver stated he didn't see anyone else present at the scene of the crash.

In the weeks that passed, Annie was treated as a suspect in the murder, and no sign of the stranger was ever found. However, the police were eventually forced to drop their case against her, as they didn't have strong-enough evidence linking her with the crime. None of Annie's clothing fibres or fingerprints had been found on Tim's body. While no one believed *all* of her story—specifically the part about someone surviving being stabbed in the neck *and* hit by a car—they *did* think someone else was responsible.

For Annie, going back to her old life was impossible. Night terrors became common, happening almost every night. Whenever she was out of the house, she expected to see *him* again, somewhere in a crowd, staring at her with his bulging eyes.

Annie soon shut down her business and moved back in with her parents. She was diagnosed with PTSD. Her days were spent indoors, with her parents urging her to start living again.

But she couldn't.

Annie just couldn't shake the feeling that the stranger wasn't done with her yet—that he would return at some point and finish what he'd started.

Worst of all, no one fully believed Annie about what had happened. That made her feel more alone. Even though she lived with her parents, she truly had no one to turn to.

All she did was exist, waiting for him to show up again.

Six months after her experience at the lodge, someone wrote to Annie. Someone that *did* believe her: Dr. Antone Bellingham.

The man said he had files of similar cases, and that he dearly wanted to talk.

FURTHER NOTES FROM DR.
BELLINGHAM

From the files of Dr. Antone Bellingham

From my detailed research, I've uncovered many instances over the years of these... entities. These things that show up, with no rhyme or reason, and invoke absolute terror in their targets.

Compiling information on them hasn't been easy. The entities don't have a collective name as far as I'm aware.

However, there are some patterns. Once a target is chosen, a kind of 'haunting' of that person takes place. These hauntings do not centre on a building or area, but on the unfortunate victim themselves. For example, one case took place in a rental property, with no prior reports of strange activity. That victim's violent death was big news for a while, and the case remains unsolved. Similarly, I have evidence of people leaving what they assumed was a haunted house, only for the strange happenings to continue. Death soon followed.

As much as I've searched, I can find no links between the

victims, other than the strange dreams they had while targeted. Dreams they can never fully remember, it seems.

It is as if these people are just picked at random—plucked out of the ether to suffer. It could happen to anyone. Again, fleeing doesn't help. If the victim runs, the entity follows.

It isn't just the target that is at risk, either, but those close to the victim. One case I know of centres on a couple who were targeted. The wife's parents were killed along with her while the husband was away.

Since then, however, the husband has been reported missing. I believe he met a similar fate to his wife, though I am uncertain.

The length of suffering isn't consistent, either. Some cases I've researched take place over a period of months, some years, and some only days. In almost every case, however, the victim ends up dead.

Almost.

I know of only one case that is different. The victim there actually survived. Of course, no one believes her story. But I reached out to Miss Annie Hearn, and she spoke to me, telling me everything. While I'm sure she encountered one of these entities, I don't understand why she was allowed to live and the others weren't. I continue to correspond with her in the hope of finding out more.

I'm not the first to link many of these cases together over the years, but I may well be the most persistent. I won't rest until this threat, obscure though it is, is fully documented.

People need to know that at any time, any place, one of these... things... could target them.

My work goes on.

Dr. Antone Bellingham.

VOICEMAIL TRANSCRIPT

THE FOLLOWING TRANSCRIPT IS FROM A VOICEMAIL LEFT FOR Dr. Antone Bellingham. The voice belongs to Annie Hearn and takes place two weeks after her last conversation with the doctor.

Dr. Bellingham? It's me, Annie. You need to help me! Please! He's... he's back! He's outside my bedroom door. My parents are already dead. I've called the police, but I know they won't get here in time.

I... I didn't kill Mum and Dad. I need people to know that! To know the truth. Please, you have to... wait! Oh God, he's... He's coming.

    <CREAKING SOUND OF AN OPENING DOOR>

Oh God! Oh God, no, he's here! No! Keep away from me! Keep away! No! Noooo!

    <MISS HEARN CAN BE HEARD SCREAMING. EXCITED GIGGLES. CALL CUTS TO STATIC>

THE END

INSIDE: PERRON MANOR

Sign up to my mailing list to get the FREE prequel...

In 2014 a group of paranormal researchers conducted a weekend-long investigation at the notorious Perron Manor. The events that took place during that weekend were incredible and terrifying in equal measure. This is the full, documented story.

In addition, the author dives into the long and bloody history of the house, starting with its origins as a monastery back in the 1200s, covering its ownership under the Grey and Perron families, and even detailing the horrific events that took place on Halloween in 1982.

No stone is left unturned in what is now the definitive work regarding the most haunted house in Britain.

The novella, as mentioned in Haunted: Perron Manor, can be yours for FREE by joining my mailing list.

Sign up now.

www.leemountford.com

OTHER BOOKS BY LEE MOUNTFORD

The Supernatural Horror Collection
The Demonic
The Mark
Forest of the Damned

The Extreme Horror Collection
Horror in the Woods
Tormented
The Netherwell Horror

Haunted Series
Inside Perron Manor (Book 0)
Haunted: Perron Manor (Book 1)
Haunted: Devil's Door (Book 2)
Haunted: Purgatory (Book 3)
Haunted: Possession (Book 4)
Haunted: Mother Death (Book 5)
Haunted: Asylum (Book 6)
Haunted: Hotel (Book 7)
Haunted: Catacombs (Book 8)
Haunted: End of Days (Book 9)

Darkfall Series
Darkfall: Deathborn (Book 1)
Darkfall: Shadows of the Deep (Book 2)
Darkfall: Crimson Dawn (Book 3)

ABOUT THE AUTHOR

Lee Mountford is a horror author from the North-East of England. His first book, Horror in the Woods, was published in May 2017 to fantastic reviews, and his follow-up book, The Demonic, achieved Best Seller status in both Occult Horror and British Horror categories on Amazon.

He is a lifelong horror fan, much to the dismay of his amazing wife, Michelle, and his work is available in ebook, print and audiobook formats.

In August 2017 he and his wife welcomed their first daughter, Ella, into the world. In May 2019, their second daughter, Sophie, came along. Michelle is hoping the girls don't inherit their father's love of the macabre, but Lee has other ideas...

For more information
www.leemountford.com
leemountford01@googlemail.com

ACKNOWLEDGMENTS

Thanks first to my amazing Beta Reader Team, who have greatly helped me polish and hone this book:

James Bacon
John Brooks
Nicole Burns
Mary Cavazos-Manos
Karen Day
Sally Feliz
Doreene Fernandes
Domenic Fiore
Jenn Freitag
Ursula Gillam
Vicky Gorman
Clayton Hall
Emily Haynes
Dorie Heriot
Lucy Hughes
Marie K
Dawn Keate
Jon R Kraushar
Paul Letendre
Katrina Lindsay
Diane McCarty
Leanne Pert
Cassandra Pipps
Carley Jessica Pyne
Gale Raab

Laura Rafferty-Aspis
Justin Read
Nicola Jayne Smith
Rob Walker
Sharon Watret

Also, a huge thanks to these fantastic people:

My editor, Josiah Davis (www.jdbookservices.com) for such an amazing job as always.

The cover was supplied by Debbie at The Cover Collection.

(www.thecovercollection.com).

I cannot recommend their work enough.

And the last thank you, as always, is the most important. To my amazing family: my wife, Michelle, and my daughters, Ella and Sophie—thank you for everything. You three are my world.